THE
MURDER
MYSTERY

BOOKS BY ALICE CASTLE

THE
MURDER
MYSTERY
ALICE CASTLE

bookouture

Published by Bookouture in 2022

An imprint of Storyfire Ltd.
Carmelite House
50 Victoria Embankment
London EC4Y 0DZ

www.bookouture.com

ISBN: 978-1-80314-486-3
eBook ISBN: 978-1-80314-485-6

To Ella and Connie, with love

ONE

Beth Haldane peered anxiously into the hall mirror, on tiptoes as usual. She wasn't after perfection. There was no time for anything fancier than the speediest swipe of make-up. She had to get her son Jake off to school, and then get herself – yikes – to her first day in her new job. She waved the mascara wand and hoped for some magic. There. The intelligent grey eyes staring back betrayed not a single jitter. Though the rest of her reflection, she thought a tad harshly, you could easily have met hanging over a stable door. She had the uncompromising thick dark fringe of a Shetland pony, and a pensive oval of a face. And, indeed, the sturdy build and short stature that so often goes with the breed.

If she did have an equine air, it was that of the prettiest little pony that ever stole the show from a prancing white stallion. But a nimble brain and sparkling eyes were scant comfort when you longed for legs up to there and a well-behaved mane. Still, Beth was happy enough in her hide. She smiled at herself encouragingly, and tucked a clump of fringe tidily behind her ear. Inexorably, it sprang back. Giving up, she took a deep breath. 'Jake! School! We're leaving NOW.'

She rattled the front door chain off and clicked the lock decisively; today she *absolutely* meant business. In seconds, the tiny house was shaking as nine-year-old Jake thundered down the stairs, one small beloved boy rivalling the din of a tank battalion on ops.

She shut the door on the chaos of breakfast dishes, books, Lego and odd socks. Normally, everything would have been left pin-neat, but getting to her work debut on time was top priority. It would have been nice if someone had been around to wish her luck. Jake knew about the job, of course, but if he thought about it at all, it was as an eccentric hobby to fill her hours while he got on with the really important stuff at school. She looked back wistfully at the house – then noticed their black and white cat, Magpie, in the window. Was it her imagination, or did Magpie twitch her tail? Beth had decided to take that as a little good luck wish, when the cat stared right at her, shot up onto her hind legs and started clawing at the window – almost as if trying to get Beth to come straight back home again. Beth felt a moment of pure dread. Magpie had never done that before. What on earth did it mean? Maybe she shouldn't have changed her to that dry cat food?

But there was no time to worry about that now. The morning sun slanted generously onto window boxes of purple and yellow primulas as they turned into Dulwich Village. It had rained overnight and the street looked as though it had been through the express rinse cycle of some celestial washing machine, windows sparkling, pavements pristine. As they passed Bartley's, the florist on the corner, Beth breathed in deeply to catch a waft of the early hothouse hyacinths, fat stems crammed into black buckets, alongside acid yellow daffodils and supermodel-spindly catkins. Five minutes more and they were at the charming Hansel and Gretel redbrick building, criss-crossed with yellow London stock brick, which was Jake's school – the Dulwich Village Primary. She left him at the gates, as boy protocol demanded.

Gone were the days when she could accompany him into the classroom, even hang up his coat and settle him at his desk. Now, every morning, she felt a pang at the thought that it might be the last time he'd deign to hold her hand as they walked along. Many of his friends took off on their scooters and were at school before their mothers had time to fire up their huge 4x4 cars. The mummies still turned up at the school gates – but that was just to chat, and deliver forgotten sports kits, packed lunches and instruments. There was no need to chide a child for forgetfulness if you had time on your hands. Even the women who did work seemed to play at it, like suburban Marie Antoinettes. Beth knew she shouldn't be bitter, but it was hard not to resent her situation. She sometimes felt she was the only woman in Dulwich who had to pay her own credit card bill. Which was probably why she always left the card at home.

She said a few hellos and was fobbing off a well-meant enquiry about the recent half-term break – no, they hadn't spent it whizzing down a Swiss mountain, like everyone else – when, with relief, she saw her friend Katie Green waving. Katie was normal. Yes, she did have a lovely husband with a good job (Michael was something important in publishing), and she did only work part-time, but she was passionate about her job as a yoga teacher. She also managed not to nag Beth about her own lack of fitness regime, and she had a lovely normal son, too, who was Jake's greatest friend.

The two women kissed on both cheeks – the basic Dulwich 'hello' – and Beth said quickly, 'I'd love to catch up but I've got to dash...'

'I know, I know, first day today. Just wanted to give you this.' Katie pressed a bulky envelope into Beth's hand. 'Now off you go, knock 'em dead. Oh, wait, seen Belinda?' she said, nudging Beth and looking over to where a tall woman was holding court with the largest group of mummies. The spring sunshine glinted off perfectly tousled blonde hair and the equally shiny metal clasps of a new handbag, the size of a well-fed toddler. Beth raised her eyebrows at Katie. That bag must have cost more than her monthly mortgage payment. Which was looming.

All that was going to get a lot easier, thought Beth as she hurried away from the school, crossing the road at the traffic lights, saying a brief 'hi' to a couple of mothers running late, kids straggling behind them like reluctant ducklings. She picked up her pace down Calton Avenue. Normally, she'd admire the pocket handkerchief gardens she passed, but today her thoughts ran in only one direction.

Against stiff competition, and much to her surprise, she'd landed the job as assistant archivist at Wyatt's – in her view, *definitely* the best school in the area, though the dinner parties of Dulwich chewed this topic over endlessly. The job wasn't going to solve all her money woes at one stroke, but it was certainly going to help. And what's more, she loved Wyatt's and was hoping that Jake might somehow squeak in; she then might *possibly* be able to scrape together the fees when he had to leave the Village Primary.

He was now in Year Five, the calm before the storm. Year Six was action stations. As soon as the school year started in September, parents all over the UK performed daredevil contortions to get their children into the secondary school of their choice, fighting catchment areas, dwindling places, and each other. It was life-or-death stuff, nowhere more so than Dulwich, where there were a huge number of high-achieving, determined parents – each one with a uniquely talented and very precious child – all jostling for a tiny clutch of places in the prestigious Dulwich endowment schools. Beth hated the thought of what was to come. But, like any hapless conscript, she was in the thick of it whether she liked it or not.

Wyatt's was the boys' endowment school, set in magnificent grounds sprawling alongside London's South Circular and dating from the sixteen-somethings. The College School was its counterpart – an offshoot of the original foundation, set up 250 years or so later with the newfangled idea of educating girls. The grounds were less impressive, the buildings not nearly as lavish – but the results were terrifyingly good. Both schools were riding high in the league tables, and together they were the main reason why Dulwich was such a sought-after area. Houses never, ever changed hands here for less than a million. No wonder the local garage only sold Audis.

Beth often thought that buccaneering Thomas Wyatt, the schools' founder, would have thoroughly approved of the affluence of his old stamping ground. In his youth, this Flash Harry made glittering fortunes overseas; his interest in children was apparently confined to fathering, rather than educating, them. But he had returned to his beloved Dulwich just in time to expire, and left the lavish pot of money which allowed the two schools to flourish to this day. Fortunately for Beth.

The gates of Wyatt's said everything they needed to about money, privilege, aspirations and even education, in squiggly wrought iron, held aloft by immense redbrick pilasters. Beth took a breath to steady herself before going in. Groups of boys rushed past her, shining with intelligence, youth, confidence, and the odd pimple. They reminded her of racehorses waiting for the off at the Grand National. She had never felt more of a Shetland pony, dusty after her walk and knee-high to these thoroughbreds, but she dismissed the self-doubt briskly. Yes, she did have a place here, and a very necessary job to do.

Strangely, for such an organised and successful school, the archives were in a woeful state. When she'd been shown them briefly at her interview, she had been taken aback. Some might have scratched their heads at a school having archives at all, but Thomas Wyatt's legacy was more than just money for a good education: it was a tangle of deeds, transfers, maps and titles. Much of the material was in boxes, following successive moves from office to cupboard and building to building, as the schools acquired property, weathered wars, and finally split into two as the years rolled by. Some of the records had gone to the College School site, as part of a detangling process which had never quite been fully achieved. There were also huge volumes of them left at the Wyatt's site. And what little was in the right place looked as though it had never been put in the right order. She had her work cut out.

As usual, she worried about being found out – she'd never dealt with archives before and was still amazed, and even puzzled, to have landed the job. She quickly scanned the letter clutched in her hand. It confirmed her appointment and told her the drill for her first morning. She must have read it a dozen times, she pretty much knew it by heart, but looking again gave reassurance. After signing in at the porter's lodge, she was to stop at reception to pick up her official pass from Janice, the school secretary, in the main school building. She remembered Janice from her interview – mid-thirties, pretty, warmly competent.

Beth trotted up a flight of stairs to the main entrance, pushed with some difficulty through a heavy wooden door with mirror-bright brass inlays, and was suddenly plunged into a cool and echoing entrance hall, all wood-panelling, smooth flag-stones and icing-sugar cornices on the ceiling miles above. She sniffed – floor polish, books and the faintest tang of adolescent boy. Turning sharp right off the main corridor, as laid down in her letter, she found herself in reception, where Janice held sway behind a countertop which glowed like a freshly peeled conker.

Beth hurried over pale, velvety carpet – which would not have been her top choice with hundreds of muddy shoes on the premises – past a pair of lush, low sofas and a coffee table bearing just one discreet prospectus. A flatscreen TV flicked silently from sporting triumphs to stratospheric A level results, showing why there was no need for a hard sell. Wyatt's was effortlessly perfect, with the subtext that your child would be, too, if only you could crowbar him in here.

Janice, in a pink cashmere sweater accessorised with a welcoming smile, was the cherry on the top.

'Beth! Welcome to Wyatt's. One of the family now,' she said, springing out from behind her burnished counter to give Beth the regulation double Dulwich kiss. 'Glad you're joining us. It's a big school, but we're only a small team behind the scenes; you'll soon get the hang of who everyone is. And it's lovely and quiet today. Lots of classes are out on school trips – we call it field day. Great way to start.'

'Oh? It seemed pretty busy coming in...' said Beth.

'Probably just the last-minute rush of sixth formers trying to beat the bell,' said Janice. Beth was relieved – perhaps that explained why they'd all been so enormously tall.

'Now, I'm just wondering who you already know at the school? You'll already have met Tom Seasons, the bursar, at the interview; and Dr Jenkins.' Janice paused, then rushed on. 'Tell you what, come and find me at lunchtime and I'll introduce you to a few of the others then. Now, here's your security pass, you'll need to swipe that to get through the doors to most of the buildings. Do you know where you're going?'

Beth swallowed. She couldn't altogether remember where the archive office was, but in the face of so much bright competence, she wasn't about to admit that. She smiled, assuring Janice she knew the way like the back of her hand, and was soon outside again and negotiating her way through the last straggles of teenagers making for the sixth-form centre and the Science buildings.

Just as she was wondering if she'd missed the turning leading to the far-flung archives block, she spotted her new boss,

Dr Jenkins, clad in a mustard yellow tweed jacket. He'd been wearing the very same thing at her interview. It had stuck in her mind for all the wrong reasons.

'Alan! Alan...' she called, breaking into a trot and rapidly catching up with the elderly man. He seemed miles away. It wasn't until she had put a hand on his arm that she got his attention. 'Hi, Alan, er, Dr Jenkins... it's Beth, Beth Haldane. Your new assistant?'

The archivist appeared startled at being accosted, and peered over half-moon spectacles. It seemed to take him an age to place her.

'Ah. Yes. The lovely Ms Haldane. Yes, yes, I remember,' he breathed. Then his small black eyes seemed to be running all over her like beetles. Oh dear. She'd had a few misgivings at the interview, but she had decided he was just of that generation which didn't find it easy to treat women as equals. She was sure she could cope with it. And she needed the job.

Now, suddenly, she wondered how this was going to work. There was no longer the comforting presence of the bursar, Mr Seasons, or the human resources manager, Geoff Something – Geoff *Trainer*, she remembered – sitting solidly between her and Jenkins, as there had been at the interview. It would just be the two of them sharing the archive office, which she now recalled as pretty cramped. Jenkins was still staring fixedly, and not even at her face. Had she made a terrible mistake?

'Now, I'll just show you in, then I have to go and meet... Well, let's just say I have an appointment this morning,' said Jenkins. And he started up a wheezing commentary on what all the nearby buildings had previously been used for over the years, as they meandered along.

Beth fervently hoped she wasn't going to be tested on this monologue. She was trying to memorise the route – and keep well out of Jenkins' way as he lurched along with little consideration for her personal space.

'Nearly there now,' he said, peering at her again for just that moment too long, with eyes that seemed to take the scenic route up and down her legs.

Dr Jenkins swiped his card to enter the unprepossessing building, which was little more than a portable office, though on two floors. The ground floor was given over to spare tennis nets, cricket stumps and great orange nylon nets of footballs, with a narrow passage left clear, leading to a set of metal stairs. They sidled past the sports kit in silence, climbing the rickety stairs to the top floor and a small lobby that seemed to grow increasingly narrow, as Dr Jenkins stared again, seeming to take forever to root about in his pockets for the key. Unlike the entrance door downstairs, with its swish modern entry card system, the archive office door had a simple old-fashioned lock.

Finally, he found his bunch of keys, then began fiddling with the keyring. 'Now, I'm going to trust you with my spare, but don't you go losing it, young lady,' he said, brandishing the key right in her face and giving her a sidelong smile.

'I think I can manage to keep it safe,' said Beth, just about resisting the temptation to roll her eyes, as Jake would definitely have done. How old did Jenkins think she was? And with how many brain cells? What a pain the man was. They hadn't even started their first day's work together and she was already telling herself to think of the salary at the end of the month.

The whole work thing was so tricky these days, she reflected. She knew she wasn't alone in struggling to make ends meet.

It was all very well that her roster of little freelance jobs could now be dignified with the title of 'portfolio career'. It sounded glamorous, but in her eyes, this was how employers justified paying a pittance. She'd stuck it out because, as a single mother, it made sense for her to work from home, giving her the flexibility to be around when Jake needed her. And she had little choice. In theory, the dribs and drabs of money she made –

editing a website, contributing copy to a local magazine, selling
the odd feature to a newspaper – just about added up to a
normal salary. On a good month.

Sometimes she didn't sleep. Worries crashed in on her in
the early hours, and only deep breaths and natural optimism
kept her going. The Wyatt's post was going to make a difference. It was a job with regular office hours, which already felt
grown-up. All the other work, she'd decided blithely, she would
keep on and just cram into weekends or evenings, when Jake
was tucked up in bed.

She still felt pretty thrilled she'd landed the job at all,
despite her lack of any specific archive experience. There must
have been better qualified candidates among the fifty or so
applicants they'd had. It was quite a mystery. But then, she
loved solving puzzles, from crosswords to deciphering Jake's
shocking handwriting. And she'd be very well placed to solve
both conundrums: why they'd hired someone without much
archive experience; and why the archives were in such a mess in
the first place. In the meantime, they'd obviously seen something in her. She was going to repay that faith by giving it her
best shot – no matter what her boss was like.

That jolted her back to the present. The archives door was
swinging open. Jenkins was shuffling off back down the corridor
after pressing the unpleasantly warm key into her hand, and
Beth walked into the room alone. Immediately, something
tickled her nose. All that paper. It was a fusty smell, true, but
she had always liked the soft powdery scent of age. It was a
small room – a box, really – with floor-to-ceiling shelves.
Cartons were stacked everywhere, obstructing what space there
was. One small window, high in the wall, let in a little light on
this fine spring day. A desk was positioned beneath it, already
strewn with a mass of papers, a brown old apple core (probably
the source of some of the smell), some sweet wrappers and a
muddle of coffee mugs. Positioned behind it, amidst the sea of

boxes, was what looked suspiciously like a fold-up card table, of the type Beth's grandparents had used for games of Bridge, and a basic steel-framed chair.

The contrast with the spacious, welcoming plushness of the school's reception desk couldn't have been more marked, but Beth smiled. This suited her better than a lot of swanky furniture. Besides, aesthetics was neither here nor there. She was interested in the contents of all these boxes, the information, the time and the secrets they contained, not their surroundings. *My kingdom*, she thought to herself. But what, exactly, was she supposed to be doing in it, she wondered.

Though she had talked airily at her interview about various kinds of systems, and there had been some vague mention from Jenkins of indexing certain records and the huge care and precision this would take, she had been expecting a bit of direction. Presumably, Jenkins had a plan, and work that he specifically wanted her to do. Otherwise, why hire her in the first place?

She pulled out the chair and sat down at the green felt-covered table, realising as she did so that she was squashing the envelope Katie had given her, still in her coat pocket. She stood up, slipped off the coat, looked around in vain for somewhere to hang it, and slung it over the back of her chair. She smiled at the wobbly writing on the envelope, and opened it up. It was a card, featuring a bunch of yellow daffodils with Spiderman looming menacingly above them. The daffs had been dashed off, but the Spiderman was lovingly worked. No prizes for guessing which theme had been at Katie's urging and which was Charlie's unique contribution. Inside, it said simply, 'Good Luck Beth, love Charlie, Katie and Michael X'.

Charlie was Jake's partner in crime, and Beth was touched that he'd spared a few moments from Minecraft to make her this offering – or, rather, impressed that Katie had managed to unplug him from the game and bribe him into doing something so thoughtful, especially involving flowers. Jake, she was sure, wouldn't recognise a daffodil if he trampled on one, let alone consent to draw one. She propped the card on her rickety work-station and switched on the laptop.

She was glad to see that this, at least, reflected the swishness of Wyatt's public face, and not the state of its archives. Within a few seconds, she was connected to the school's intranet, and could see timetables for every class and a run-down of all the important staff meetings of the day. What she couldn't see, and had no idea about, was the whereabouts of Jenkins. Shouldn't he be here, showing her the ropes? She wasn't yearning for his presence, mind you. She'd just get on without him.

Right. First things first. The inbox, towering to the side of the laptop. There was a huge clutch of letters referring to Wyatt's boys who'd served in the First World War; there was a lot of correspondence with the other endowment school, either requesting documents or explaining why they couldn't be lent. There was a fascinating, if crumbly-looking, piece of parchment right at the bottom of the pile. It was, Beth rapidly decided, all the stuff left behind by her predecessor because it was either too difficult or too fiddly. Well, she liked a challenge. And fiddly was no problem at all.

It was nearly three hours later when she looked up again. She'd been quietly working away, making some progress with getting all the First World War documents into date order, taking careful notes of questions to ask Jenkins when he reappeared, and she'd been through the emails. But now, she realised, she was starving and also needed the loo. Jenkins hadn't thought to show her where the nearest ladies was, and she might as well seek out an early lunch while she was at it.

Carefully shutting down her computer, she collected her bag, remembered the key Jenkins had grudgingly entrusted her with, and locked up the archive office. For the first time, muted playtime shouts could be heard from outside, where it sounded like the sixth formers were already letting off steam. She rattled quickly down the metal stairs. It was a lot easier getting past all the sports supplies without Jenkins lurching too close to her.

Shutting the door firmly behind her and checking she had the all-important swipe pass to get back in, Beth made her way back across the asphalt to Janice and the reception desk, dodging clumps of children as she went. As she walked, it struck her how odd it was that Jenkins hadn't returned. Well, she knew nothing about his working methods. Maybe he considered it good practice to leave a brand-new colleague completely alone for half the day? She should count her blessings. It wasn't as if she was desperate to have him sitting cheek by jowl with her anyway.

She caught sight of a sudden flash of fuchsia pink jumper to the side of her, behind the sixth form centre. It had to be Janice. Maybe she had decided not to have lunch with her, after all? Beth felt a stab of disappointment. She had enjoyed the solitude of her morning's work, but she could certainly do with a bit of socialising in her break. She wondered whether to follow the pink, but then reasoned Janice might not be the only person wearing that colour today. It was a big school, as the secretary herself had pointed out.

She turned the corner, only to run slap into a huge bear of a man coming the other way. They whirled round as he fought to get his balance, ridiculously grabbing her shoulders briefly, as though to steady his six-foot-plus bulk on her tiny five-foot-not-much frame.

'Oh, I'm sorry,' she said – the automatic English response to someone else tripping over her and then using her as a Zimmer frame.

'Do excuse me...' said the man, releasing her and managing to get himself upright. Oh God, it was only Dr Grover, the headmaster.

'Ah, it's our new archivist, isn't it? Ms Haldane? May I call you Beth?'

Dr Grover, like all teachers, seemed to have an amazing knack for remembering names. They had only met for five minutes, as part of her courtesy tour of the school on her interview day, though of course she had already known all about him. Every Dulwich mother did – especially those dying to get their children into Wyatt's. While no one could pretend that Wyatt's had ever been failing, it was true that the school's star had burnt still brighter since Thomas Grover, with his double first in English from Cambridge, had breezed in. His trademark dove grey, chalk-striped, double-breasted pinstriped suits, worn with primary-coloured Hermès ties, were hardly radical fashion statements. But in a sea of sober lawyer and banker daddies, Grover stood out as that tiny bit more flamboyant... a touch more 'Wyatt's'. And his magnificent height and stature – think of a very tall Winnie the Pooh – made him seem almost Falstaffian.

The fact he was popular with staff and children alike helped, as did the searing intelligence plotting an effortlessly upward path for the school. Depending on which schools' guide you were reading – and in Dulwich, they were pored over much more often than any Booker Prize winner – Wyatt's was now either in the top twenty-five or top fifty schools in the UK.

'Dr Grover, good to see you. Yes, well, I'm the *assistant* archivist...' Beth started, then flushed as she realised it was hardly politic of her to correct the headmaster on their second meeting, and particularly not when he'd accidentally promoted her.

'Splendid, splendid, great to meet you again, and let's schedule a proper chat soon, talk to my secretary, must dash now but have a great first day, and welcome to Wyatt's.'

With that, Grover was off, striding purposefully. He seemed to be heading towards the spot where Beth had caught that tiny glimpse of pink a few minutes before. She collected herself, then decided to press on and see whether Janice was in reception after all. But was she still going the right way? Being whirled bodily about by the headmaster, of all people, meant she had lost her bearings for a moment.

She hurriedly glanced around. There was a narrow passageway here, between the sixth form centre and the Science block. Yes, that must be a shortcut. She'd just nip along it... Blast! She realised it came out almost back where she had started, at the big rubbish containers which flanked the perimeter fence, leading back to the archives outbuilding.

She paused for a moment, taking stock and looking around, deciding she had to seriously regroup if she was ever going to get any lunch, with Janice or alone. Then, as she turned, something caught her eye. Something she could just see jutting out from under one of the wheeled bins. Something which really shouldn't have been there.

It was a foot.

Or, to be more precise, a leg, ending in a sock, an inch or two of exposed very white flesh, and a sturdy black shoe. Not quite believing what she was seeing, she walked forward a little, to get a better view. Was someone under the bins? Was it some kind of prank? Maybe the children playing a strange trick... But there were no children anywhere near this area. She could still hear muted breaktime sounds, but a long way off. She craned forward more, then stopped abruptly. It couldn't be!

But it was.

What she could see was a body, crumpled between two of the dumpsters. She couldn't see the face; it was in shadow, and there seemed to be a cloth over it. But she could see the jacket. It was tweed, and a horrible, and horribly familiar, mustard colour. Except where it was stained and stiff. With dark red blood. There was more blood, the colour of a fine wine, pooled lavishly around the body, too.

It was Alan Jenkins, her boss.

TWO

No wonder Dr Jenkins had never come back to the office, was Beth's first, ignoble thought. If he had ever needed an excuse for his cavalier behaviour towards a new colleague, the universe had given him a permanent 'get out of jail free' card.

Then, crashingly, she felt the shock of the situation. He couldn't really be *dead*, could he? But it seemed that he could.

She stood, frozen in horror. Dr Jenkins was equally silent and still. The blood around him was like a dark mirror, reflecting the clouds in the spring sky, the only things that moved in the scene.

Beth was conscious of that feeling of hyperrealism you get when catastrophe has struck. She seemed to be seeing colours more clearly – especially mustard yellow and wine red – and the seconds ticked by, in time with her heartbeat, which she could now hear pounding in her ears. She didn't realise she was shaking until she saw her own hand reaching for her phone. But who should she call? The school? The police? She pressed every button before realising the battery had died.

Now she was truly in a state of panic. She thought she should probably check whether Jenkins really was dead or not

before doing anything else, but she knew better than to disturb
the body or mess up the crime scene. She edged a tiny bit closer
but then gave up the attempt. She couldn't face getting any
nearer to the splayed form and, besides, his preternatural stillness and the lake of blood on the ground around him were
telling their own grim story.

She reached out a hand towards his foot but couldn't bring
herself to actually touch it, feeling all the time that she would be
violating Dr Jenkins' privacy, his dignity, and probably all kinds
of CSI laws about DNA transfer. Part of her was also waiting
for a roar of angry disapproval from the supine figure. She didn't
know whether she would have been more terrified or relieved if
he'd suddenly sat up and started shouting. But there was no
reaction, no moaning, no movement at all. Just a deep and
ominous silence. The phrase 'dead as mutton' came to her. He
was as inert as anything in the chilled cabinet at the big Sainsbury's in Dog Kennel Hill.

Beth knew someone was supposed to stay with the body,
but she couldn't do that at the same time as relaying the news.
She considered shouting for help, but what if some of the children came to investigate? She'd hate them to see this. Just as the
slightly pointless dilemma threatened to overset her in a way
which the actual death hadn't, salvation came lumbering round
the corner, complete with a squeaky wheel.

'Wossisen?' said a stout woman in a blue overall, pushing a
trolley laden with a large urn, cups, saucers and covered plates.
The trolley shrieked to a halt as Beth struggled to make sense of
the dinner lady's words, which were made all the more exotic
by the Silk Cut clamped to her lower lip. Pushing the heavy
trolley was a two-handed job.

'Wossappened?' the woman persisted. Tufts of fierce red
hair were bursting out from her white catering hairnet, and she
narrowed her eyes suspiciously at Beth.

'Um, well... I'm not sure...'

'Fark!' the woman shouted suddenly, catching sight of the spreading pool of blood and skittering sideways with the trolley. There was a clatter of china and the cigarette fell from her lip, coming to rest about a metre from Dr Jenkins' inert foot. It said a lot for the dinner lady's respect for the dead that she didn't immediately pick it up and pop it back into place. 'Well, ee's a goner, innee? Fark me sideways.'

No thank you, thought Beth primly. But the shouting had brought her back to herself. The best thing was for her to get help at the main school building as quickly as possible, now that there was someone to stay with the body. She'd aim for reception. There would be people there who'd know what to do, including the lovely Janice, and it was also probably the only spot she could reliably find in her current state.

'Can you stay here, please, while I go and call the police?' she asked the woman.

'Whotcha, mad? Nah. Not stoppinere on me own. Yegorrabe jokin. Ang on. Ear!' the woman yelled out deafeningly across the playing field.

A figure in the far distance – one of the grounds staff, Beth guessed – started running towards them. Then a lanky boy in jeans and a T-shirt came round the other corner and stopped short, his face blanching as he took in the odd assembly of Beth, the dinner lady, the distant groundsman and, last but not least, Dr Jenkins. He yanked an earbud out and said, 'Wow'; eyes round in a face that suddenly looked absurdly young.

'Gappy, innit?' said the dinner lady, accurately sizing up the newcomer as one of the gap-year students who helped out at the junior school before heading off to uni. He nodded silently, and swallowed, his eyes skittering nervously to Dr Jenkins, the blood, Beth, and rapidly away again.

Beth got him to promise to stay put with the dinner lady, and the groundsman arrived, panting. She left the trio firing up a medicinal Silk Cut each, and standing awkwardly like guests at a truly lamentable cocktail party.

An hour later, Beth was ensconced in one of the back offices behind reception, hands clamped around a cup of sweet tea produced by a wan but still efficient Janice. She closed her eyes, and immediately a vision of red-splattered yellow tweed rose up. If her hands hadn't been holding the cup, she knew they would still have been shaking. Dr Jenkins was a stranger, and on their brief acquaintance she hadn't warmed to him, but she was near to tears. He had looked so ungainly, stuck there between the bins, like some forgotten rubbish himself. Poor, poor man. Beth shook her head. He surely hadn't deserved that. Had he?

'All right, love?' said the police constable sitting opposite her, painstakingly transcribing her statement. She nodded briefly, but she wasn't all right. Not really. This had to be the worst ever start to a new job. She knew it wasn't all about her – a man had died, for goodness' sake – but part of her was rueful. From the moment she'd run into reception, pale, wild-eyed and gibbering about a dead body, all the Wyatt's staff had been eyeing her curiously. She'd wanted to make an impression. But not this one.

Yes, there had been sympathy. And Janice had been wonderful and given her a hug, then sat with a cosy cashmere arm around her as they waited for the police to arrive. But Beth was conscious that a great calamity had come to Wyatt's – and she was somehow stuck right in the middle of it.

The school had been going from strength to glossy strength for hundreds of years, then she had arrived. Suddenly, there was a dead body on the premises and the place was full of police cars. It all seemed surreal. There was a SOCO van right outside the building, and other police cars kept piling in; she could tell from the monotonous blue flashing outside. The hum of the school continued, but everything was out of joint. A tragedy had struck here, and you could feel it in the lowered voices and darting glances.

Beth was surprised the school was still open, but perhaps it was too difficult to send the children home, now that so many parents – even in Dulwich – were working. And she didn't suppose for a moment that there was a mechanism in place to deal with a situation like this. Jake's little school had a snow protocol, where every parent at the top of a class list had to call the one below, and so on. But not even super-smooth Wyatt's was going to have a Sudden Death List ready to roll.

The police constable's radio burst into life with a ferocious crackle of static. Beth was amazed he could understand what on earth the control station was saying, it was so garbled. Then two words jumped out of the babble. 'Body' and 'knife'.

She eyed him nervously. 'Do you need to go and find... something?' she said, not sure whether she should let on what she'd heard. Accidentally eavesdropping on a police radio was another situation that she wasn't equipped for.

'No, that's fine, miss. There's a team out in the playground dealing with... all that,' said the constable. 'Now, if we could just go over one or two points again, if you're feeling up to it?' He was looking at her as though, like a Victorian heroine, she might need to avail herself of a chaise longue and some smelling salts at any moment.

She sat up a little. 'Of course, I'm just not sure how much I can really help. I hardly know... knew... Dr Jenkins. It was my first day at work.' Despite herself, she knew her bottom lip was wobbling. She bit it.

'And you're sure that's who it was?' said the constable, leafing back through his notebook. She nodded silently.

No one had asked her the cause of death, and she didn't like to broach it herself, but she had seen a lot of blood. Now this mention of a knife over the police radio. Jenkins couldn't have fallen on the knife by accident, surely? He had been lying on his back, although his face was covered. For the first time, she wished she'd got closer and been able to see what it was over his face. But the fact he'd been covered up certainly implied there'd been a second person present when Jenkins died.

Unless he'd pulled something over his own face as he expired? No, ridiculous. So, with the knife, the covering, the blood... the whole thing was beginning to look a lot like... murder. This time she was beginning to feel distinctly nauseous.

'Now, you don't look too clever,' said a man in the doorway. It was a deep voice, with a trace of an Irish accent.

Beth looked up quickly, brushing strands of fringe out of her face. She could feel her forehead was clammy, her upper lip prickled with sweat. She knew her appearance didn't matter a jot, yet somehow she felt she'd been caught out, found wanting. All right, she was a bit dishevelled – was it any wonder? How would he feel if he'd just stumbled on a dead body? she thought crossly. Then she realised that, though he wasn't in uniform, this was definitely a policeman. He'd strolled in as though he was in charge – because he probably was. And he stumbled across dead bodies for a living. Or at least found murderers.

She glanced at the constable opposite, who had also straightened himself up and was now looking alert and expectant, a tiny bit like a dog who's been promised walkies. This new arrival was clearly the boss. Well, good. She might get to go home soon, then. So far, there had been very little sense of urgency since the police had arrived. The whole operation had been concentrated on locking things down, keeping adults from leaving the school, cordoning off the playground as much as was possible, and then waiting.

This man, it seemed, was who they had been waiting for. Already the atmosphere had changed. Maybe it was his outdoorsy air, but there seemed to be more life in the stale office now. He was wearing a dark navy peacoat and, from the ruffled dark blond of his hair and the colour in his cheeks, it looked like he'd hiked across country to get here. That seemed very unlikely, but the speculation was helping Beth's wave of sickness to pass.

'You need some oxygen, let's take a bit of a walk,' said the man decisively.

She immediately glanced at the constable, who closed his notebook eagerly and looked ready to fetch his lead and come too.

'Take a statement from the bursar and the head now. I'll be back in a while,' the man ordered, dismissing the deflated officer, then turned back to Beth. 'I'm Detective Inspector York. Harry York,' he explained. 'Now, let's get you sorted.'

He held her coat for her and she struggled a bit to put it on, then nearly forgot her handbag. It had been quite a day. Suddenly she wondered what the time actually was. Jake! She had to pick him up at 3.30. It was after 2 p.m. already.

'Don't worry, you'll be away in time to get your son,' said York, seeing her worried glance at the office clock. Beth wondered for a moment how he knew about Jake, then mentally kicked herself. He was the police. He knew it all.

'So, I don't want to drag you through everything again, but it would be really helpful if you could just take me through the events of the morning. I know you've had a shock,' said York, holding the heavy main door open for her.

They emerged by the rectangle of lawn in front of the Grand Hall. It was the most perfect patch of grass she'd ever seen, its stripes rivalling Wimbledon. Not a single weed or bald patch marred its smooth green surface. Today, its effortless perfection seemed incongruous. Blue lights still flashed from the police cars flanking the long windows of the Grand Hall, and a uniformed officer stood at the entrance to the playground, his high-visibility jacket garish against the muted red brick of the venerable school buildings.

Beth had already digested the inherent contradiction in what York had said – he didn't want to drag her through events, but he did want a complete run-down of what had happened. She sighed just a little as they strolled back and forward and she told him everything. Well, almost everything. She wasn't sure if she should mention that flash of fuchsia which she might – or might not – have seen, and she also didn't say anything about her own burgeoning dislike of Dr Jenkins, which had been cut short by the discovery of his body. He was dead, and wasn't there that whole thing about not speaking ill?

But it seemed that York had sensed something in her account. He listened attentively and scribbled a couple of notes. Unlike the constable, he didn't feel the need to capture every syllable of her tale. His first question was, 'And what did you actually think of Dr Jenkins? Did you know him? Like him?'

'I didn't know him at all, really. I'd only met him once before this morning, at the job interview, and today I was barely with him for ten minutes. I don't know anything about him as a person.'

Beth knew her equivocating was telling its own story. She might as well be honest.

'There was something about him that was a bit...' 'A bit what?' York was alert.

'Well, old-fashioned in his attitudes.'

York looked baffled. She tried again. 'He didn't seem very politically correct.' 'You mean he was racist, homophobic, what?' York asked.

'Nothing like that... It was the way he kept looking at me... It was a bit Jimmy Savile, if you know what I mean.'

The penny finally dropped. 'He was leering at you?' York clarified.

Beth nodded gratefully. 'I was pretty certain he was. There

was something sleazy about him. I'd only just met him, though. Maybe I was imagining it,' she said, trying to give the dead man the benefit of the doubt.

'But you don't think you were?'

She took a breath. 'No. I don't.' Why not say it? York would hear it from other sources, even if she were discreet herself. A man like Jenkins who, even on two minutes' acquaintance appeared to have no respect for boundaries, had to have a track record. It was the kind of thing that women had once had to take with a pinch of salt, but she was pretty sure that nowadays there would at least have been gossip in the staffroom about his behaviour.

'Interesting,' said York.

'Has anyone else said anything?' said Beth, hoping for some corroboration. 'So, what time was it when Dr Jenkins left you?' York turned the subject neatly. Beth thought back, her forehead wrinkling under the thick fringe.

'It can't have been much after nine o'clock, maybe ten past, something like that? I tried to get here a few minutes early – well, it was my first day – but getting a security pass and so on ate up a bit of time. I caught up with Dr Jenkins on the way to the office. He was in the playground already, and he walked me to the building and then right up to the archives office door. He opened it with his key, but he didn't go in. He gave me his own spare key, from his keyring. And that was it. I didn't see him again until – well, later, by the bins. You know. It all seems like weeks ago now,' she added quietly.

York looked at her with narrowed eyes. 'So, he went out, basically, and never came back? He was gone for what, several hours? And you didn't wonder where he'd got to? Or think to go and look for him when he didn't come back to the office?'

'Well, yes, I did wonder what he was up to, because I wasn't really sure what I was supposed to be doing. It was my first day, as I've said, so I had assumed he'd go over things, give me an idea of what his expectations were, certainly give me a couple of things to get on with. As it was, I didn't quite want to go searching for him and asking a lot of questions. I mean, he had a perfect right to be having meetings and so on without me. I had no idea what his daily timetable was.

'I thought it was *really* strange that he'd just gone off,' she carried on, 'but I wanted to show that I could get on with the job myself. After all, it was one of the things that kept cropping up in the interview, and it was even in the job ad: "Must be a self-starter, able to work independently".

'I suppose I thought it might be a sort of test, leaving me like that. I didn't want to come over as, well, needy,' said Beth, frowning. 'Also, I had absolutely no idea where he would be, so I couldn't actually go after him... it's a big school... and he could have gone anywhere, been talking to anyone...'

It was York's turn to frown. She wondered if he'd spotted the way Jenkins had played on his new assistant's inexperience. He'd basically left her entirely to her own devices – presumably for his own good reasons. Maybe he'd only intended to be out for a moment or two; maybe he just didn't want anyone else around. Maybe he hadn't actually wanted an assistant working with him in the first place.

'As he went off,' Beth continued, 'he said he was meeting someone, and then he changed that to saying he had "an appointment". That's a bit odd, isn't it? I'm not sure what the difference is, really. Maybe an appointment is more... official? He didn't say who with, or I would have told you, of course. On the other hand, maybe he was just planning to be away for five minutes or so, and then someone, er, something, well, you know, then whatever happened, happened.'

'Either scenario is perfectly possible,' said York evenly.

'I suppose it will depend on time of death and things like that?' said Beth.

'Yes, very much so.' York smiled blandly, giving nothing at

all away. 'Now, back to when Dr Jenkins left you, at around ten past nine or thereabouts. He didn't give any indication about who he was meeting? What was his manner when he was telling you? Was he matter-of-fact, nervous, relaxed?'

'I suppose I'd have to say he was a bit... secretive. He could have told me who he was seeing, if it was a work thing, and he could have explained what it was about. It would probably have been useful information for me. As it was, I had no idea what he was up to or why. Maybe he realised that if he had said a name, the chances were I wouldn't recognise it anyway, as I hardly know anyone yet. Or maybe he just wanted to be mysterious.

'I suppose I got the impression that he didn't think he owed me any explanations – I was just an underling, and why should he explain himself to me? But I don't know that. All I really know is that he didn't say, and I wasn't really in a position to ask.'

'Why do you say that?'

'Well, again, it was my first day on the job. I couldn't really have cross-questioned him about what he was doing, could I? Even if he'd been an approachable sort of person. And he wasn't. Or, at least, he wasn't a person I wanted to approach,' she qualified.

'Did he make you feel welcome?' York wondered.

'Well, no, not at all. I don't know whether the leering thing was something he tried on with everyone or... what, really, but it didn't exactly make me feel at home, if you know what I mean. I don't even know if he wanted an archive assistant in the first place, or whether the school just decided he needed one because the records are in such a mess,' said Beth.

'But presumably you can sort all that out quite quickly, if everything really is in such a state? You're a trained archivist, aren't you?'

'It's definitely in a state, I'm not imagining it,' said Beth. 'But that's just the thing,' she added miserably. 'I'm actually not trained at all. You can do a postgrad qualification in archives and records, or you can have hands-on experience, or have worked in a library or public records office. But I don't have any of that; I just have a history degree. I'm more of a researcher than a records person, though I am really organised. My background is in journalism. I was thrilled when I got the job, but I was surprised too. It all feels... well, a little out of my comfort zone,' she admitted.

York smiled reassuringly, but she could see his mind was ticking over; no doubt he'd get someone to look over the CVs from the recruitment process. If there had been candidates with more obvious qualifications, she wondered what that would say about Jenkins, or whoever had a say in recruitment?

Beth didn't know if she should go ahead and speak her mind, but York's stillness encouraged her to carry on. 'I think, having just arrived this morning, I can maybe see the school a bit more clearly than someone who's been around for years, and a couple of things surprise me.'

'Oh, what are they?' York's slight smile was encouraging.

'Well... The records are in such a mess. I was warned there was a lot to do, but they've had a full-time archivist here for ages – Dr Jenkins himself. He's been here for quite a few years, I think; I don't know how long exactly, but he certainly gave the impression of knowing the school inside out, as though he'd been here forever, knew everyone... you see what I mean? So why hadn't he sorted things out? And also, if the archives are important enough to be maintained by two people, why are they stuck out in the playing fields in a glorified shed? The rest of the school buildings are pretty plush. It's... odd.'

Beth felt better for getting these observations out, though she wasn't sure if York had really been listening. He didn't acknowledge her comments and now he was squinting at his phone. She wondered if it would be incredibly rude to look at her watch. She was yearning for home now, for normality. And for a good solid hug with Jake. She knew he was in no danger – he was nowhere near Wyatt's, and had been safely tucked away in his own cosy little primary all day. But there had been a sudden death here. She needed to see him.

'Could I ask you something?' she said, suddenly.

York raised his eyebrows, neither permitting nor preventing.

'Was it... murder? There was a lot of blood... And I heard one of your colleagues talking about, well, a knife...'

York's mouth compressed into a thin line. 'We're not saying anything officially yet. You'll understand that I can't go into details. We need to inform the family. I don't suppose he mentioned anyone to you?'

Beth shook her head.

He scanned her face quickly before continuing, 'I would appreciate it if you kept this quiet at this stage. It's going to be hard enough for us once word gets out, and we need to use whatever advantage we have to find out as much as we can before people know.'

Beth smiled for the first time in what seemed like years. She had idly been wondering if York lived locally. Now she knew for sure he didn't. Otherwise, he would have realised that, minutes after Dr Jenkins met his maker, the whole of the village would have known something was afoot.

This was Dulwich, after all.

THREE

Beth wasn't surprised, the following morning, to get the call announcing that Wyatt's would be closed. It would be a lot easier for the forensic team to do their work without nearly a thousand schoolchildren milling around metres away from the crime scene. Not to mention the fact that few Dulwich parents would be happy with their precious offspring so close to a grisly murder.

She felt sorry for Dr Grover – how on earth could he spin this? With a twitch of his Hermès tie, he would be more than capable of persuading parents that everything was fine if, say, the GCSE cohort dropped a couple of grades. But violent death? Right on the premises? During the school day? If anything, ever, was going to dent Wyatt's reputation as first among equals in the endowment school stakes, it was this. Their rivals, the College School, had never had a staff member removed feet-first from the premises in a body bag.

Even if her job had been temporarily shelved, Beth still had her hands full with Jake. She was worried he would have somehow heard about the murder, but the evening had been calm, and then he woke her with a bombshell of his own: a dinosaur project, which she hadn't even known was looming, had to be given in by 9 a.m.

After suppressing some epic expletives, she had cobbled together an eleventh-hour effort – a plastic stegosaurus shoved into a shoebox full of green tissue paper moments before they left the house – and they just made it to school on time. Jake was not great about telling her this stuff beforehand. Mind you, she hadn't interrogated him to winkle out vital information on school stuff for a while. She'd been distracted, by the preparation for her job interview, getting the job, and now dealing with the fallout from the world's worst first day.

Beth spent a few fruitless minutes trying to point out to Jake that his projects would be much better if he mentioned them to her in advance. He responded that his dinosaur was brilliant and that he was bound to win all the prizes, then ran off ahead without a care in the world.

She loved his confidence, but she just knew some of the kids would be turning up with porcelain brontosauri that their mothers had fashioned then fired in kilns purchased specially for the purpose. If they could have cloned the actual dinosaurs in their pristine Dulwich kitchens, some of these mums would have. Even the more lackadaisical among them would probably have hand-knitted a pterodactyl or two.

Beth sighed. She didn't want to think of herself as competitive – yet nor did she want her son to be trounced by a rival whose mother had too much time on her hands. But last night she'd had way too much to think about. She'd managed to sleep, thank goodness, despite worrying that mustard and red visions would keep her up all night. But she had spent the entire evening mulling over the whole business. She was looking forward to discussing it all with Katie – she needed her friend's perspective.

She wasn't that surprised to see the crowd of mothers outside the primary gates was thicker than ever this morning.

Jake's dinosaur project deadline was quite a draw, even without a murder down the road. There would inevitably be some mothers – Big Bag Belinda included – who would be desperate to get a look at the other mummies' – sorry, children's – efforts. Beth hadn't been expecting the reporters, though. There was a straggle of them, staying a safe distance away, thanks to the reassuring presence of a police constable standing squarely in the sea of mothers.

In a way, she felt she'd missed a trick. If anyone knew the inside track on the death at Wyatt's, she did, and with her journalistic background, she could have sold the story in a trice to one of the papers. Heaven knew, she needed the money. But that would have been disloyal. After only one day at work, she was part of Wyatt's, and a betrayal would have felt grubby.

She was glad not many of the mums realised she was now working at Wyatt's. Katie was one of the trusted few, and she elbowed her way through the throng to give Beth a sympathetic hug. They'd spoken, briefly, the previous night, but the homework/bedtime routine was so all-consuming – especially for single-handed Beth – that they'd barely scratched the surface.

Beth passed the Jurassic shoebox to Jake, and Katie handed over a bag sprouting a jungle of newspaper foliage. Thank goodness, Charlie had obviously made this one himself.

With the boys safely waved into school, Katie turned to Beth. 'Jane's? Cappuccinos?'

Jane's was the newest, and most popular, of the Dulwich cafés. As such, it was rammed night and day with mummies with buggies, mummies with toddlers, mummies with school-age kids, and also mummies who'd achieved total drop-off and needed to celebrate that with coffee, too.

'Could we go somewhere a bit... quieter?' said Beth.

One of the problems with Jane's was it was so full you needed to shout to make yourself heard, and Beth really didn't want to be yelling about yesterday's events. They quickly agreed to go to a much smaller and less public café, the Aurora, which was just round the corner from the main village thoroughfare, yet managed to be a world away in terms of popularity. The service was iffy and Katie didn't rate their coffee – perfect, today, to keep other ears at bay.

Sure enough, the café was almost deserted as they took their seats in a corner and ordered.

'This better be worth drinking dishwater for,' muttered Katie, as the waitress stomped off to the kitchen, where Beth suspected she would be making fake 'coffee machine' noises while spooning instant granules into two cups for the worst cappuccinos within a mile radius.

'Well, what do you want to know?' Beth said. Unconsciously, her shoulders sagged a little.

'I'm sorry, Beth. I feel awful,' said Katie, reaching out a hand and patting Beth's. 'I'm just being curious about the death, instead of realising it's been horrible for you. What a start for you!'

'I know, right? The next time someone tells me their job is complete murder, I won't know whether to laugh or cry,' said Beth, instinctively lowering her voice as the waitress bustled back and plonked two coffees on the table.

As they watched, the meagre centimetre of foam on the top of both cups sank without trace, leaving sickly grey-brown liquid. Katie closed her eyes as if in pain. Beth shrugged and took a sip anyway. At least it was hot.

'So, what do you think actually happened? Was it like being in *Midsomer Murders*?' Katie was sitting on the edge of her chair.

'Exactly like that, apart from there not being any thatched cottages, quaint villagers or sinister squires in the vicinity.' Beth laughed.

'Well, apart from Dr Grover himself,' Katie speculated. 'I've always thought his looks are a bit too good to be true...'

'I'm sure there's a step or two between being handsome and being a cold-blooded killer.' Beth raised her eyebrows.

'Don't tell me you don't find him attractive?' Katie said.

'He's maybe an inch or two too tall for me,' said Beth. But her face immediately fell. It felt a bit too soon to be joking.

Katie caught her newly sombre mood. 'So, it was definitely murder, then?' she asked in a low voice, glancing around.

'The police inspector was very discreet but I think it must have been. I can't see any way Jenkins can have had an accident, flat on his back like that, which would have caused so much blood...'

'Euuww,' said Katie, screwing up her delicate features.

'Well, yes,' said Beth. 'But you did want the gory details. And they are – really gory. He was stabbed. It's the only explanation I can think of. When I shut my eyes, I just hear that line of Lady Macbeth's, you know: "Yet who would have thought the old man to have so much blood in him?"'

'God, how dreadful,' said Katie. 'I wonder how his wife is taking it.'

'His wife? You know her?'

'Well, yes, sort of. She started taking one of my stretch classes about six months ago.'

'What's she like?' said Beth, agog.

'Well, she's a funny one, really. She's one of those older ladies who looks really cuddly, you know – lots of cardies and florals, and she's quite smiley. Everyone's idea of the perfect granny. She looks friendly, but I get the impression that she's really not at all. She doesn't mingle much with the rest of the class – apart from the bursar's wife.'

'Which bursar?'

'The Wyatt's one – you probably know him now that you're in with that lot. Anyway, Mrs Jenkins – Ruth is her first name – is always tagging along with the bursar's wife. Now *she's* quite nice, very well-turned-out, blonde, and very good at yoga. But

Ruth Jenkins, she's not really what I'd call a yoga natural. She's a bit more, well, cylindrical, shape-wise, you know.'

Beth, who did know only too well, was newly sympathetic towards Mrs Jenkins. Marriage to Dr Jenkins can't have been fun. Now she'd been horribly widowed, and even her yoga style was under attack.

'Do you know if she works?'

'Not every day, or she wouldn't be at my class, I suppose. I think she has something to do with our school, Charlie and Jake's, I mean. I've seen her in there. She never says hello to me, though she must recognise me. And I don't know what she does. Some kind of office job, maybe?'

Beth was surprised, but made a mental note to check. 'Anything else strike you about her?'

'Nothing I can really put a finger on. I'd sum her up as aloof,' Katie said, stirring her coffee with a frown.

'Mmm. Sounds quite different from Jenkins. He wasn't nearly aloof enough. Like I said on the phone, a bit of a perv. I wonder how they got on?'

'No idea. Never saw them together. I don't suppose she'll be coming to the session today, but her friend might. I'll let you know if I find anything out. Is there any reason you want to know, or is it just idle curiosity?'

'It's mostly just being nosy. I mean, he was supposed to be my boss. I didn't take to him. But obviously not enough to do him in. You know me. I don't like secrets and mysteries. I'd like to know what happened. But also, I am a bit worried, because I'm the person who found the body.'

'Well, that's appalling, but it's not as though it was your fault. You were just there.'

'Yes, but don't you see? The police always suspect the person who found the body. Half the time, they're right to. Because the only reason someone *finds* the body is because they've just killed it...'

'Present company excepted, I assume!' said Katie.

'You see, even you're sounding a bit suspicious,' said Beth, cradling her cup again, as she had yesterday in the office when the constable's questioning was going on and on. 'You can imagine what it's going to be like at Wyatt's. Nobody's said anything, of course, but I was already getting some sideways glances. The only thing they know about me is that I started work on Monday at nine a.m. and my boss promptly died a gruesome, violent death. It's not a great introduction to the place, is it? Some of them are bound to think...'

'What? What are they going to think? That you took that job on purpose just to attack a complete stranger? No one can really think that, particularly once they've met you,' said Katie, looking at her friend affectionately.

Beth, from her mop of shiny dark hair and worried grey eyes, to her tatty 'day off' jeans and little pixie boots, was the last person anyone would suspect of murder most foul. She might frequently be guilty of stressing out, she overthought things on a daily basis, she could be a tad clumsy, but violence? Never.

Beth put down her coffee cup a little too hard, and half the remaining liquid sloshed onto the table. They both set to with napkins to mop up.

'I'm such a klutz!' Beth groaned. 'I don't know, Katie, look at all this. I'm a wreck,' she continued. 'I'm the obvious suspect. The only suspect, as far as I know. People are bound to be wondering. I would myself, if I were in their shoes. I bet that's just going to get worse, until they find whoever did it.'

'What about the police? Surely they can set everyone straight, tell them you were nowhere near?'

'But don't you see, Katie? They don't know where on earth I was. No one knows. I don't have an alibi. I was stuck in the archive office, on my own, for three hours. I didn't see anyone... and no one saw me. I don't even know what the time of death was; the policeman was so tight-lipped. But it doesn't really matter because I've got no alibi at all for any of that time.'

Katie was silent for a minute, absently stirring her coffee dregs. Then her sunny nature shook off the gloom. 'On the other hand, you have absolutely no motive, either. You didn't know Jenkins. Had you ever met him before?'

'Only at the interview, and I wasn't alone with him at all. If I had been, I would have noticed the leering more, and... well, I would still have taken the job, but I would have been a bit more prepared for him yesterday.'

Katie looked thoughtful. 'They won't think you stabbed him because he was perving at you, will they?'

'God, I hope not! He didn't do anything, after all; he just made me feel uncomfortable. It's not punishable by death yet. I'd be more likely to have a quiet word with him – excruciatingly embarrassing though that would have been – than take him out to the bins and stab him.'

'They don't know that, though, do they? They might think you're a completely militant feminist or something. "Death to the defiler", and all that,' Katie mused.

'Oh cheers, thanks for that. Even my best friend thinks I have an excellent motive. Would you mind keeping an eye on Jake for me while I'm in prison for twenty years?' said Beth.

'Oh, don't be silly, I was just thinking out loud. They're going to take one look at you and realise you couldn't stab the plastic film on a ready meal, let alone a fully grown pervert.' Katie was matter-of-fact as ever.

'God, I hope so. Mind you, that makes me sound so limp. I mean, I really don't think I could kill anyone in cold blood – but say he was attacking Jake? I might be able to then.'

'Well, maybe don't mention that to the police,' said Katie briskly. 'Let's stick with the wouldn't-hurt-a-fly and didn't-know-the-victim-anyway angle – both of which are true. I hope you won't be officially under suspicion. That could be horrible.'

'I know. Maybe I could have had some sort of ancient grudge against him... Who knows? That's why I'm beginning to think... Katie, this may sound crazy, but I think I've got to try and clear my name. At least, try and find some other people who would have had a motive to kill him. Then maybe one of them will turn out to have been in the playground at the right time. After all, someone really did murder him – and it wasn't me.'

They looked at each other, eyes wide. 'But how on earth will you start?' said Katie.

'Well, maybe with Mrs Jenkins. If anyone understands why somebody wanted him dead, it'll be his wife – or her best friend. Listen, I've got an idea. Jake's at school, I can't go to work, I'm not in the mood to tackle any of my other jobs – what time is your stretch class?'

Two hours later, Beth was lying on a yoga mat, wearing the best impromptu exercise gear she could dig out at short notice – an ancient T-shirt and pair of leggings that had seen far better years. She loved Katie's yoga school. It had a fantastic location, on the first floor above one of Dulwich's most exclusive – read, most expensive – boutiques. It was a large whitewashed space, very New-York-loft-apartment in spirit. There was a bank of open wooden shelving at one end for mats, bolsters, foam blocks and other mysterious yoga accoutrements. An office and a tiny loo clustered at the other end of the room. All the splashes of colour in the room came from Katie's clientele's expensively curated fitness clothes. Everyone either arrived ready-changed or was so body-confident that getting into the latest gear from Sweaty Betty or Lululemon in front of the rest of the class simply wasn't an issue.

Beth, naturally shy, had felt self-conscious as the assorted Dulwich ladies shrugged out of their skinny jeans and then wriggled into equally skinny Lycra pants, flashing a good deal of lightly tanned, expertly depilated flesh. Luckily, this particular class wasn't too advanced and she was loving the stretches, even if she sometimes found she was listing like a creaking door to the left while everyone else glided effortlessly to the right.

Technically, she was a spring chicken – most of this group had at least ten years on her. But they were all in great shape, with barely a love handle breaking their smooth Lycra-ed lines as they raced through the movements with precision. Katie, in her element, was correcting a posture here, offering encouragement there, nipping from lady to lady.

As she hovered over the woman next to Beth, she looked meaningfully at her friend. Beth nodded quickly, hoping Katie wasn't being too obvious. She took a quick look when everyone else was absorbed with their downward dogs. So, this must be Mrs Jenkins' best friend.

Beth spent the rest of the session working out how best to approach the woman. Unfortunately, all the thinking wasn't helping Beth's own performance. She was giving only part of her mind to the routine, and it didn't seem to be the sporty part. As they got to the tricky chair pose, her lack of attention got the better of her – she stumbled forward and, to her mortification, collapsed onto Mrs Jenkins' friend.

She flushed beetroot and whispered her apologies – the rest of the class was politely ploughing on, despite the disruption – but at last she had her entrée. As the class wrapped up and everyone began to collect their bags from the side of the room, she had the perfect reason to apologise again.

'I feel such an idiot... in fact, I've been a bit shaky since yesterday,' she said, not having to embroider her flustered act too much; the whole business genuinely was still so raw. 'I had a terrible first day at my new job at Wyatt's.'

As she had expected, this was enough to get her companion's full attention. She was the Wyatt's bursar's wife, after all.

'Oh, were you there when...?'

'I was. I actually found the body,' Beth said, lowering her voice and looking around to see if they were being overheard.

Sure enough, a couple of the women turned away and started determinedly talking among themselves. She wasn't at all surprised. Murder didn't happen every day, did it? Not in lovely, leafy Dulwich.

'You must be the new archive girl,' said her companion quietly.

'That's right, I'm Beth,' she said, immediately sticking out her hand. She felt if she could establish a connection, she might root out a lot more information. Her hand was shaken, reluctantly.

'Judith. Judith Seasons. I'm a great friend of, well, was a friend of Dr Jenkins – and his family, of course,' she said quietly. Her still-glossy, expensively blonded hair was tied back in a ponytail, and her skin glowed from the recent exercise. She might be in late middle age but, as they said in Dulwich, sixty was the new forty-with-fillers.

'Is there anywhere we could go, just to have a quick chat?' Beth saw alarm flicker in Judith Seasons' eyes. 'In case you have anything you want to ask me,' she added quickly, as though extracting information on her own account was absolutely the last thing she had in mind.

'Well, I was about to...' Judith Seasons appeared to be on the verge of thinking up an excuse when Katie popped up, having rolled all the mats and stacked them neatly in double-quick time. Everyone else had disappeared while they had been talking.

'I don't suppose you two could do me a big favour and just stick around for a few minutes, could you? I have to quickly pick up, er, something, from the suppliers. You can sit in the office, there's two lovely comfy chairs there. Thanks so much, see you in a minute... or two...' said Katie, shutting the door behind her.

It was masterful. Beth owed her friend a big coffee – and a much nicer one than this morning's effort. 'Well, she was in a hurry, wasn't she?' said Beth, shaking her head in mock-astonishment and ushering the other woman towards the tiny office at the side of the exercise studio.

'Let's make ourselves comfortable. She'll be back in a second, I'm sure. So, you were saying, you and the Jenkinses are friends? It was so awful, I still can't believe it,' said Beth, completely truthfully, as she sat herself down on Katie's office chair and Judith perched reluctantly on the other.

'So you were the one who actually found Alan, er, Dr Jenkins?' said Judith, curiosity overcoming her obvious qualms. 'That must have been ghastly.'

'Yes, yes, it was,' said Beth, swallowing.

'Do you mind if I ask... Would it have been quick?'

Beth glanced at Judith and saw her anguished expression.

Beth shrugged. 'To be completely honest, I have no idea. The police haven't told me anything at all... All I know is what I saw, but I'm sure it would probably have been quick,' she added, a little unconvincingly.

She was pretty certain that the large pool of very dark blood meant Jenkins had lain by the bins, bleeding away quietly, for quite a while. On the plus side – if there was one – he hadn't seemed to have thrashed about much, as the pool was undisturbed, which probably meant he'd been unconscious. Beth shook her head to banish the images from her mind.

'How is his family taking it? He was married, wasn't he?'

'Yes, yes, he was married. His wife is devastated. Poor Ruth,' said Judith Seasons, but her delivery was formulaic. There was none of the tension in her now that there had been when she'd asked about Alan Jenkins' death.

Beth was suddenly alert. Now that she thought about it, if

Katie's husband was suddenly killed, would Beth be prancing around at yoga the next day, or would she be by Katie's side, handing out tissues, making cups of tea and offering the few snippets of comfort she could? How good a friend was Judith Seasons? Beth was beginning to think the answer was not a very good one. And could she scent another conundrum too? Was Judith Mrs Jenkins' friend, or was she – hard though it was to believe – keener on *Dr* Jenkins?

'I expect, er, Mrs Jenkins, is being questioned by the police,' said Beth.

'Questioned? Why would they question her? She wouldn't have anything to tell them. She had nothing to do with it. He'd had breakfast, then gone off to work like always, and that was... that,' she said, eyes suddenly glittering with tears.

'Would Mrs Jenkins have been at home?'

'What? No, not on Mondays; she would have been here, at yoga. She works part-time, but she has Monday mornings off. The session is at nine, and then we walk round the park afterwards, and we sometimes have lunch... but...' Judith Seasons had been recounting her normal timetable as though by rote. Then she tailed off.

'What is it?' asked Beth.

'Well, that's our usual routine, we've been doing it forever. But in fact, Ruth couldn't make it yesterday. It's only just struck me. It's been such a shock, you see.'

Beth nodded sympathetically, while silently willing Judith to carry on with the story.

Obligingly, Judith seemed to shake herself out of her reverie.

'I got a text from Ruth just before the class, saying she was ill – her hay fever had suddenly started playing up. She's a martyr to it every year,' said Judith in the bored tones of someone who had never had a reaction herself. 'She was going to catch up with me in the park, if it stopped. But she never came.'

Beth tried not to show her excitement. It looked as though Ruth Jenkins was going to join her in the previously horribly exclusive no-alibi club. 'So, when did you hear the news?'

'Oh, it would have been about three or four p.m. Ruth rang me. I could hardly understand what she was saying at first. Then, when I *could* understand, I couldn't believe it. Well, you know,' said Judith, looking bereft again.

'Had you known Dr Jenkins long?' Beth asked gently.

'Oh, years,' said Judith, sighing. 'You know, he was a wonderful man, so scholarly. Brilliant mind. He'd been at Wyatt's for quite a while, but before that, he'd been doing something quite hush-hush, if you know what I mean. MI5 or MI6, something like that. Terribly important. The Cold War, and all that. He was really high up in Intelligence, you know. But, of course, he never really spoke about it.'

In that case, how did you even know about it? thought Beth, but she said nothing. Fascinating to think the leering dinosaur she'd met was the man of mystery she was hearing about now. Move over, James Bond.

'And now we'll never really know. What a loss, what a loss,' Judith crooned in distress.

'Awful,' chimed Beth automatically, but she must have hit a wrong note somewhere because Judith snapped out of her elegiac mood.

'But, of course, I was more Ruth's friend, really,' she said quickly, the visceral distress quickly hidden beneath the veneer of the well-bred, leisured lady. She rummaged in her handbag for a calming moment before bringing out a tissue and pressing it carefully to damp eyes. Her immaculate eye make-up had hardly budged, despite the strenuous stretch class and her obvious distress about Dr Jenkins.

'Oh yes, Ruth and I have known each other forever. Our

children were at Wyatt's together, but they're grown up now, with children of their own.'

'Oh, you have grandchildren? And where are they at school?'

'Wyatt's, of course,' said Judith, looking at Beth as though she were mad. 'Ruth and I both have granddaughters in Year Two. Our daughters' children. The prep school is co-ed, you know.' Her smile was tremulous. 'Ellen will be broken-hearted about her grandfather,' Judith added, and tears threatened again.

But, with a determined movement, she swallowed the emotion. Clearly, if she was going to do any proper crying over Alan Jenkins, it was going to be on her own terms, in private. Whatever she felt was too jagged and raw to be displayed in public.

'Can I get you a glass of water?' Beth asked sympathetically.

The offer was batted away by a hand heavy with diamond rings. 'I'm fine, dear. Now where on earth has Katie got to? It's high time I left.'

Beth agreed. She needed to get on, too, though she was increasingly daunted by her investigation project. Judith Seasons had shown there was a tangle of generations involved, all probably – save for the grandchildren – with potential motives for bumping off the awful Jenkins.

And, if he really did have a career as some sort of spy behind him, there could be a whole bunch of oligarchs and assorted evil world leaders champing to get him as well. Though, surely this idea that he was an older, creepier Daniel Craig was madness? True, if he was ex-MI5, he'd need a convincing cover story. Maybe he was a brilliant actor. Beth considered it for a moment. No. She was sure she hadn't been imagining anything. Maybe he was more careful with family and friends. Or, could it just be that Judith, thirty years her senior, had different expectations of men – and a very rosy, not to say fanciful, view of Dr Jenkins? No doubt he'd loved drop-ping hints about his own importance – Beth could completely see him doing that, even if genuine involvement in spycraft was stretching it too far.

At that moment, they heard trainers on the stairs. Two seconds later, Katie bounded into the room, glowing with health and looking like her own best advertisement. Immediately, Judith Seasons' posh hairdo and careful yoga kit looked a little overdone.

'All sorted. Thanks so much for holding the fort, I really appreciate it.' Katie smiled widely at both women.

There was a polite mumble of 'not at alls' as Beth and Judith Seasons collected their belongings. Beth tried to be as quick as possible, so she could follow the older lady out, but by the time she'd changed shoes, the downstairs door was clanging shut on Judith's retreating form. No prizes for guessing that Judith was extremely glad to get away from her questions.

'Did you get anywhere?' asked Katie.

'You're amazing, Katie, thanks so much. That couldn't have been better organised if we'd planned for weeks. I'm a little bit further. You won't believe this, but I really think that Judith and the horrible Dr Jenkins could have been an item.'

'No! The perv? And my lovely Judith? Are you sure?'

'Well, she didn't admit anything, but there was an under-current...'

Beth was still wondering what on earth Judith Seasons saw in Alan Jenkins later that evening, as she sat with Jake at the scrubbed kitchen table. Supper had been cleared away, Jake had been dragged through his homework, and it was the time of day when they usually played a card game together before the bedtime routine kicked in. Tonight, as a special concession for well-memorised spellings, Beth was allowing Jake extra screen time. Little did he know that this was because she was desperate to get online herself. She needed to do some serious digging into the life and times of Dr Alan Jenkins.

There was something horrifying about the ease with which you could find stuff out these days, she thought, as she rapidly compiled a dossier of hard facts to add to all the speculation and wild surmises she'd been making. Once life had revolved around tiny communities, where everyone had known each other's business. Now, no one had any idea who their neighbours were – unless they decided to delve. The internet was the modern village well. With a few persistent dips, and a lot of cross-referencing to make sure, you could find out anything about anybody.

It all boiled down to this: Jenkins was an Oxford graduate who'd had a long career as a civil servant before joining Wyatt's a few years before. Even James Bond would probably put 'civil servant' down as his job when he had to fill in an application for car insurance – unless Moneypenny did that for him – but Jenkins seemed to have eked out his own career in the relative safety of the Department of Education rather than in the wilder reaches of the security services.

Judith, if she ever decided to google him, was going to be very disappointed. That's not to say it hadn't been a distinguished career. He'd finished up with an OBE and then immediately fallen into the Wyatt's archive job. This was puzzling. Depending on what he'd actually done at the Department of Education for all those years, archive management seemed like a sideways move. But, as his children – and now grandchild – went to Wyatt's, he undoubtedly knew the school backwards.

It looked like a straightforward case of Dulwich influence. Jenkins had been friendly with the bursar's wife for years – presumably he was close to the bursar himself as well. It didn't take a genius to see how Jenkins had snaffled the Wyatt's job.

Beth went through the bath, bed and book routine on

autopilot, and thankfully Jake was tired and cooperative for once, without his usual million questions and bottomless bag of delaying tactics.

As she smoothed his dark hair and then turned out his light, Beth sighed. She couldn't complain about Dulwich influence herself. The only reason she and her boy were sitting pretty in their own little house in Pickwick Road – a stone's throw from Jake's primary and the endowment schools, and right behind the village itself – was because the estate agent was a friend of a friend and had tipped her the wink before the property hit the market. There was no way she could have afforded more than the asking price, had there been the usual Dulwich feeding frenzy.

These Pickwick Road houses, mostly three-bedroom properties (though a few had managed to cram in extra bedrooms with cunning loft conversions), were full of odd angles and tended to be pretty snug, but she loved hers. It was a sanctuary for her and Jake, and she didn't care if it was the scruffiest house in the road; which it was, by a long way. He had just enough space in the garden to kick a ball, if he didn't mind it bouncing straight back at him at high velocity; she had a spare room for her brother Josh's sporadic visits; and space enough to think and dream. It was everything they needed.

Probably her own job at Wyatt's had come about, indirectly, through Dulwich influence, too, she reasoned. Though she had no connection with anyone at Wyatt's now, and had gone to school herself in nearby Blackheath, her brother had been at Wyatt's and her mother, Wendy, was still living in Dulwich, playing Bridge with anyone who was anybody, which no doubt included a few endowment trustees. Anyone looking in at Beth from the outside would say that this south London apple had not fallen far from the tree.

In fact, Beth knew that few gales had blown through the orchard she was blessed to have grown in. If it had not been for the death of her beloved husband, James, seven years ago now, when Jake was a rambunctious toddler, she would have had the cushiest life ever.

James, James, she reflected. If Mrs Jenkins was feeling a tenth of her sorrow, now, then Beth's heart truly went out to her. James had been so young and had so much to live for. She still shuddered at the thought that a few headaches and a dizzy spell or two had led so rapidly to his death in a hospice. If only he'd been a bit more of a moaner. If only she had been on the case. If she'd just googled his symptoms straight away... Who knew a brain tumour could hide its terrible, aggressive strength for so long under such a weedy bunch of ailments?

But what-ifs were worse than useless. They robbed her of perilously acquired serenity and acceptance, and robbed Jake of the stable, emotionally balanced mother he needed. If you only had one parent, it had to be a good one.

Thoughts of James coloured Beth's world in bittersweet hues and, though her sleep was not too disturbed, she was glad to shake off the duvet in the morning and leap – or stagger, perhaps more accurately – into a new day.

It wasn't until she was trailing back home from dropping Jake at school, planning to spend the next few hours on her other neglected writing projects, that she suddenly stopped dead in her tracks. The bursar. He had a motive. If Judith Seasons had been having an affair with Dr Jenkins, then Tom Seasons, Wyatt's dependable, reliable, jovial bursar, had an excellent reason to stab him.

It was the first time Beth had come up with a decent motive for the killing. Tangled tales of MI5, oligarchs and a huge extended family fell away when set next to an easy explanation like jealousy. All right, certain parts of her theory were still so flimsy as to be positively diaphanous – she had no real idea whether Judith was sleeping with Dr Jenkins; it was just her intuition jangling. And she also had no clue at all whether Tom

Seasons was the psychotically jealous type. Again, she'd only met him briefly at her job interview, where he'd been as nice as pie, in a steely sort of way. He'd asked searching questions, he'd listened politely to her answers and, ultimately, he'd given her the job. He'd even asked her, at the end of the session, whether she had any questions to ask. She was kicking herself, now, that it had never once occurred to her to ask whether he ever felt a red mist descending, or whether he was unhealthily fixated on faithfulness in a long marriage. Her lame query about car parking permits just didn't cut the mustard at all.

Mustard. That made her think, again, of Jenkins' tweed. If she hadn't been the one to find the body, would she have felt such a deep connection to the whole business? But she still would have been horrified that violent death had been so close, without her knowing until she'd stumbled across it. That made her wonder what would have happened if she had left the office earlier that day and run across the murderer herself. Would she have been the one to get stabbed, instead of Jenkins?

The idea sent shivers down her spine, but it only made sense if it was a random murder, a madman roaming the playground searching for a victim. That didn't seem to be the Wyatt's way. Everything in the school was thought-through, and this murder seemed that way, too.

If it was personal all along and Jenkins was the intended victim, would she have been killed anyway, just because she was in the wrong place at the wrong time? It was terrifying, and the underlying cause for all her uneasiness. She just had to find the murderer as quickly as possible. Jake could have been orphaned that day. Beth knew her brother and her mother would do their best to fill the void for Jake if anything did happen to her, but she had a duty to look after herself, for his sake. The murderer was still out there – and she could be in danger.

That, and the fact she was without an alibi for the crucial

times, had to drive her on. A prison sentence could take her away from Jake almost as effectively as the murderer could.

If she had died in that playground, either with Jenkins or instead of him, there would have been another suspect, though. Someone else would eventually have stumbled across them. Who else had been around? No one, when she virtually tripped over the corpse. The dinner lady and the gap-year student – but they had popped up a safe few minutes after she had. But, yes, she had seen Dr Grover just *before* she'd made her grim find. She'd run right into him. What had he been doing there? As headmaster, he had a right to prowl the playground as freely as he liked, but she didn't believe he had time for aimless wandering. The more she thought about it, the odder it suddenly seemed that he'd turned up there, of all places, just before her macabre discovery. And the flash of hot pink in the distance – Janice, surely, in that delectable cashmere sweater?

Had she even mentioned these two facts to the policeman, Harry York? She wasn't sure. And they might be crucial. She fumbled around for the card York had given her. But, like everything in this house, from Jake's homework to her own front door keys, it vaporised as soon as she started to look for it. Having patted down all her coats and peered in vain through the stack of newspapers – overdue for recycling; a sign in itself that she was slipping from her normal OCD-esque standards of housewifely efficiency – she couldn't find it anywhere.

She brushed her fringe resolutely to one side. It sprang back, masking those clever grey eyes.

She smiled faintly. There was only one thing to be done.

FOUR

The mighty gates of Wyatt's were technically closed again today – but just to pupils, surely? The headmaster and the bursar were bound to be on site, and so Beth could be there, too. Ostensibly she would be offering her support and getting on with her job. But, while going through the motions of being a helpful new broom, she could try and find out whether Seasons had been anywhere near the back playground at the right time on Monday. She could also establish exactly why the head-master and the school secretary had been milling around just before she'd found the body. And if she didn't manage to get any further with her own investigations, she could mention the whole thing to Inspector York, in the hope that he could take it further.

With all the might at his disposal – loads of constables, plenty of vehicles with flashing lights, SOCO folk with white suits, and so on – he'd be able to get at the truth.

The trouble was that the thought of going back to the little archive office – so close to those bins – was horrible, to say the least. Perhaps she could just hang out in the main reception area, with other people safely around, and see what she could glean. All right, it was a little sketchy around the edges, but it was definitely a plan. Sort of. She was nearly home from Jake's school already, but she turned round sharply and marched all the way to the gates of Wyatt's before too many shards of doubt could creep in.

There was a constable on duty at the gates, but Beth saw with a flash of pleased recognition that it was the one who'd originally questioned her. She smiled and he opened the gate for her.

'Expecting you, are they, miss?' he asked. She opened her mouth to tell a whopping lie, then luckily his radio crackled into life and she got away with just a wave.

The grass in front of the school was as smooth and green as a billiard table, and Monday's battery of emergency vehicles had been resolved into a single police car. The headmaster's sleek silver Volvo was in its usual reserved spot, right by the door. It was the perfect choice for Dr Grover. Outwardly discreet and reliable, it was also eye-wateringly expensive and luxurious – like his ties – and it cunningly referenced those wonderful Scandiwegian detective drama series that Dulwich parents tended to get addicted to. All too appropriate at the moment.

Acutely conscious that her constable friend might well be watching, Beth plunged forward through the main front door to reception and its reassuring hub, Janice.

Any building which usually accommodates hordes of bodies seems to teem with silence when empty. The Wyatt's entrance hall, always imposing, positively dwarfed Beth today. The place echoed at every step. An abandoned school bag was lying in the corridor, spilling books. She stooped to pick it up, stuff the books back in. Suddenly, a bell shrilled out of nowhere and made her jump a mile. It was just the pre-programmed signal for the end of a period, she realised, when her thudding heartbeat returned to normal. Did someone want the reassurance of routine, even in these most un-routine times?

As the bell died away, Beth heard raised voices. Rounding the corner into reception, she saw Janice and Dr Grover, both red-faced and angry. The reception desk between them seemed to be the only thing stopping them from coming to blows. They both turned to her, and she felt their fury redirect itself at her.

'Sorry, I just found this bag in the hallway, thought I'd bring it in... Its owner will miss it when school gets restarted...'

Both of them looked sceptical, and Beth could hardly blame them. It was beyond the bounds of credibility that she'd take it upon herself to come in from home just to act as an impromptu lost property monitor. She bumped up her excuse. 'And I wanted to see what I could do to help today. I am part of the staff now, after all. This must be such a difficult, awful time...'

'That's very thoughtful, but the school is closed today. The best thing you can do is go home, let the police do their job and sort this thing out as soon as possible,' said Dr Grover, switching effortlessly from beetroot crossness to his usual ebullient charm.

'Well, actually,' said Janice, looking at Grover through narrowed eyes, '*I* could really do with some help. The phones are ringing off their hooks and no one else has thought to offer any sort of back-up.' On cue, her mobile started to trill and Beth heard another, more distant ringing start up in the back office.

'That's no problem at all, happy to help,' said Beth. 'As long as it's fine with Dr Grover?' she said quickly, remembering who was employing whom.

Dr Grover gave her a brief smile and then flicked a look at Janice, who was suddenly ostentatiously busy with her phone. 'Of course, of course. I must be getting on,' he said, turning on his heel. If he'd been a less imposing figure, Beth would have said he flounced out. She raised her eyebrows at Janice.

'We're all a bit emotional, I'm afraid,' Janice said. 'It's been a very difficult few days. It's an absolute tragedy for the school. And for Dr Jenkins' family, of course,' she added.

'It must have been really tough on you,' said Beth. Secretly, she thought it had been a whole lot tougher on the archivist, his family, and even herself as the official corpse finder, but she wanted to get into Janice's good books. Janice was the font of all wisdom – and unless Beth was way off course, there was something up between her and the headmaster. She'd just interrupted a massive tiff. It seemed a lot more passionate than any falling-out over supplies of paperclips or forgotten memos ought to have been, even under the current stressful conditions.

Could it have been an assignation that had brought them both to that out-of-the-way spot behind the sixth form block on the fateful day at around noon? She could see a large diamond-studded wedding band on Janice's finger, and Dr Grover was famously married to a willowy actress – the only factor that kept most of Dulwich's divorcees at bay. But when had being married ever stopped people? True, if it ever got out, there would be a fuss; not least from the disappointed divorcees. This was a potential scandal, but was it a motive? Beth thought probably not. Wyatt's wasn't a church school, after all.

Nevertheless, Beth smiled sympathetically at Janice, hoping she'd want to unburden herself. For a second, she thought it might work. Janice gave her a tremulous glance. Then her phone bleeped imperiously. The eye contact was broken. Janice prodded at a few keys.

'Oh God,' she said. 'It's that same mother again, texting this time. She's left three messages already. She's beside herself; I must get back to her.' She sounded a little choked, and Beth had an ignominious hope that she'd still crack, sob the whole story out on her shoulder, then ring the mother back later. But Janice was made of sterner stuff. She swallowed, then pinned her professional smile back firmly in place. 'If you wouldn't mind answering the phones in the office, I'll just ring this lady right back. We're just saying, there's no danger to the pupils, the police are near to sorting everything out, and the school will be reopened as soon as possible.'

'Really? Are the police close to finding whoever... did it?'

Janice sighed. 'Seriously? I have no idea. They're not telling us... me... anything. We don't even know yet officially that it was murder. As you can imagine, the parents are going nuts. But we're Wyatt's. It's under control; it's going to be fine. No, it actually IS fine. *Everything Is Fine.* That's your mantra.'

Beth smiled, then took herself off to the small back office. She picked up the nearest phone while settling herself in a chair. 'Good morning, Wyatt's?' she answered calmly.

Over an hour later, after talking in reassuring tones to what seemed like the full one thousand anxious mothers, Beth got her reward. Tom Seasons, the bursar, strolled into reception. She remembered him from her interview. Though only of middling height, his burly former rugby player's physique had felt intimidating as they'd sat politely round the small table discussing record-keeping. He was still exuding that same impression of scarcely contained force now. Resting a meaty forearm on Janice's shiny countertop, he leant forward to chat. His shirt and tie were rumpled, as though he'd prefer to have been in a rugby jersey, getting stuck into a scrum. Though Beth could see him clearly from her vantage point, peering over the top of a state-of-the-art widescreen Mac, Seasons didn't seem aware of her presence at all.

'Busy morning, Jan?' he asked, his slightly battered good looks crumpled into a worried smile, his fingers tapping the walnut surface restlessly.

'You can say that again,' she said, sighing. 'What's the situation for you?'

'It's highly concerning,' he said, ramping up the tapping.

Beth, behind her computer, winced involuntarily. She hated it when perfectly good words were distorted for no good reason.

But she mustn't become irrationally prejudiced against the bursar, just because he tortured the English language.

Meanwhile, he carried on self-importantly. 'We need to get this wrapped up as soon as possible, get open, back on a level playing field. It's not good for the school, or for any of us. You won't believe this,' he said, suddenly bending even closer to Janice.

'What?' She was agog – and so was Beth, straining to hear behind her Mac.

'I've had two parents this morning pulling their children out.'

Beth relaxed. While undoubtedly serious for Wyatt's, this was not the kind of revelation she was interested in. Janice, however, was outraged.

'No! That's ridiculous! That's such an overreaction. Why would they even do that?'

'Well, nerves. Their precious children, the possibility that a homicidal madman is prowling the playground...'

'But that's crazy, it isn't like that at all...'

'*I* know that. *You* know that. But the parents don't know Jenkins was a grade one bastard who was begging to get stabbed, do they?' said Seasons viciously.

Beth, who'd been holding her breath, dropped her pen with a clatter. Janice simultaneously breathed out a warning. 'Tom!' Seasons immediately looked over Janice's shoulder for the first time. Beth obligingly poked her head out from behind the Mac. Her cover was blown.

'Oh, it's... er, Beth, isn't it?' he said blandly, darting a furious look back at Janice. 'What are you doing in today?'

Beth smiled, and was about to answer, but just then the phone rang again. 'Wyatt's, how can I help you?' she said smoothly. Just as she'd hoped, Seasons' attention was diverted back to Janice.

'Does she know anything?' he said softly.

Beth, unpardonably inattentive to the worried parent on the end of the line, strained for Janice's response, but couldn't hear a word. Seasons ambled off, ostentatiously raising a hand to her in farewell. She ducked her head down automatically, too late, and then wished she'd insouciantly waved back. Now he knew she'd been watching him. Oh well. She turned her attention back to the mother on the line, and did the best she could to reassure her that her son was in absolutely no danger – though she wasn't that sure she believed it herself.

It wasn't until lunchtime, umpteen calls later, that Janice took pity on Beth. 'Look, let's get away from the phones for a while and get something to eat. You're looking shattered – and I definitely need a break,' she said. She switched the answering machines on and they left reception, Janice locking the door behind her. 'Everyone's got pass keys, but you can't be too careful at the moment,' she said.   ·

'Are you scared?' Beth said, as they entered the staff canteen. It was eerily deserted, as she might have expected, but there were covered trays of sandwiches left out for the skeleton staff working today, along with a Thermos each of coffee and tea and jugs of orange juice, with bottles of water in the chiller. There was a basket of fruit and some packets of crisps and snacks laid out on the central table. You could never accuse Wyatt's of being unprepared. It was as though elves had left them a little feast, and then vanished, thought Beth.

Janice shrugged a little listlessly, and they browsed for a while, making their selections. Beth hoped Janice wasn't going to be professionally tight-lipped. Here she was, tête-à-tête with the person who knew more about the school than anybody else. It was the perfect opportunity to get somewhere at last. Plus, frankly, Beth genuinely did find it frightening, rattling around in this huge place, just the two of them. The head, the bursar and a bunch of police must be tucked away somewhere, but they were not making their presence felt. She looked expectantly at Janice.

'Well...' said the other woman reluctantly. 'Yes, it does all feel very odd. Alan's been... well... killed. Right here. I'd known him for years. And no one's been arrested... yet. It's surreal.' Janice shook her head a little.

'Who do you think it was?' said Beth, in little more than a whisper. It was absurd, but she looked around her even though she knew there was no one else there. But the shutters were coming down on Janice's normally friendly face.

'We don't know yet whether it was even murder, maybe it was a heart attack, some sort of accident—'

'Oh, come on,' Beth broke in. 'I saw the body, remember? That was no accident, unless he fell face-forward onto a knife, then rolled onto his back and covered up his own face himself before dying.'

Janice looked at Beth in fascinated horror. 'Is that...?'

'Sorry, I probably shouldn't have said anything,' said Beth, contrite. She really hadn't meant to come out with all of that. It was just that she'd spent the morning trying to airbrush the situation for the sake of the parents. She couldn't stand there pretending to Janice as well. There had to be some honesty about what had happened, didn't there?

But she was conscious that Inspector York had told her to keep the circumstances of the death to herself, and she hadn't wanted to shock poor Janice either; the school secretary had known Jenkins for years, and might have been fond of him. You never knew. She did hope that her indiscretion, now it was out there, might tempt Janice into some reciprocal confidences. She let the silence lengthen, allowing Janice to make up her own mind about what she would and wouldn't say. It was an old journalistic trick. Some people found silence so uncomfortable that they would rush to fill it – saying more than they had bargained for.

'The thing is,' said Janice, after a brief struggle with herself, 'Alan wasn't a particularly popular member of staff. Well, not with any of his women colleagues,' she added, giving Beth a meaningful look.

So much for being fond of the man, thought Beth. 'You mean the, er, leering thing?' she suggested tentatively.

'So, he had started that with you.' It wasn't a question. Janice didn't seem at all surprised.

'Well, he didn't do it so much in the interview, or I wasn't *that* conscious of it then. It was only when I saw him on Monday... Even then, we were only together for a few minutes really, but let's just say that I *was* completely aware of it that time.'

'Yes,' said Janice heavily. 'It was such a pain. Well, some people found it more than a pain. Luckily, he was stuck out in that shed most of the time... sorry, I mean the archives office.' She smiled. 'So, he didn't get much chance to annoy people. But, of course, he was around at lunchtime and so on... It was mainly the younger girls who just couldn't stand it; women his own age maybe gave him the benefit of the doubt. Times have changed. And I tend to hear all the moans. Everyone complains about everything to me.' Janice was now unmistakably glum.

'Well, no one will be whingeing about him any more, that's for sure,' said Beth. 'You don't think any of the people he'd hit on would actually *stab* him, though, do you?'

'I'd seriously doubt it,' said Janice. 'No. People just used to avoid him. It's not like anyone had to be stuck with him, when they could just walk away. Honestly, he could clear a room in seconds flat.'

'Of course, I *would* have been stuck with him... in the *shed*,' mused Beth. It was another awful thought. Not only was she the one to have found the body, not only was she alibi-free, but now she actually had a pretty strong motive – one every woman working at Wyatt's would be able to point out to the police. 'I'm basically going to be the number one suspect.'

Janice looked sympathetically at Beth. 'Come on. You'd only just arrived; you didn't have time to hate him yet. It's probably something entirely different, if it really was murder anyway.' She seemed to be trying her best to slip back into the undoubted comforts of denial, before remembering she'd just been told in no uncertain terms that it definitely was a suspicious death. She wasn't spinning the situation for the parents now. She met Beth's eyes.

'All right, it *was* murder. But maybe it was... oh, I don't know, some random mad person who'd got into the premises? Though that wouldn't be good for the school either. I mean, we don't want anyone to think that we could have one of those awful US-style massacres here. Maybe it was someone from his past *before* he joined the staff.' Poor Janice was scurrying around for an explanation that didn't involve Wyatt's. But, given that he was a Wyatt's employee who'd been murdered on Wyatt's premises during a Wyatt's school day, she was having trouble.

'Did any of the men dislike him? They'd be more likely to be violent, wouldn't they?' Beth was trying to inch Janice round to a discussion of the bursar, who, judging from the word he'd used to describe Jenkins, was not a fan. But the other woman instinctively recoiled from anything that might reflect badly on Wyatt's, determinedly reinterpreting Beth's suggestion.

'Mmm, you mean a casual labourer? Or a kitchen supplier?' she said, brightening up considerably. This was the perfect solution – someone who hadn't breached the defences designed to keep the Wyatt's children safe, and wasn't part of the inner sanctum either. A hired hand who could well be mad, bad or dangerous to know, without besmirching Wyatt's recruitment policies.

Beth sighed. 'Why would they stab Jenkins, though? Don't

they say victims usually know their killer? The bursar didn't seem to have any problem thinking someone had a reason to kill Jenkins, did he?'

One look at Janice's suddenly blank face showed how hard Beth was going to have to work to get her to discuss the bursar's fruity language, let alone the possibility of a perpetrator with a motive other than mental illness.

'I suppose we have to remember it wouldn't be right to cover anything up, just for the sake of the school's reputation, would it? There is such a thing as justice?' Beth tried.

Janice nodded, but it was clear she was unconvinced. Abstract notions came a poor second to the interests of Wyatt's. 'I think Jenkins was probably just in the wrong place, at the wrong time.'

'Talking of timing, I actually bumped into Dr Grover just before I found... Dr Jenkins,' said Beth, a little tentatively.

'Oh, did you?' said Janice blandly. 'He's amazing, isn't he? Such a brilliant head, so inspiring. Probably wanted to check you were doing all right on your first day,' she said.

Beth smiled politely, marvelling at Janice's diplomacy. She'd been yelling at Dr Grover just a couple of hours ago, not showing the faintest sign of finding him amazing. 'And I thought I saw *you* just before I saw him,' she continued.

'Oh, maybe, I'm always pottering about somewhere, running errands, for my sins,' said Janice airily. Hmm, thought Beth. Which of your sins exactly? But, short of getting out the thumb screws, she couldn't see how to push this further.

She resigned herself to getting nowhere and set about her delicious sandwich instead. Say what you like about Wyatt's, they did make a lovely lunch.

FIVE

By the time school reopened on Thursday, Beth felt that she was an old Wyatt's hand. Nothing fazed her any more about the place – buildings, children, or even the parents milling around the grand entrance gates. Thank goodness, there was no sign of reporters anywhere in the village now. 'Murder at posh school' had dominated the headlines for a couple of days, but terrorists in Europe and a Tory minister entangled with a dominatrix had hit the news since. And in the fickle world of the media, new stories trumped old every time, particularly when developments stubbornly refused to occur.

Beth had left work shortly after her rather fruitless lunch yesterday, and had immediately been plunged into Jake-world. There hadn't been a minute during the usual treadmill of home-work-supper-bed, and by the time all that was done and she had polished off a bit of neglected bread-and-butter work for her other clients, her own bed was calling her relentlessly. She now felt the weight of unshared information dragging her conscience to the ground. She needed to see Detective Inspector York and tell him about Dr Grover and Janice. She wasn't sure if she needed to tell him about her indiscretion yesterday over the cause of Dr Jenkins' death, though. She'd play that by ear.

Her businesslike stride across the playground faltered a bit as she spotted the bursar charging towards her across the netball courts with an old rugby player's determination. He was still number one suspect in her book, and she hadn't forgotten the visceral loathing with which he'd spoken of Jenkins yesterday. She managed a watery grin, though, and he smiled heartily in return.

'Ah, Beth, glad I caught you,' he said. 'Just wanted to say, there'll be a staff meeting at lunchtime. Just to run over a few of the issues brought up by... recent events.' She looked into his slightly bloodshot blue eyes but he appeared quite nonchalant about equating grisly murder with the resolutely bland word 'events'. 'There'll be sandwiches, of course,' he added as he swerved away, as though that made it all right.

The one thing that worried Beth about going back to work, really worried her, was passing the spot where she'd found Dr Jenkins. But, as she came near, she realised nothing lacked an aura of menace like a well-tended children's playground. There was no scene-of-crime tape anywhere, and the bins had been relocated to some other distant corner of the extensive grounds. There was not a drop of blood in sight, thank goodness. The place looked utterly nondescript. In fact, if she hadn't been pretty sure the crime had been committed within a stone's throw of the back of the archive building, she couldn't even have sworn she recognised the spot.

In a way, it was pitiful that such a significant event could be effaced so effortlessly. There was no lingering atmosphere at all, no Jack the Ripper-like sense of dread enveloping the chain-link fence, the smooth grey tarmac, and the playing fields stretching out, beautifully green and flat, beyond. Good, she decided, and turned away to find the archive door pass. She jumped a mile as a hand descended on her shoulder.

'Jesus,' she said, clutching her throat. Her handbag crashed to the ground, scattering possessions far and wide.

'Here, let me,' said Inspector York, bending to help. He was wearing dark chinos and a navy linen jacket today, all the better to blend in with the smartly dressed teachers, she supposed. His soft-soled shoes explained why she hadn't heard him coming up behind her. Scary, given the murder. She definitely needed to be more aware.

She immediately dropped to her knees, scrabbling for her scattered things, knowing there'd be horrors she didn't want on display. Sure enough, as well as a confetti of crumpled tissues and till receipts, he passed her a shaming jumble of Twix wrappers and shrapnel-hard Haribo.

'Kids,' she said, trying to make a joke of it. He raised his eyebrows.

'Could we have a word inside?' he asked.

Her hand shook a tiny bit as she swiped her card, and she led on silently through the storeroom and up the ringing metal stairs. She fished out her key and got the door unlocked on her second go.

The small office smelt more strongly than ever of paper. And if there had been no trace of Jenkins outside, here – in what had so recently been his domain – his presence was everywhere. An old jacket swung from the hook on the back of the door, the mouldering apple core she'd spotted on his desk so long ago – *was it really only on Monday?* – was busily composting itself, and the whole masculine, neglected air of the room screamed of Jenkins. His computer had been taken away and there was a film of fingerprinting dust over everything, including the apple core.

She was relieved to see her own laptop was still in place, though there was powder over that too. She gazed about her, trying to work out what else had changed, if anything. She didn't know the room well enough to be sure. The towering piles of papers and boxes of folders looked much the same as when she had last seen them, but she had the vague sense that something was missing.

In some ways, having a second person in the small office did a lot to dilute reminders of Jenkins. It also made Beth all the more aware of the inspector's height and muscular presence. She supposed policemen had to be fit, for chasing people and so on, but there was no need for him to be *this* large, she thought illogically. He was making her feel very small and also very out of shape. Once they were both seated – she taking Dr Jenkins' larger chair, because it was closer and she didn't want to edge past him in this confined space; the policeman perching incongruously on the little typist's chair, its castors creaking in protest – there didn't seem to be room to breathe.

Beth looked expectantly at York.

'Look, we've been through the initial stages of the enquiry. As you can see, we're checking Dr Jenkins' computer. Now, you had only just started here, hadn't you?'

Beth nodded.

'We felt on balance there was no need to take your laptop away. Our tech guys had a look and it seems clean.'

Beth wasn't surprised. She hadn't been in the job long enough to work out how to bypass the school's firewalls and break out into the internet, though she suspected every teenager in Wyatt's could do it in seconds. On Monday, she had just been pootling around on the school's intranet, which couldn't have been more anodyne, while trying to work out what on earth she was supposed to be doing. The poor IT worker who'd had to check on her browsing history, used to a diet of extreme porn and terrorism, must have died of boredom exposed to the term's cricket fixtures.

Finding out what her job entailed, though, was going to become much more of a problem, now that she was the school's only archivist and had no one to tell her what was needed. She was going to have to make some big decisions. On her own. It was actually going to be fun. She would genuinely be gaining quite a lot from Jenkins' death. Unless, of course, the school decided she was woefully underqualified for the job and got someone else in.

'Did you happen to get a glimpse of Jenkins' working methods? See the kind of sites he was accessing?' York brought her back to the matter in hand.

Beth was surprised. 'I told you. He didn't even come into the office with me. He just unlocked the door, gave me the spare key, and that was it. That was the last I saw of him – until, erm, later. He didn't explain what I was supposed to do, or how I was supposed to do it.'

York and Beth silently glanced around at the wall of boxes bearing down on the space. 'This must be pretty daunting,' York conceded.

'Well, it is, to tell the truth,' said Beth. 'But it's quite... an opportunity, I suppose you could say. I'm hoping to talk to the bursar about it later. He was involved in the interview process, so I'm thinking that may well mean he knows what I'm actually here for,' she said wryly.

'There's plenty of stuff to sort through, isn't there? I suppose I'm asking you to flag up to me if you find anything you think might be... relevant,' said the inspector.

'Relevant? To the murder? You think the motive might be here somewhere?' Beth looked around her again. She picked a stapler up from the desk, absently brushed the fingerprinting powder off, and started to fiddle with it. It was an alarming thought that the key to the murder could be lurking here, not least because it was going to take her a long time – who knew how long? – to unearth everything concealed in these boxes. But it was most certainly in her interests to find anything at all that hinted at a reason why Jenkins had to die. After all, if she couldn't offer the police an alternative, and if they didn't stumble across anything themselves, they were left with her as the most obvious candidate for the unwanted role of killer. She clacked the stapler open and shut while her mind raced.

* * *

York looked at Beth, reached over and took the stapler out of her hand. He could do without that clicking while he was trying to think. You didn't have to be a mind-reader to see the woman was worried. Her nails were bitten. And her bag had been full of the kind of junk wrappers which indicated someone too anxious to eat properly. It was quite possible that she thought they were going to arrest her at any second. But looking at the situation objectively, she had hardly been in the place five minutes, and there were no immediate indications that she'd known the victim beforehand.

True, she could be an opportunist psychopath. Or she could be a stalker, and they might be about to find that her bedroom wall was papered with covert shots of Jenkins she'd snatched with a long lens – but York doubted it. That reminded him: he'd better ask if they could pop round to her house. This afternoon right after work would be ideal, giving her less of an opportunity to rip down the shrine before they got there, he thought, smiling to himself.

York carried on, as he sometimes did on a case, dreaming up possible motives. Maybe she could have engineered all this, the job, the proximity, in order to bump off Jenkins for some reason lodged deep in both their pasts. But it was a bit baroque. It must be clear to her, and everyone else, that so far the police didn't even have a ribbon of evidence, let alone enough rope to fashion a decent net.

She might just, quite sensibly, be twanging with anxiety because there was a killer around and it *wasn't* her. He'd post a constable round the back here, near where those damn bins had been, he decided. She was a bit off the beaten track in this archives shed, or whatever they called it, and until they knew what the hell was going on he didn't want to take any chances. He didn't want the only observant and helpful person he'd met so far in this stupidly plush school to come to a sticky end. It wasn't chivalry, he told himself, looking at the small figure, anxious eyes peeping back at him from behind her long fringe. It was expediency.

Beth, meanwhile, was noticing that she hadn't been corrected when she used the word 'murder'. 'So, it's definite now, is it? Dr Jenkins was actually murdered?'

York inclined his head. 'Yes, it's officially a murder enquiry. OK, I'm going to leave you to it now, but here's my card,' he said abruptly, getting to his feet and trying to stretch a bit. His legs felt cramped, thanks to the folding chair. 'I want you to call me if you remember anything that might be useful, or if you find anything I need to know about.'

'That reminds me' – Beth shifted uncomfortably on her seat like an anxious schoolgirl – 'I keep meaning to mention the fact that I saw two people, well, maybe two but definitely one, just before I, er, came across Dr Jenkins.'

'Really?' said York, sitting back down heavily on the flimsy chair, which creaked even more ominously. 'Why didn't you say before? Tell me who you saw.' His tone was sharp and he leant forward impatiently.

'I'm really sorry, it went right out of my head after everything... well, you know.' She looked more anxious than ever, her cheeks faintly flushed.

'Look, don't worry. It's good that you've remembered now. Just tell me everything, right from the beginning.' Beth darted a look at him and he smiled reassuringly, while inwardly sighing that he was going to be held up here when there was so much else he needed to get to. Nothing for it, though.

'Well, it was when I'd decided to leave the office. As I've

said, it was around lunchtime, I was hungry and I needed...
well, the loo. Strange how that went completely out of my head
when I found the, the body,' said Beth. 'I was just outside the
office here, and I was sort of wandering around trying to get my
bearings. It's a big school and my first day, as you know, so I
wasn't completely sure which way reception even was. I don't
have the best sense of direction,' she confided. York smiled reassuringly at her. 'I'd been walking for about five minutes, vaguely
in the direction of the, you know, *bins*, when I came round a
corner and ran right into him.'

'Who? Dr Jenkins?' said York.

'No. Dr Grover.'

'The headmaster?' York was surprised. 'Did he speak to
you? How did he seem?'

'Oh, he was, you know, fine. A bit rushed... He'd nearly
knocked me over, barrelling round the corner, and then he
almost fell himself. It was a bit... awkward. After that, he just
wished me luck on my first day, stuff like that. He even remembered my name,' said Beth, still impressed at the memory, her
shy, pretty face flushing a little.

I bet he did, thought York a touch sourly. 'What was his
manner, though?' he asked. 'Did he appear agitated? Breathless?
Sweaty?' He just managed to stop himself from asking if the
man smelt, and tried to get his subconscious under control.
However annoying he might suddenly find the debonair headmaster, he had to remain rigidly professional. 'Anything else at
all you can remember?'

'Well...' Beth cast her mind back. 'It was only a few days
ago, but it was what happened *next* that I remember. I knew I
should mention to you that I'd seen Dr Grover but it really
didn't seem hugely significant... though I remember being a
little bit surprised that he was in the playground at all. He must
be so busy, and it was lunchtime, as I said. I suppose I imagine

he's always hobnobbing with school governors or having really high-level meetings, not rushing around near the playing fields.'

'You're sure he was rushing?' York asked.

'I think he must have been; we both were, otherwise we wouldn't have both been so winded when we ran into each other. Oh, and before I forget, I think I saw Janice just before that.'

'Janice, the school secretary? What on earth was she doing there?'

'Well, I'm less sure I really saw her. It was just a flash of the really bright fuchsia pink colour that she was wearing that day, in the distance.'

'In the distance? Could you say where exactly?'

'I think it was over by the Languages department, but it was just for a second,' said Beth. She seemed unsure, looking at his expressionless face, whether the information was relevant or not. 'I hope I haven't wasted your time with all that,' she added.

'No, no, course not. No information is ever wasted in this sort of enquiry. Thank you. And if you think of anything else, you've got my card,' he said.

'Um, yes,' she said, searching fruitlessly on the desktop.

He handed her another with a sigh, wondering how she could have lost it in such a short time. She wasn't the only one. He got through boxes of cards every year. Just as well he kept being promoted, so they were constantly being reprinted.

'And good luck with... all this,' he said, taking a last look at her cluttered workspace as he exited. 'Oh, this is yours, I think,' he said, turning back to place the stapler carefully back on her desk. It would never do for the police to start filching office supplies. And it looked as though she needed all the equipment she could get to do this job.

* * *

Beth, alone now with the entire contents of the Wyatt's archive, looked about her, too. Where on earth should she start? It was hard to get motivated, especially with so much on her mind that was nothing to do with the archives at all. Had she done the right thing, mentioning Dr Grover? She felt a little stab of guilt, particularly at having said she might have seen Janice. She didn't want to get the woman who was rapidly becoming her best, no, *only* friend at Wyatt's, into trouble.

Eventually, she decided that tackling the archives would be preferable to worrying about the murder. It didn't take long to work out that the shelves were groaning with a vaguely chrono-logical selection of school publications, dating back to its earliest days. These would be easy enough to sort and prune. The boxes, though, were altogether more of a mystery. She pulled out the nearest one, extracted a wodge of documents, and settled down to read.

Outside, a PC took up position by the playing field fence and prepared for a very long shift, guarding what looked like, to his expert eye, an old metal shack. His colleagues were already joshing him over the police radio but, as far as he was concerned, it could be worse. It was another beautiful spring day and the deep green of the playing fields was studded with yelling figures playing rugby. All right, it wasn't Twickenham, where he spent every weekend when he wasn't working over-time on some case or other. But some of these schoolkids had promise. Knowing Wyatt's, they could be the England squad of the future. Yeah, could be a lot worse.

'All right, all right, let's come to order now,' said the bursar in ringing tones. Immediately the hubbub in the staff canteen died away and all eyes turned to Tom Seasons, standing before them in his customary rumpled white shirt, sleeves pushed up over his mighty forearms. His legs were planted stockily apart and he effortlessly dominated the room. Beth, who'd arrived just in time, recognised the stance – Henry VIII, as painted by Holbein.

Beth surreptitiously wiped a cobweb or two off her jeans. She scanned the room for a friendly face, and was relieved to spot Janice at the back. She raised her hand and got a tiny wave in return. Joining this enormous place was just like starting back at school again herself. There was the same pressure to get to grips with a whole bunch of arcane rules in no time at all, and, above all, to fit in and make friends.

'Now, I'm not proposing to keep many of you from your delicious lunches,' said the bursar, with a flash of heavy charm. 'The junior school staff are not involved in this – the police have established that no one came through the gates separating the two schools at the times in, erm, question.' There was an audible sigh of relief from a cluster of teachers to Beth's right, but Seasons was carrying on.

'As far as the senior school goes, I only need to trouble those of you who were in school for any period of time on Monday before one o'clock. I'd also like to see our middle school head, Alison Lincoln; our admissions guru, Susannah Baggs; and Janice, of course. I think that's about it. Oh, no, our new archivist as well, please. Beth Haldane.'

Beth, sensing the curious glances all around her, followed Janice and a handful of others she hadn't met before over to where Seasons was standing. It was a surprisingly small group.

'It was a field day on Monday,' said Janice in a low voice, seeing Beth looking back at the much larger contingent of teachers who were now busily getting on with their lunches, laughing and joking in obvious relief at escaping whatever the bursar was planning. It seemed a little unfair.

'A field day?' said Beth blankly.

'Yes, remember, I mentioned it when you first came to reception on Monday? No? Well, you wouldn't, I suppose, under the circumstances. It's a Wyatt's thing,' explained Janice. 'Instead of having various trips for different classes and subjects throughout the term, we have one day when most of the years go on organised days out. It just happened to fall on Monday. A lot of the heads of department were out supervising. The sixth form wasn't included, of course. Too close to exams. So, they were in school as normal.'

That was probably why Beth remembered so many strapping teenagers from Monday morning. There had certainly seemed to her to be enough kids around to constitute an entire schoolful, but then she wasn't yet used to the hustle and bustle of a busy secondary. It also occurred to her that, if you were a responsible murderer and were planning to stab someone on school property, you might choose a day when quite a lot of the pupils would be out of the way. Fewer children to terrify – and fewer potential witnesses too.

Beth looked around at the little group of her peers with interest. Unless she was mistaken, all seemed a tad nervous. No one had 'killer' written on their forehead. Damn it. It wasn't going to be easy to prove her innocence.

Tom Seasons took over again, shepherding everyone away from the now busy and noisy main hall off into a side room. Judging from the formal starched linen tablecloth at the large oval table and the framed oils on the wall, it was used for entertaining visiting speakers and VIPs.

'Let's settle ourselves down here and just chew over this business a little bit,' he said, making it sound like an invitation to a pleasant chat rather than a discussion of the brutal demise of one of their colleagues. He whisked a large linen cloth off silver trays of sandwiches in the middle of the table. 'As you can see, we won't starve to death,' he said, then coughed at the unfortunate phrase. When everyone had served themselves, Seasons looked around the table and Beth had to resist the urge to shrink from his gaze.

'Now, as you know, the police are still finishing off their questioning, and I just thought there were some areas we could usefully go over. Wyatt's, of course, is determined to cooperate fully with the investigation, and we must all offer every possible assistance to the police.'

Was it Beth's imagination, or was there a large 'but' looming somewhere?

Seasons carried on seamlessly. Despite his bruiser's build, he was an accomplished speaker, the veteran of many a parents' evening. 'The continuing success of Wyatt's, like any of the top-ranking schools, rests on its reputation. As you all know, we aim to combine academic achievement with a welcoming atmosphere...'

Here, Beth thought, he'd come to the sticking point. Sure enough, his voice changed timbre.

'I, I, well. I don't have to tell you that this current situation, and the attendant publicity, is distracting to our pupils. It doesn't, frankly, give off a welcoming impression at all – quite the reverse – and, of course, it is deeply worrying to Wyatt's families.' Then he gathered himself and carried on as though speaking to his usual audience of rapt parents.

'All of us here, as representatives and as leaders, in our various ways at the school, have a duty to ensure that this... unpleasantness... is dealt with as quickly, as sympathetically, and as calmly as possible. I shall be relying on you all. I would also like to ask anyone who has any information that may be pertinent to the investigation to come straight to me. You all know where you can contact me, and my door is always open.'

'Unpleasantness?' Beth had said the word out loud, as though in heavy inverted commas, before she could stop herself. Was she the only one here who understood that murder was more than a slight inconvenience to the running of the school? What about the fact that a man had died? Was she alone in feeling some fleeting sorrow for Dr Jenkins' passing, though she'd hardly known him and hadn't much liked him? She looked around the table, but encountered only surprise. If anyone was sad, or scared, or guilty, they were hiding it well. And if they disagreed with the bursar, they certainly weren't saying.

Beth strove to make herself clear. 'Erm, I mean, shouldn't we really speak to the police, rather than to you, Mr Seasons? If we do have any information?'

'I think it would be appropriate if we could discuss any developments at a school level first,' said the bursar. There was now no effort to conceal his aggression. 'Those who have been at the school a little longer will understand the importance of what I am saying here. There is a Wyatt's way of doing things, and I think in these circumstances it is very important that we keep the ball in play. We have a history to preserve, and I should think that you, in your job, would most definitely be sympathetic to that,' he added fiercely to Beth.

She flushed, as suddenly all eyes turned to her. It just added to her sense of unease at the direction things were taking.

It was all very well to try and keep things in-house; she understood the school's need to keep a lid on wild speculations and accusations that could damage its reputation and, heaven forfend, make it less desirable to prospective parents. But this was murder. To describe it simply as 'unpleasantness' was a wilful attempt to whitewash the situation. And the bursar, for all his forcefulness, was no policeman. Was it even safe to suggest keeping things quiet? There was a killer out there somewhere.

While Beth was mulling, one of the teachers succeeded in catching Seasons' eye. She was young, in her twenties, Beth guessed, and wearing an impeccable black suit and heels. She could have been a lawyer or a banker. Instead, she was teaching the children of many lawyers and bankers to become new lawyers and bankers.

'Ah, Miss Godfrey. Louise, for the benefit of our new girl, is head of French,' he added, with another nod in Beth's direction.

'I took my lower and middle school French groups to Madame Tussauds, with the History and Geography departments,' said Louise Godfrey. 'I had to come back to school early to sort out a double-booking with the French A2 oral exam timetable. My colleagues in the French department and, of course, some of the History and Geography teachers, stayed with the children on the trip, but the other department heads came back with me, for various reasons of their own,' she said, nodding at two colleagues on the other side of the table.

'What time did you make it back to school?' asked Seasons.

'We were back here at one p.m. I immediately went to the Languages centre to make some calls about the exams. I'm not sure what you two did?' she said, asking the others, but Seasons cut in to forestall them.

'If you weren't back until one, it's not relevant to us and we need detain you no further. We're looking strictly at the period between nine and twelve. Any teachers who returned to the school after, say, twelve thirty, may go.'

Louise Godfrey got up and, with a beaming and rather tactless smile, left the table along with the Geography and History heads, who looked equally relieved.

'Anyone else able to excuse themselves?' said Seasons, looking round the table with a businesslike air, though, Beth reminded herself, he was actually asking them if they could provide an alibi for murder.

The rest of the teachers looked at each other uneasily, then a sharp-faced woman in her thirties piped up. 'Jane and I were here at the time in question... But we were together all the time. Our classes were out on the field trip but they were being supervised by the others. We were catching up on marking in the staffroom. Does that mean we are free to leave?'

Another woman across the table suddenly brightened up

and nodded vigorously. 'I can confirm that,' she said, leaning forward eagerly.

'You may go,' said Seasons. The noise their chairs made as they scraped them back in double-quick time said it all about their eagerness to be gone.

Then Alison Lincoln, the middle school head, cleared her throat loudly. She was a sensible-looking, grey-haired woman, who must have been nearing retirement age. Her fringe was cut straight across her forehead, an inch above her eyebrows, which gave her the look of a medieval knight. Beth wondered how her hair stayed under such magnificent control, as her own fringe flopped forward and she brushed it away for the millionth time that day.

'If you recall, bursar,' the middle school head said when she had got everyone's attention, 'I had a meeting with Susannah here to discuss admissions. We have several children on the waiting list at the moment and a place has just opened up. We were discussing the right candidate. It can take ages, and it did this time.' She nodded to Susannah Baggs – a comfortable-looking woman in her forties – who smiled her agreement. 'On this occasion, it was a very hard decision to make. We had several suitable children and only enough remaining in the bursary kitty to support one of them. Of course, we had to consider so many factors—'

The bursar broke in. 'Yes, yes, we know how difficult it can be to select the right pupil. It can make such a difference to families.' He and Susannah Baggs both took a moment to look pious.

Beth felt her irritation rising at their smugness, but knew that what they were saying was all too true. Getting a bursary place at Wyatt's could be a turning point for families. The school, thanks to its founder's late-onset social conscience and enormous fortune, sponsored a number of exceptionally bright pupils throughout their whole school career, right down to supplying uniforms, lunches and money for field trips like the one they were discussing now. It virtually guaranteed that the chosen child would go on to university and a solid career, often as the first from their family to do so. Any place at Wyatt's was hotly coveted, but bursaries were gold dust with diamonds on top. Beth herself was hoping against hope that Jake might, just might, be in the running himself next year.

The bursar inclined his head and half-closed his eyes, seemingly rendered speechless for a moment by the thought of the school's – and by extension his own – generosity. He was stretching Beth's patience. While she knew the school was often a force for good, she also knew that Wyatt's, and other schools like it, owed their charitable status – with all the tax advantages this bestowed – to these acts of generosity. Sitting in this plush dining room, set in the extensive grounds of this magnificent institution, it was a stretch to believe that all Wyatt's actions were designed to benefit the less well off in the community.

Beth was glad when Alison Lincoln continued in her slightly grating, high-pitched voice. 'We weren't together for the whole period; our meeting started just after nine, but we didn't stop until probably twelve forty-five.'

'It was twelve fifty-five, I remember because I was starving,' said the rounded Susannah Baggs with a little giggle. The rest of the staff smiled politely.

'Well, I think that lets you out anyway. You are free to leave,' said Seasons. Once again, the speed with which Susannah Baggs and Alison Lincoln left the room said everything about how happy they were to be officially not guilty.

The rest of the group round the table looked at each other nervously. Three teachers and two members of the administration staff had now left. Beth, Janice and the bursar were still sitting at the table, along with three increasingly jittery-looking teachers. It looked as though every one of them was firmly in the frame.

The tense silence was broken by a middle-aged woman
dressed in a vast woolly sweater dress that failed to constrain
her ample bosom. 'Bursar, am I right in thinking you are
conducting your own investigation into this, er, death?' she said
shrilly. 'Are we all going to be asked by you where we were and
why at the time of the murder? Because if that's the case, then
I'm not sure if I really want to...'

Having started vehemently, the woman's sentence petered
out and she finished by wordlessly shaking her head, which did
huge damage to her gravity-defying bun of greying hair. She'd
only just stopped herself from registering a direct criticism of
the bursar. His face took on an even ruddier tone, while her bun
seemed to wilt deferentially. She put up a practised hand to
prop it up and out of the way, and was soon busy skewering the
edifice with a plentiful supply of emergency hairpins from her
handbag, her protest forgotten.

Beth turned to Janice, at her side, and raised her eyebrows.
'Dr Joyce, head of English,' Janice whispered obligingly.

'Clearly, the police will be conducting an enquiry and the
whole school, and the bursar's office, will be doing everything in
its power to support that enquiry. Whatever you may feel as
individual teachers' – Seasons paused here to shoot a look of
dislike at the head of English – 'it will be helpful if we make
sure that the enquiry is streamlined and concentrates on the
matter in hand without any unnecessary distractions and speculations, which could be damaging to the school and could delay
resolution of this most unfortunate matter.'

Aha, Beth was starting to understand. Wyatt's, via the
bursar, applied its super-efficient take on life to everything.
Why should murder be any different? Instead of having this
'unfortunate matter' straggling around like an unruly teacher's
bun, Seasons was planning to package the whole thing up for
the police, like a glossily produced prospectus, which would
enable them to snap the handcuffs on the miscreant as quickly

as possible, with the least inconvenience and damage to the school's reputation. Then they could all get on with the important business in life, churning out confident and supremely well-qualified fodder for the finest universities, and thus keep this quiet corner of the world turning very nicely, thank you.

Beth, who often rearranged her sock drawer in moments of stress and knew she spent way too much time bleaching the kitchen sink when she could be working, completely saw where Seasons was coming from. His restless, forceful personality meant he wanted to nail down everything he could, so that the out-of-control element (the murder!) was minimised, sanitised and, with any luck, completely eradicated. Judging from the murmurs now starting up around her, she wasn't sure if her colleagues were too happy with the idea. It was one thing talking to the police, because there was no choice. But did anyone want the bursar poking about in their secrets? Seasons, either oblivious to the unease around the table or deliberately ignoring it, was off again.

'What I'm proposing is that each of us here finds the time in what, I know, are busy schedules, especially at this time of year when the students are approaching important exams next term, to pop to my office, simply to discuss movements on the day in question. Once we have a run-down of everyone's timetables, I am sure the police will be able to go on their way.'

'Hang on a minute, Mr Seasons,' said one of the three remaining teachers – an intense-looking young man whose conventional suit had been teamed with a loud electric blue shirt. It was a small rebellion but, at Wyatt's, it counted for a lot. 'Are you seriously asking us to come to you with our alibis? Do you suspect that one of us is the murderer? One of the people *at this table*?' The last vestiges of what had been a nasty teenage case of acne glowed with indignation on his cheeks.

'I agree with Henderson,' piped up another man, slightly older than the last speaker, though still absurdly young for his dark tweed jacket. 'Yes, I was here on the day in question but I was right over in the Maths department, close to Henderson in Physics. As you all know, it's a long tramp over to the archives place from the Science block.'

'With respect, Radley, even mathematicians can take a stroll occasionally, same goes for Physics, too, Henderson,' said Seasons drily. Beth noted that, as usual, the phrase 'with respect' now actually meant 'with no respect at all'.

'Now, I'm sure you will all find this idea a little... intrusive,' the bursar continued, seated with his legs spread expansively, one leg jiggling a little with nervous energy. He leant forward suddenly, and both Henderson and Radley looked startled. 'But listen, guys, you'd have to speak to the police anyway. We all have to. None of us is exempt. Look on it as an opportunity to talk over your statement. We spend enough time prepping the students for exams, don't we, everyone? This is the same thing. It'll just help you to gather your thoughts, present your movements in a coherent fashion, and save everyone some time.'

Beth wondered if she was the only one doubting the bursar's suddenly matey tone – and also questioning what they would really get out of this exercise. The students, it was true, were being groomed to win places at the great universities. But her colleagues? What was their likely prize? Were they supposed to be aiming for a place in a maximum-security cell, to protect the school, or would they be drilled on how to slide out of a conviction? Were they being encouraged to smooth themselves away from the truth, or to confess in as likeable a style as possible?

The bursar himself, after all, was one of the few at the table who had a seriously good motive for getting rid of Jenkins. Together with Beth, of course. Ignoring the doubters, Seasons was wrapping up the meeting and getting to his feet.

'I suggest we start with you, Dr Joyce,' he said, bowing in the English head's direction. 'Would you be free to just get this

out of the way now?' He didn't wait for assent or even acknowl-
edgement, but started to stride away, before calling over his
shoulder, 'I'll email a list to everyone of when I'll expect you
over. Thanks, guys.'

Dr Joyce straggled to her feet and picked up a couple of
folders, a large bag and a very long woolly scarf, which she
wound round her neck several times despite the mildness of
the day. Meekly, she trailed behind the bursar, all trace of her
brief feisty moment gone. Beth noticed her bun had been
completely squashed by the scarf wrapping and, as she walked,
spools of salt and pepper locks started a leisurely descent down
her back.

The group of teachers seemed far smaller once the bursar's
dynamic presence was removed. Everyone started to collect
together phones and folders, and a few chairs scraped back as
people got up to go. Beth, who had a horror of public speaking,
realised she would have to commit the unpardonable English
sin of drawing attention to herself.

'Um, I'm new here, but I was just wondering if this was
normal practice?' she ventured in a wavering voice, addressing
the table as a whole.

There was a moment of startled silence and then Radley,
the Maths head, spoke up witheringly. 'Well, we've not had that
many murders on the premises, so this is pretty much uncharted
territory for us all.'

Beth flushed, but noticed how much braver he was when
the bursar wasn't there. The number two dog in the pack, to the
bursar's alpha male – in his own estimation, anyway.

Kind Janice took pity on Beth and said to the teachers, still
packing up and signalling their impatience to leave, 'Poor Beth
was the one who found Dr Jenkins on her very first day here.
This has been the most awful shock, as you can imagine.'

There was immediately a murmur of sympathy from the
table and Beth was grateful for a few supportive smiles, even

one from Radley who seemed to be thinking better of his sarcasm.

'I think we're all a bit on edge, and the fact that the bursar wants to micromanage everything isn't helping,' he admitted.

'Will you all go along with the bursar's idea, though? I mean, you'll tell him your whereabouts and so on?'

Everyone looked at her in surprise. It didn't seem to have occurred to anyone that they had an option not to cooperate. 'Well, I've certainly got no reason not to help,' said Radley defensively, and there was a murmur of agreement.

'Yes, how would that even look?' piped up Henderson, who was struggling to stuff a banana, two apples and an extra sandwich into his slender briefcase.

'Well, erm, it's Mr Henderson, isn't it?' started Beth.

'Geoff,' the scrawny teacher said a little reluctantly, 'and I think we should give the bursar all the help we can. Quickest way to get everything sorted.' Having at last shut the flap of his briefcase, he nodded at the table in general and loped off to the door, tripping over his feet slightly on the way.

It was the signal for the other teachers to remember their duties and soon the exodus was complete, leaving only Beth and Janice at the table. Her plan to get the Wyatt's teachers to question Seasons had fallen rather flat. Janice gave Beth a sympathetic smile.

'Do you agree, as well?' Beth said, but she knew the answer before Janice even spoke.

'Of course. Anything that gets this mess dealt with. Come on, Beth, you must see. It's terrible for Wyatt's.'

Beth did agree. It *was* terrible for the school. But it had been even worse for Dr Jenkins.

SIX

Once Beth was back in the archives office – she was determined she was going to call it that, no matter how many times other people might refer to it slightingly as a shed – she pondered it all again. Maybe independent action wasn't the Wyatt's way. But that didn't mean that she too had to fall in with the bursar's plans. As far as she could see, he was still the one among them who had the strongest motive in any case. What if he was just asking people to tell him their alibis so that he could work out one of his own? That would be incredibly ingenious, and there was something about its undoubted efficiency as a plan which struck Beth as peculiarly appropriate to Wyatt's.

Now, as well as a room stacked with goodness-knew-what in a billion boxes, she also had quite a cast of characters who were possibly in the murder frame. While so far only one – the bursar – had a motive, this lunchtime's little gathering had shown that there were four other people among the staff on the school premises at the crucial time, who had all known Jenkins, and might very well have reasons of their own for wanting the man dead. She checked her laptop for the bursar's email and saw that her own appointment to tell him her (lack of) alibi was this afternoon at 2.30. Well, she thought, looking about her as she sat in lonely splendour. She could make that meeting with no problems at all. Since the demise of Jenkins, her time in the archives was all her own.

The email list was just what she needed, as it detailed the names and departments of everyone who'd been round the table at lunch. She felt she was beginning to get people sorted out – Sam Radley, the defensive Maths head; Geoff Henderson, the skinny, nervous Physics teacher; and Dr Regina Joyce from the English department, for example. Susannah Baggs, in charge of admissions, and Alison Lincoln, the head of middle school, were now both off the hook.

She opened up a new document on her laptop and tapped in the heading, 'Suspects'. As well as Dr Joyce the English teacher, Radley the Maths head, and Henderson from Physics, there was the bursar, the headmaster himself and Janice. She added in 'Grounds staff? Catering people? Friends/enemies of Jenkins?'

Sighing, she decided that the more she looked into it, the more people sprung up as possible murderers. She needed to start eliminating them, and quickly, or her investigation would go under before she had even begun. The fact that the bursar was working on his own version, too, made her even more determined to carry on. There was something about his bullish, rugger-bugger persona that made her suspicious. He was clearly an intelligent man – was that touch of boorishness just an act? She also strongly believed that he had a credible motive. So far, in her investigation, he was streets ahead of the competition. The trouble was that there was so much competition. How on earth could she find out which of the catering staff and groundsmen were on duty, and whether they had a realistic reason to polish off Jenkins, for example?

She was tussling with this thought – oblivious to the sea of unopened boxes all around her – when the phone rang. It was Inspector York.

'Just wondering if I can fix a time to visit you at your home this evening. A few questions I need to get cleared up. I was thinking around six p.m.?'

Beth thought fast. That was after Jake's supper, if she managed to get organised for once and have it on the table as early as possible, but it was before the bedtime rigmarole kicked in. It wasn't convenient, but it wasn't impossible either.

'That's fine,' she said. 'I was just wondering...'

'Yes?' York asked.

'Have you thought about all the groundsmen? The gardeners? The caterers? Could it just have been one of them?'

'That would be very convenient for Wyatt's, wouldn't it? Just a hired hand, no one who really counts in their eyes. But the fact that it was what they call a field day on Monday makes that virtually impossible. The catering staff were around early in the morning, but left just before nine after making a lunch of sandwiches for the reduced school population expected that day. Two of the caterers were signed back in by the porter at twelve fifteen when they returned to serve – but the body had already been discovered by then. As you know.'

There was a pause, then York rushed on. 'Apparently, the pupils remaining on site see field day sandwiches as a huge treat, a bit of a picnic. Meanwhile, the whole grounds team was occupied with a revamp of the tennis courts right over at the far end of the playing fields. No one left the group; they stuck together all morning. It was supposed to be an all-day job, so there was no one on the main school premises at the crucial time. The porter was in his lodge, which we can see from the CCTV images—'

'CCTV? I'd forgotten the school has that. Surely that must show everything that went on that day... even the killing?'

'Well, it would,' said York drily, 'if the network extended

over the entire school premises. But it seems that some areas are not considered worth scrutinising. Coverage becomes patchy away from the main school buildings, and by the time you get to the vicinity of the archives office, I'm afraid there isn't a camera in sight.'

'Not even on the perimeter fence? I would have thought that would be worth keeping a watch on. Even if they don't care about the archives, they should be worried about burglars coming across the playing fields into the school?'

'You'd think. But no, the area is camera-free.' York's heavy silence indicated what he felt about the arrangement. 'So, we have hours of pictures of the main part of the school, and just the odd angle from the parts we actually need on this occasion.'

'Oh. Oh dear,' said Beth.

'Yes. Not your problem, though. See you at six.' York snapped back into businesslike mode. 'See you later,' agreed Beth.

As she put the phone down, she caught sight of her watch. Nearly 2.30. She'd almost missed her appointment for her second encounter with the bursar that day. She collected her bag, locked the office carefully, and sprinted for the main building. She flashed a quick smile at Janice in reception as she passed, and arrived at Seasons' office on the dot.

'Ah, Beth,' said Tom Seasons as she stuck her head round the door. She'd taken a few deep breaths outside to compensate for her scurrying and hoped she didn't look too rosy-cheeked. 'Sit down, sit down,' he added genially.

She settled herself opposite him and admired, as ever, the school's effortless plushness. Seasons' desk was a substantial chunk of mahogany. Framed pictures of his smiling blond family were much in evidence, while a large sash window looked onto the immaculate lawn, like a silken scarf in emerald green, fronting the school.

Seasons frowned at his Mac for a few moments, tapping

away importantly, before hitting the off button with a flourish and turning to Beth. She felt she'd been treated to a marvellous performance of the busy man generously finding time for an underling. But, she reminded herself, it was he who had called her here. She was actually finding time for him. She smiled neutrally and brushed her fringe away, her keen grey eyes locking briefly with Seasons'.

'Now then, Beth, let's just get this done as quickly as possible and we can all get on with more important things, can't we?' he blustered.

'More important?' said Beth, surprised, before she could stop herself. She'd already seen, from the bursar's cold treatment of Dr Joyce, the English head, how much he hated having his actions questioned. But, on the other hand, she really couldn't see how putting a few hundred years' worth of school play programmes into chronological order could be seen as more important than establishing who had killed a colleague. Much as she loved her job, of course.

She was quite relieved when the bursar didn't acknowledge her interruption at all, but just swept inexorably along in what must be, by now, quite a well-practised routine. He would have seen at least a couple of the others on his list already.

'So, all we need to establish is your whereabouts in the school between eight thirty and eleven thirty...'

'Eleven thirty?' said Beth. She hated to interrupt, yet again, but unless the bursar had better information than her, he'd arbitrarily narrowed the time down by half an hour. 'I found Dr Jenkins at just a few minutes after twelve. And I was with him at nine or a little after, and he was fine then...'

Again, the bursar acted as though Beth had not spoken, merely smiled and said, 'So. Your whereabouts?'

Beth collected herself and recited mechanically. 'I arrived at the school at about eight forty, went to reception, collected my swipe card, went to the archives office, met Dr Jenkins on the way, he took me to the door of the office and then left at a few minutes past nine. I stayed in the office, working, until just after twelve when I left to find a loo and some lunch, and stumbled across... Dr Jenkins... dead... at maybe five past twelve, round by the bins.'

Seasons appeared to wince, though Beth wasn't sure if it was her mention of death or of the bins. Neither was really very Wyatt's. But she couldn't help that. Now, having trotted out her story, she reached down for her bag.

'Now, Beth, we're not quite finished yet. There's no rush, is there? I'm asking everyone this, and I'm appealing with them to be as frank as possible,' said Seasons, fixing her with unwavering blue eyes and leaning forwards a little, his hands lightly clasped on the desk. She wondered if his leg was jumping away under the desk as it usually did. He reminded her of a rather unconvincing politician, able to control parts of his act, but not all of it all the time. Though heaven knew, there were enough of them in positions of power. Phony sincerity seemed to win hearts, minds and votes more often than seemed possible.

Seasons put on a particularly grave expression. 'Why do you think Jenkins was killed?'

'Why do I...? I have no idea. I hardly knew the man. Who on earth *would* have a reason to kill him?' Beth couldn't resist asking this very pointed question, staring hard at the bursar as she did so. 'I certainly don't know why someone could have felt so strongly about him. I would have thought you would know that a lot better than me.'

For a moment, the bursar's eyes narrowed with pure anger. It was a bit like the look he had suddenly flashed at the hapless Dr Joyce. But seconds later, his features had morphed back into a bland smile.

'I'm asking everyone, Beth, it's nothing personal at all,' said Seasons at his most urbane.

Beth got to her feet. 'Murder is personal, in my view,' she

said, and left the room. It was a great exit line, and she was rather proud of herself. The feeling lasted all of a minute, until she was passing reception again. What was Janice doing, lying across the countertop like that, her face hidden by her hair? And where was that drip-drip sound coming from? Beth looked closer. Something was gently streaming from the beautiful burnished counter onto the pale velvet carpet, where a rich red lake gathered. She had a horrible moment of déjà vu. It was like the bins all over again. She opened her mouth, and began to scream.

SEVEN

Beth's cheeks burnt painfully that evening as she remembered those terrible moments, gazing at the prone form on the counter, certain that kind, smiley Janice – her only friend at Wyatt's – had been viciously slain; victim number two of the murderer on the loose.

Her scream had echoed in her own ears – only to be joined by Janice's voice, also yelling. But not in her death throes. No, she was loudly complaining. 'Damn, all my sweet chilli sauce! That blasted Waitrose delivery man must have known it had split.'

Janice promptly straightened up and abandoned her sprawling attempt to scoop the sauce back into its plastic pouch.

Sure enough, now that Beth had tottered closer to the counter, she could smell the sharp, sweet scent of the gloopy sauce, so different from the iron filings stench of blood. Even the pool at the foot of the counter was the wrong colour – too pale a scarlet, and much too richly flecked with Waitrose's delicious combination of fresh chilli seeds and oriental herbs and spices. Beth clutched the counter with a trembling hand.

Janice looked up from the sticky mess, wiping dripping

hands on a tissue. 'Sorry, Beth, I think I gave you a bit of a turn there. I'm just so annoyed. It's not the first time this has happened. And I'm not even supposed to get the shopping delivered here. It's just so convenient when we're doing long hours. Quick, help me get the bags out of sight?'

Beth slipped round and started shoving the Waitrose bags into a coat cupboard in the backstage area behind reception. By a cruel twist of fate, there was no Waitrose anywhere in Dulwich. Residents were forced to go online or venture as far as Beckenham or Bromley to bag a taste of the grocery high life. The shopping was hastily stuffed away by the time the bursar rampaged out of his office to see what was afoot. Both women stood nonchalantly in front of the counter, blocking the mess on the floor.

'Everything all right here?' said the bursar, small blue eyes darting back and forth, jaw thrust forward.

'Mmm,' said Janice, trademark warm smile perfectly in place. 'I was just explaining to Beth about the period pad machines in the teachers' loo in the sixth-form blocks. So, they get refilled quite regularly with maxi pads...'

As expected, even this glancing reference to women's matters worked like extra-strength kryptonite on the burly Seasons. He retreated quickly – though quite why talk of vending machines would make the new archivist scream like a stuck pig was never explained.

She had overreacted hugely – her nerves were still badly jangled by Monday's horrible events, that was plain, thought Beth, as she cleared up slowly after supper. As usual, Jake had massacred a plate of fish fingers, the lavish encrustation of tomato ketchup mixing with the chilli sauce in her mind's eye, but also taking her back inexorably to the scene of the crime itself.

The splotch of chilli sauce on the pale carpet had been swiftly vanquished by Beth's skill with a stain, then the remnants covered by a small Persian rug Janice had filched from a music practice room. The blood at the crime scene was a different prospect. She remembered the way the clouds had floated past in that great incarnadine pond.

She scrubbed away at the plates as she thought. The kitchen was so tiny that she had decided not to give up precious space to a dishwasher. They hadn't needed one as a family of three and now, with only the two of them, it really didn't seem worth it. But on days like this, it meant that either she used a tankful of hot water scrubbing at these dried clots, or she left the plate to soak, and risked coming back to a sinkful of gory red water later on.

The doorbell punctured her gloomy musings. As she ripped off her Marigolds and dried her hands on a tea towel, she realised that the caller was going to be Inspector York, that she'd forgotten all about his visit, and that the house was a tip. Her beloved black and white cat leapt up from her comfortable spot on the wicker kitchen chair as though she'd been poked with a cattle prod, and scarpered through the cat flap with a bang. Magpie didn't discriminate; she hated all visitors to the house equally. She'd be back later, once the coast was clear of strangers.

Beth wasn't worried about Magpie; it was more the fact the place was a mess which left her flustered. Somehow, in her quest to get life under control after the death of James, during the taxing years when Jake was just a baby, she had started to equate tidiness with an ability to cope. Certainly, she knew she now felt as though all was right with the world if her house was tidy. It was a bizarre illusion but it had sustained her through some tricky times. Now she cast an anguished look around at the scattered school books on the table, the remnants of their meal in the kitchen, and even at her beloved son, sprawled in front of the telly, enjoying to the full the short window he was allowed with his beloved Play-Station.

* * *

Inspector York, bringing a gust of early spring chill into the small hall with him, looked around and smiled involuntarily. It was a beautiful house, immaculately kept, yet with all the warm signposts of family life – a jumble of coats, rebellious trainers poking out from a bench – making him feel there was no real rush to return to his own sterile flat. His job took him to all corners of south London, and this was the cosiest he'd felt in months.

Ostensibly, he was there to assess whether Beth could have any motive for bumping Jenkins off. As well as the hidden stalker shrine which, now that he was here in Beth's neat and pretty house, he was slightly embarrassed to think he had ever considered, York was on the alert for giveaways to a sudden influx of wealth. If there was evidence of blingy watches, or a new car in the drive, it might suggest a motive. Equally, suddenly falling on hard times could precipitate violence, too. He wasn't going to prejudge the situation – he never did – but he was pretty sure he wasn't going to find anything like either extreme here.

As he walked in, he trod inadvertently on a well-worn trainer, hailing – if he wasn't mistaken – from Primark. Beth's handbag, lying by the bench, was, to his admittedly inexpert eye, nothing wildly special either. The place seemed to be in what estate agents described as 'excellent decorative order' but it was by no means fancy. Case pretty much closed, he thought. He could have turned on his heel, saved himself some time, got back and made a start on the pile of paperwork that had already mounted up since Monday, but...

'Would you like some tea? So sorry about the awful mess! I'm afraid you sort of slipped my mind.'

'I'll try not to take that amiss,' said York with a smile. He realised he was parched. 'Tea would be great.'

Beth reached out a hand for York's peacoat, looking surprised at how heavy and large it was. She cast around for somewhere to put it, then arranged the coat over the bannister as neatly as she could and bustled to the kitchen.

York followed slowly along the narrow passage between the bannister and the sitting room wall, admiring Jake's artwork, stuck in Ikea clip frames, which adorned the pale yellow walls at regular intervals. The boy was no Picasso, but he certainly had gusto. The kitchen, at the end of the passage, was small but pin-neat. He felt enormous as he loomed by the fridge, amused that the usual gathering of random fridge magnets was here dragooned into neat rows, pinioning the school notices he usually saw flapping and dog-eared.

* * *

'Do sit down,' said Beth, busying herself at the kettle with her back to him, organising mugs. She rapidly stuffed the one emblazoned 'Sexy Mother' – a birthday gift from Katie – right at the back of the cupboard, before getting out the tea bags and milk. The kettle was old and made a terrible din when boiling.

When she turned round again, he had disappeared, and she peeped into the hall in alarm before hearing squawks of excitement from Jake in the sitting room.

York had plonked himself down on the sofa, taken the other, scarcely used, game controller, and the two were now jointly fighting aliens, or whatever the awful foe was, with all their might. Beth opened her mouth to announce bedtime, then shut it again. As well as all the real, day-to-day anxieties she faced, she sometimes indulged in worrying about the 'optional extras' that the Sunday papers got so exercised about, like the lack of a male role model in Jake's life. There was her own beloved brother, Josh, but how often was he around? And, crucially, was it enough to stop Jake joining gangs or getting teenage girls pregnant when the time came, which could be any day now, depending on how often you watched scary documentaries on Channel 4? Reluctant to break the spell, she plonked the tea on the kitchen table and went back to the washing-up.

An hour later, and Jake was miraculously tucked up in bed while Beth and York settled down to talk at the newly gleaming kitchen table with fresh mugs in front of them. Beth had been anticipating a Herculean task in settling her son for the night after the excitement of extra time and a co-conspirator on the PlayStation, but wily Jake – suspecting that good behaviour this time around might allow the ground-breaking treat to be repeated – had been better than gold.

'I'm glad you came,' said Beth. York looked over at her tired face and opened his mouth to reply, but Beth rushed on. 'Because, I don't know if I'm speaking out of turn or not, but something's going on at Wyatt's that I think you should know about.'

She'd been rehearsing what she was going to say while she'd scraped the last of the ketchup stains off the supper plates, while the 'boys' were playing, and her words now came out in a bit of a rush.

York was intrigued. 'Go on,' he said, sitting back in the surprisingly comfortable chair, a cheap online knock-off Beth had found of a 50s design classic, currently taking the kitchens of the intelligentsia by storm.

'Well, today, the bursar – that's Tom Seasons – called together all the teachers who were on the premises at the right times on Monday, and basically has asked us to go through all our movements with him.'

'Hmm. Sounds like he's doing my job for me. Or Hercule Poirot's?' said York with his usual hint of a smile.

'Doesn't that make you angry?' said Beth, amazed at his imperturbability. If someone had peremptorily decided to put her own archive in order, say, she'd be furious, she thought. But actually, not *that* furious, because it was beginning to seem more and more like an impossible task.

'Angry? No. But, of course, I do wonder why he's doing it, and what he hopes to gain from it.'

'The other thing is that the timings he's asking for seem a bit off. I reminded him that I'd seen Dr Jenkins at just past nine and then found him a little past twelve, but he wanted to know about eight thirty to eleven thirty.'

'That's interesting,' said York, but to Beth's disappointment he said no more on the subject. 'I think I'd like a list of the teachers who were in the right place at the right time, so to speak. Could you email it to the address on my card?'

Beth immediately looked around, panic-stricken. She had a bad feeling that she'd just stuck his latest card in the recycling. York sighed inwardly again and silently handed over another. 'What did you make of the teachers, incidentally?'

'Oh, it's hard to say, they're all very different, of course, but still all very *Wyatt's*, if you know what I mean. I got a few impressions – the English teacher seemed a bit scatty, and I don't think the bursar likes her. Radley, the Maths guy, seems very touchy, maybe a bit aggressive – though I don't mean *stabbing* aggressive, of course. The head of French – Miss Godfrey, I think – got herself off the hook and was absolutely delighted, and then flounced out and left the rest of us looking as guilty as sin, somehow. But since I don't know any of them properly, and didn't know Jenkins either, it's impossible to say who might have wanted to do something that awful.'

'Of course, it doesn't have to be a teacher, anyway,' York said, sipping his tea appreciatively.

'Doesn't it? I thought the grounds and catering people had been ruled out? That's what you said this afternoon,' said Beth, astonished.

York gave her a steady look and, as usual, refused to confirm, deny or elucidate. She suddenly felt very tired. All this restraint was admirable, she supposed – but it didn't get her much further.

'Well, let's think, if we exclude the teachers, I suppose there's still the bursar himself, not to mention the head, Janice, even *me*... but I didn't do it, obviously!' she said, looking up at York in alarm. Had she accidentally managed to implicate herself even further than her alibi-less, corpse-finding state already did? But York was smiling gently, amused rather than poised to clap the handcuffs on her.

Beth paused for a moment. Maybe it was time to come clean about her yoga session with Seasons' wife.

'Um, on Tuesday, I happened to be doing a yoga class in the village with the bursar's wife, Judith.' Was it her imagination, or did York suddenly snap to attention? It wasn't his posture, which remained relaxed. But there was something about his gaze which, she realised, indicated that his alertness levels had shot from a languid 4 to a hyper-vigilant 10.

'Oh yes?' he said.

'Yes, she's very agile, I must say, really brilliant at some of the more difficult poses, she must have been practising yoga for years.'

York didn't say that she was spouting irrelevant nonsense. But she still tailed off into silence. He wasn't sitting there to enjoy an eager discussion of middle-aged ladies' prowess at keep-fit. 'Did you have a chance to discuss the killing?' he asked evenly, as though he was pretty sure what the answer would be.

'Well,' said Beth, turning her mug around in her hands nervously, 'it turns out Mrs Seasons was good friends with Dr Jenkins. *Very* good friends was the impression I got, if you know what I mean,' she added, her cheeks flushing pink. 'You know, she's the only person I've met who seems even a tiny bit sad that he's dead. And she told me all kinds of stories about him working at MI5 – which don't seem to be true.'

'And you know that because... you checked him out yourself?' York asked heavily.

'Well, yes. I know you're going to say that I shouldn't poke around in this... and I know that I can't find out as much as the police can, you must have much better sources of information than just Google and a bit of persistence. But having, well, *found* Dr Jenkins, I do feel I'm involved. He may not have been a nice man but it was so pitiful seeing him there... and, of course, there is the fact that I haven't got an alibi and, erm, well, all the rest of it...' Beth mumbled, not wishing to reinforce the case against her.

'There are plenty of other people in the frame; there always are. No shortage of suspects at all,' said York, taking a sip of tea.

Beth wondered briefly whether that was meant to be reassuring. To her, it sounded a little as though the leafy lanes of Dulwich were now being prowled by multiple potential murderers. Not a comforting thought at all.

'Did Mrs Seasons say anything else?' he asked.

'She did mention that she usually sees Mrs Jenkins on Monday mornings, but that she couldn't make it this time for some reason... meaning, I suppose, that she doesn't have an alibi either?'

'Don't worry about Mrs Jenkins, we'll get round to her in good time. And I'm glad you've said what you have about *poking around*. That means I don't have to tell you what a seriously terrible idea it is to meddle in a crime like this – you already know.' He took a look around the sparkling kitchen and hall as he stood and finished off his tea, his gaze lingering on one of Jake's splashy paintings. 'You have a lot to lose,' he said, plonking the cup down firmly.

Beth stood, too, and the house suddenly seemed tiny again as he strode into the hall, plucked his coat off the bannister and shrugged into it.

'Thanks for the tea. Take care now,' he said meaningfully, then he smiled as she opened the door for him and he was off out into the cold night. Promptly, the cat flap in the kitchen pinged as Magpie sauntered back in again, as though nothing had happened and she hadn't spent the last few hours skulking crossly in the garden.

Yes, she did have a lot to lose, thought Beth, catching her own serious gaze in the slightly-too-high hall mirror. That was why she didn't want to risk being accused of the crime, if no one else emerged as a credible suspect. It was all very well York saying there was no shortage of people in the frame. But, from where Beth was standing, there didn't seem to be nearly enough of them.

What the policeman didn't seem to understand was that Dulwich was a very small place. It wouldn't be long before gossip got round, linking her to the crime. In a way, she was surprised that there wasn't tattle about it already – though she supposed she would probably be the last to hear. She couldn't afford to become Dulwich's favourite prime suspect.

What would happen to Jake, if she were arrested? Logically, she knew that her mother and brother would always step in. But fear drove out reason. She had to carry on *poking around*. And no amount of well-meaning warnings was going to stop her.

EIGHT

It was Friday already and they were coming to the end of the strangest working week Beth had ever had. She had done hardly anything worthy of the name of work – she kept shifting papers around her tiny office, but, diligent though she usually was, the murder now weighed more heavily on her than the need to justify her pay packet.

She had to talk to Dr Jenkins' wife. Yes, there were the three teacher suspects, but they were all being cross-questioned by the bursar, and she couldn't see them taking kindly to going over their movements with another amateur. She might as well follow up on her conversation with Judith Seasons and see if she could get the measure of Mrs Jenkins instead.

Taking a look around the cluttered office, she decided she'd be doing everyone a favour if she packed up Jenkins' belongings – *effects*, they called them, didn't they, once someone was dead? – and returned them to the grieving widow. It would give her the perfect excuse for a nice little chat which, with any luck, would shed some light on Mrs Jenkins' mysterious behaviour on the fatal morning. Not to mention clearing a tiny bit of space in her ridiculously cramped office.

Beth picked up the nearest carton, unceremoniously upended it on a bare patch of floor, and let the dusty contents spill out. She kicked the pile into some sort of order without bothering to read any of the documents, though under a couple of inches of the now familiar back copies of school magazines from the 1970s, she did notice a few much older-looking ledgers and documents tied up with discoloured tape.

She started stuffing the empty box with all the things that could easily be identified as belonging to the late Dr Jenkins. In went a moth-eaten pullover; a rather nice leather shoulder bag which, on inspection, seemed to contain only old copies of *The Times* – folded down to the cryptic crossword page (mostly at least three-quarters finished and certainly suggesting he was less than dedicated to his work); a scarf in what looked like an ancient take on the school colours; a pair of well-used tennis shoes; a dog-eared John le Carré paperback (maybe the source of his MI5 tales); a stash of chewing gum; five rolls of Polo mints; and several packets of Benson & Hedges cigarettes. There was also a stack of well-used Moleskine notebooks, bristling with receipts, and a ragged sheaf of bank statements.

Beth, after a brief struggle with herself, decided she really needed to go through these herself before handing them over. She could always say they had been stashed away in a drawer blocked by one of the boxes, if anyone wondered why she'd held them back. A cursory glance at the chaos in the archive office would help anyone believe that could be true.

Technically, she supposed she shouldn't be leaving the premises during the school day, but with Jake to look after once school finished, it was now or never if she wanted to beard Mrs Jenkins. And, after only a few days in the job, she was now pretty convinced that no one else in the school had the least interest in what happened in the archives office anyway.

She almost laughed out loud as she contrasted her expecta-tions of her shiny new job with the reality which had confronted her, right from the off on Monday. She'd been looking forward to careful, methodical hours, sorting, categorising, marshalling facts, doing the thing she did best – bringing order. Instead, from the moment she turned up, she'd been faced with a sort of casual indifference to her role. Everyone else referred to the place as a shed, and the more she thought about it, the more even Jenkins' attitude to her had seemed offhand and resentful.

From Jenkins' own point of view, she supposed she had burst into his kingdom, and would soon be shedding light on his laziness and complete failure to get a handle on the archives. If anyone had had a motive to do away with someone on Monday, it was probably him garroting her, as his cover was about to be blown. But things had fallen out very differently. She now felt that, by trying to find out what had really happened, she was not only sticking up for Jenkins (however little he may have deserved it) but also fighting for the archives themselves. They had clearly been neglected for years. Well, all that, she pledged, was going to change. She was really going to start getting to grips with this room, she thought, as she looked around the crowded and cobwebby space. Just as soon as she'd got somewhere with Mrs Jenkins.

With that, she picked up the large box and breezed out, carrying it in front of her as though she was on legitimate urgent school archive business, whatever that might mean. She passed a few teachers (not her Prime Suspects, as she'd begun to think of them) and legions of children without a query or barely a raised eyebrow, nodded to the porter in a very important way, and was out through the Wyatt's gates before she'd even paused for breath. She could only hope Mrs Jenkins would be as accepting.

It was a perfect English spring day. A fresh coolness was tempered by fingers of gentle sunshine, which stroked the bobbing daffodils and bright blue grape hyacinths dotted in gardens along her way. All the houses in Dulwich Village looked as though they'd been freshly painted to greet the new season, and she wouldn't have been altogether surprised if they actually had.

It hadn't been hard to ferret out the Jenkins family address in Gilkes Place. It was at the top of Dr Jenkins' bank statements, and Beth knew the road well. It was close to her own home, though the houses in Jenkins' road were infinitely bigger and more stately than in her little street. Gilkes Place lay curved like an encircling arm around the back of the St Barnabas parish hall, which was a quaint building with a triangular-shaped roof, like a ski chalet suddenly dropped from a mountain top into comfiest suburbia. She had very fond memories of the hall itself, as she'd taken Jake there every Thursday morning for at least a year for one of his first toddler groups. It was where she'd met Katie.

As she rounded the corner into Gilkes Place, she leant the box on a handy wall for a moment to catch her breath. If she hadn't been carrying such a massive chunk of cardboard, she would have thoroughly enjoyed the stroll. The box had been useful as a prop when she'd exited the school, but now she was cursing all its unwieldy angles and the way its contents slopped from side to side with every step she took.

She lifted it up again with a little sigh. Not far to go now. The road was a cul-de-sac and even the birds seemed to have been fitted with silencers to preserve the hush. These houses were gorgeous, and very rarely came on the market. She wondered – acknowledging she was being horribly 'Dulwich' as she did so – if the Jenkins' place would have to be sold now. There would be a feeding frenzy as soon as it hit rightmove.-com, that was for sure.

The houses in the short road were all different in style, though each one was signalling solid middle-class values and unassailable affluence. Jenkins' home sported a green pocket handkerchief of lawn outside – not quite up to Wyatt's billiard-table smoothness, but not far from it – which was roped off from the street by dinky short white posts with a painted chain slung between them. It wasn't Beth's style – the post and chain arrangement served no purpose but would require loads of work to keep it blindingly white – but it was eye-catching and high-maintenance, which were definitely Dulwich virtues, she had to admit.

All this observation was taking the edge off her nerves as she stood, box in arms, contemplating Jenkins' house. Even though she didn't want to be hefting the box around forever, now that she was here, Beth was reluctant to ring the bell. What on earth was she going to say to poor Mrs Jenkins? Wasn't she intruding terribly? And what the hell was she hoping to achieve by this piece of nonsense?

As usual, letting the negative voice in her head have full rein for a minute helped Beth convince herself that she was right. Yes, she did risk making an utter fool of herself. But on the other hand, she needed to clear herself of the imputation of murder. Her choice was either to wait what was likely to be a very long time for the police to sort everything out according to today's elaborate protocols, or to get on and do it herself. If she could bring up Jake, pay her mortgage and put food on the table, she could do this simple thing and barge in on a grieving widow, couldn't she?

She took a deep breath, marched up the crazy-paving path, plonked the box at her feet, and rang the brass bell on the shiny pillar-box red door. With any luck, no one was in. There was a long pause, and Beth really thought her wish had been granted. Suddenly, she was disappointed, and stooped to pick the dratted box up again. Now she'd have to carry the blinking thing all the way back.

Then she heard the unmistakable sound of someone stirring inside. Her heart started thumping, and she ran a hand over her hair, pushing the Shetland pony fringe out of her eyes. It flopped inexorably back into place just as the door opened.

'Miss Brown!' exclaimed Beth in shock. It was Jake's Learning Support teacher – a little more red-eyed and rumpled-looking than usual, it was true, but the same reassuringly motherly figure Jake had been getting extra reading practice from every Thursday this year.

'I don't understand,' said Beth. 'What are you doing here, Miss Brown? Where's Mrs Jenkins?' She couldn't help rising onto her tiptoes and looking behind Miss Brown into the gloom of the hall.

Was Mrs Jenkins a friend? Was the kindly Miss Brown comforting the new widow? Beth's thoughts whirled. Miss Brown, in burgundy wool trousers and a fawn cowl-necked sweater, and seeming less cuddly than usual now that Beth looked more closely, was still gripping the front door. She sighed and spoke quickly and quietly, her voice strained.

'I *am* Mrs Jenkins. I go by the name of Brown at the Village Primary, because I started there before I married. People get used to the name. Not that I quite see why it concerns you?' Her eyebrows made perfect half-circles against her pallor.

Beth was astonished. She'd had no idea that Jake's Miss Brown and Dr Jenkins' widow were one and the same. She felt silly. But she hadn't made the connection at all. It was a common enough name and, it sounded ridiculous, but she had never thought for one moment about the woman's life outside the school. She did remember she and Jake had bumped into the teacher in Dulwich Park, back in September, and had said their hellos, but Dr Jenkins hadn't been anywhere in evidence. And besides, that was months before she'd got the Wyatt's job. She wouldn't have known who Jenkins was anyway at that point, even if he and Miss Brown/Mrs Jenkins had been skipping around the park together hand in hand. She did wonder whether Katie had known, but if she had, she would have told Beth. Wouldn't she?

She felt quite disconcerted, but maybe the fact she already knew Miss Brown – or Mrs *Jenkins* – however slightly, might work in her favour now and help the older woman to open up. She could but hope.

'Oh! Well, I have a little boy at the school. Don't you recognise me from parents' evening? His name is Jake. I'm his mum, Beth Haldane. He's in Year Five. At the Primary. As I said,' said Beth, beginning to babble as Mrs Jenkins continued to look unrelentingly blank.

'You read with him on Thursdays,' she added a little desperately.

Mrs Jenkins heaved a sigh and seemed to come to a decision. 'Well, I'm sure we can talk *at school* if you've got concerns about how he's getting on. I'm afraid I can't chat now,' she said with a brief smile, then prepared to close the door.

Beth rushed into speech, determined to prevent this opportunity from slipping away. 'I'm very sorry to have troubled you, Mrs Jenkins. This is really odd, but I haven't come about Jake at all. I've come about your husband.'

'Oh.'

Mrs Jenkins' tone was curiously flat, but her hand dropped from the door.

'I actually just started working with your husband... He appointed me as assistant archivist...'

'Oh, did he?' Again, Mrs Jenkins' tone was flat, but there was a spark of something in her eyes at this news. Was it dislike? 'Well, I don't see what that has to do with me. I'm sorry, I do need to get on. There's such a lot to do...' She tailed off, flashing that meaningless social smile again. As far as she was concerned, that was that.

The last thing Beth wanted was to see that shiny pillar-box door shut in her face. She had to try and get inside the house and interrogate Mrs Jenkins – as sensitively as she could, of course. She racked her brains for anything, anything, which might give her a pretext. She started to talk fast.

'Um, well, I don't know if you knew this, but the police have been going through everything in the archives office and I thought that might well mean you hadn't wanted to pick up his things from work. I thought I would save you the trouble of coming to the school. It must be very difficult... in the circumstances...' She knew she was rambling and she knew Mrs Jenkins, listless as she was, was running out of patience.

Beth picked up the box and brandished it in front of her, hoping it looked too tempting to slam the door on. She even rattled the contents a little, like someone trying to entice a pet. 'I've brought some of his things round for you. I wondered if you'd like them. And, well, I really thought you should have them back.'

For a minute, Beth wasn't sure whether Mrs Jenkins was going to ask her in, but when she saw the size of the box, the older woman sighed. 'I've got a bad shoulder; I can't lift that great big thing. Well, I suppose you'd better bring it in, whatever it is.' There wasn't much enthusiasm in her voice.

Beth followed the older woman into the dark hall, which led off at the end into a large square kitchen. It was immaculate but somehow cheerless, dominated by unfashionable dark-stained wooden units, lavishly patterned wall tiles, and a moss green paint which seemed to suck out the light. The only sign the room was ever used was a plate lying on the draining board, with an apple on it. Mrs Jenkins had been in the middle of peeling it. Now it was going gently brown, like that withered core in the archives office.

'What a lovely house, have you been here long?' asked Beth brightly, hoping to dispel a bit of the gloom by simply refusing to acknowledge it.

Mrs Jenkins looked around. 'It seems a long time,' she said

heavily. 'This is all much more Alan's style than mine. He wasn't into change, to put it mildly. I won't offer you tea. I expect you're in a rush.'

'Oh, actually, tea would be great. I don't have to be back for ages and I haven't had a cup all day,' said Beth enthusiastically. As it was only 11 o'clock now, she was making herself sound like a hardened tea addict, but that was plausible enough, she thought. She was British, for goodness' sake. A cup of tea was *always* going to be lovely.

Mrs Jenkins sighed but filled the kettle and switched it on automatically. The mugs she unearthed from a cupboard were dark brown. Beth recognised them as being the same as the ones from a huge service her grandparents had had dating from the 1970s, bristling with gravy boats and vegetable tureens, which had infested all their kitchen cupboards and which she had heartily loathed. Whenever she'd stayed at her grandparents' house, they seemed to be entertaining and she remembered feeling left out upstairs alone as they and their friends shrieked late into the night. This pattern was now back in fashion, but still horrible, she reflected. She wondered if it was original, or had been bought recently in a bid to be trendy. Her money was firmly on the former option.

Mrs Jenkins stirred milk into both cups slowly and brought them over to the heavy oak table, with their matching saucers – naturally – and an oval platter of hard-looking Rich Tea, Beth's least favourite biscuits. She placed them on a lace table runner that bisected the shiny wood. Her face was still blank and unsmiling. Either Mrs Jenkins had been firmly under her husband's cheerless thumb and was devastated by his death, or Beth had got her all wrong and she was far less warm and maternal than she'd seemed at that parents' evening. Beth dragged out one of the oak kitchen chairs and sat down facing her.

'I expect you're wondering what Dr Jenkins was like to

work for,' said Beth gently. Mrs Jenkins looked at Beth. It was clear that, whatever she had been thinking, it wasn't that – and that her actual thoughts were far darker than anything Beth could guess at. She must miss him terribly, thought Beth to herself. Poor lady. She seemed so different today from the cosy figure she remembered. Well, it wasn't surprising that she would be affected by the murder of her husband, but she seemed depressed rather than sad.

'Actually, I hardly knew your husband really. It was my first day when... well, you know,' Beth tailed off. 'But he seems to have been held in great esteem at the school... I'm sure he'll be much missed...' She shut up as she realised that she was spouting platitudes which did not fit Dr Jenkins at all. He didn't appear to have been held in much esteem and no one seemed to miss him in the slightest – apart from the widow's supposed best friend, Judith Seasons, who had given the impression of being altogether too keen on the man.

She needed to start again. 'Shall I just show you what I've packed in the box?' Beth made to get up and fetch the carton, but Mrs Jenkins stopped her.

'No! No, don't do that. I'd rather go through everything... in my own time. You know.'

'This must have been the most dreadful shock,' Beth said sympathetically. 'Are you sure you're all right here on your own? Is there anyone staying with you?' She looked around, but the house had a peculiarly deserted air. 'I think you're friends with Mrs Seasons, aren't you? I expect she's been round?'

'How did you know about her?' Mrs Jenkins was roused from her torpor for a moment.

'I could ring her, if you like,' said Beth, edging round the question and hoping to get Mrs Seasons' number, though she supposed it would be fairly easy to find it at school.

'No, don't ring her,' said Mrs Jenkins firmly. 'I'm fine on my own. I really am. I just need to... think things through a bit.'

It was an odd comment. It certainly didn't sound to Beth like the standard thoughts of a grieving widow. It was more as though Mrs Jenkins was struggling to come to terms with a seriously substandard tumble dryer, rather than having her life's partner snuffed out in... well, not exactly his prime, but still with a reasonable amount of time on his side. Beth, who had previously thought of the woman as a gentle, patient teacher Jake seemed happy enough to trot off to once a week, realised there was a whole other Mrs Jenkins or Miss Brown – she wasn't even sure what to call her now – who had remained hidden. She wasn't sure she liked her. She definitely didn't understand her.

She tried again. 'Maybe I could call your family, then?'

'The family? Nooo,' said Mrs Jenkins, shaking her head vigorously. 'No, no, they shouldn't be here, absolutely not... Oh, it's all been so difficult. You wouldn't understand,' she said, fixing Beth suddenly with an anguished look. That glance made Beth realise how little eye contact they'd had since she had been in Mrs Jenkins' home. Had the woman been deliberately avoiding her gaze? Or was she just consumed with her own misery – or depression?

'Try me,' said Beth. 'I might understand more than you think. My husband died, too.'

'Oh, did he? I knew you were on your own with your son, but I'm afraid I assumed you'd just had one of these splits. Well, it's the modern way, isn't it? Families don't stick together any more, not like they used to. It's not that I approve or disapprove, you understand,' said Mrs Jenkins carefully. 'One can't discriminate, and of course my duty is to the children, whatever their backgrounds. But it does make everything so difficult. Two sets of PE kits, homework always left in the wrong house, all the confusion on who's picking who up from school; the poor mites. They do suffer. They're so mixed up. Divided loyalties, you see.

Most of that is caused by people moving on, in one way or another. Not by death.'

'Well, in my case, it was... death. So, it means I do understand. Exactly how you feel,' said Beth, tentatively reaching out a hand across the table, where Mrs Jenkins was fidgeting with the small lace table runner, her wedding band gleaming against the dark oak.

The more that Beth's fingers extended, the more Mrs Jenkins retreated, taking the table runner with her and pulling the oval platter of biscuits across the table. Beth gave up the effort and Mrs Jenkins stopped dragging, leaving the biscuits mercifully still on the table.

'You don't understand! Nobody could. How on earth could you think that you do?' hissed Mrs Jenkins in a low voice. She was now pleating the lace runner in her restless fingers, creasing it badly then attempting to smooth it out. 'All those years... year after year after year... with Alan,' she finished.

'I'm so sorry, I didn't mean to...' Beth didn't quite know how to apologise, because she wasn't sure how she'd offended. Mrs Jenkins, once again, seemed to be metres deep in some sort of murky past that only she could see. Beth wondered how on earth she was going to get the subject round to Monday, and Mrs Jenkins' whereabouts at the crucial time when she should have been performing sun salutations with Judith Seasons.

Now that she thought about it, the women didn't seem very well-matched as yoga partners. Seasons was willowy and athletic, while Mrs Jenkins was of a more comfortable build. More importantly, Judith Seasons was every inch a modern woman who might be sixty-something but wasn't going even into middle age without a massive fight, let alone embracing a comfortable retirement. Mrs Jenkins, meanwhile, seemed to be firmly mired in the past, from the dated décor of her home to her attitude to family life.

Beth looked at the woman, who'd now picked up a Rich Tea

and was mechanically munching her way through it, transparently miles away. It looked like something she did many times a day. She was pretty sure Judith Seasons would not have been seen dead with a biscuit, even one as cheerless as a Rich Tea. But having radically different attitudes to carbs didn't mean the women couldn't be friendly, she supposed.

'I could easily call Mrs Seasons...' Beth mentioned her again and hurried on before Mrs Jenkins could protest. 'I know you usually see her on Mondays, but you didn't see her this week, did you? Were you busy on Monday?'

'I was at the school... Meetings. It's always meetings now. Strategy, targets, you name it... ridiculous. And they change the name about once a week too – Special Needs, Learning Support. Children used to be fine, or they were plain backward. At least we agreed on that. Alan and I,' Mrs Jenkins clarified.

Beth paused, suddenly realising Mrs Jenkins had unceremoniously dumped her own Jake in the 'backward' bin. She wasn't happy with that. A slight reluctance to read, which the school had assured her would be ironed out in months, was not the same as being 'backward'. She could feel her hackles rising, and knew she was going to find it very hard, now, to stop herself from heartily disliking Mrs Jenkins. Anyone who disparaged Jake wounded her to the quick. It was also rather horrifying that someone working in this sensitive department should have such outmoded ideas. But, Beth supposed, at least Mrs Jenkins had had that in common with her husband. They both seemed to be dinosaurs, in their own different ways.

Beth marvelled that, all year, she'd thought this woman was such a lovely teacher and a really nurturing figure for Jake. There was none of that on display here, only a decided coldness and a frightening kind of deep, rather sinister depression which worried her – for Mrs Jenkins herself, and for all the children in her care. Mind you, she was at home, which Beth supposed meant that either Mrs Jenkins or the school itself had signed her off, realising that tackling lively nine- and ten-year-olds was not the best thing for her at the moment. That was a relief, at any rate.

It didn't really seem a good idea to leave Mrs Jenkins alone with her sombre thoughts, much as she was beginning to dislike her. Beth was just wondering what on earth to do when the doorbell rang. Mrs Jenkins now seemed utterly sunk in gloom, so Beth trotted to the front door herself and opened it.

On the doorstep was the beautifully blonded Judith Seasons. Her hair shone in the spring sunshine and seemed blinding against the darkness of the hall. 'Oh, it's you – the girl from yoga, isn't it?' Judith said, visibly taken aback. 'What on earth are you doing here?'

'I just dropped some of Dr Jenkins' belongings round... from the office, you know, at Wyatt's,' Beth said. Lowering her voice, she added, 'I'm glad you're here. I don't think Mrs Jenkins is in a good place.'

'Well, of course she's not,' said Judith Seasons, shaking her head at Beth's stupidity. 'Her husband has just died, you know. No doubt you have to get on,' she added pointedly, looking back at the still-open front door. 'I'll take care of her now.'

Beth loitered in the hall for as long as she could, hoping to hear some significant interplay between the women, but the most she got was a slightly distant, 'Oh, it's you, Judith,' from Mrs Jenkins.

'Yes, dear, I'll just put the kettle on. And I don't think we need any more of these biscuits, do we?' bustled Judith Seasons. Beth felt genuinely sorry for Mrs Jenkins.

Back in the archive office later, and doing a desultory sort-out of the contents of the carton she'd emptied earlier, Beth reflected on two things. First, no one had noticed her absence from her post at all. She could have been elsewhere all day long and she wasn't sure that anyone would have found out, or even cared. Secondly, her meeting with Mrs Jenkins hadn't been completely wasted. She had at least established where the woman was on the crucial morning. And Beth was quite proud of the way she'd managed to talk her way into the gloomy, oppressive house and then get some answers.

This led Beth to an important conclusion. She'd had her doubts about pursuing her own investigation into Dr Jenkins' death, and she hadn't forgotten York's warning last night, about the possible consequences of meddling. But she had a very good reason to persist. She was still the number one suspect, as far as she could see.

Today had also taught her the important lesson that she had the liberty to carry on investigating. No one could call her job exactly pressured. At some stage, she imagined, either the headmaster or the bursar was going to decide to remember she was there and do something about her role. But until that happened, there didn't seem much to stop her pootling about as much as she saw fit.

This made her feel guilty, as she was taking the school's money (not that she had been paid yet) and, so far, could not be said to have earned it. It went against the grain. Beth was a hard-working person and really enjoyed getting her teeth into something. She resolved she would *definitely* do some proper archive-type work tomorrow. But until then, she was going to concentrate on the mystery right in front of her.

First of all, she had to establish whether Mrs Jenkins really had been at a meeting at the infants' school. It was easy enough to say something like that, just to put everyone off the scent, but had she actually turned up? Beth supposed the police were able to check things like this in a matter of moments, and normally she'd have a very difficult time following in their footsteps. But handily enough, Beth had a good excuse to call in on the

Learning Support department after picking up Jake that afternoon.

She was privately still fuming about Mrs Jenkins' description of her son as 'backward'. Although the woman hadn't directed this harsh definition entirely at Jake, Beth was finding it very difficult not to take it personally. But she didn't want him to fall further behind with his reading. So, it made perfect sense to pop along and double-check that he'd be getting his session next Thursday, even if it wasn't – and she really hoped it wasn't – with Mrs Jenkins. How hard was it going to be to drop some sort of question casually into the conversation which would nail down the other woman's whereabouts once and for all?

So, at the Village Primary that afternoon, Jake sulkily scuffed his new shoes in the playground while Beth went about her mission. She wished fervently she were either sheltering behind a nice, official uniform, or that she was a more outgoing type. If she had been, say, an uber-mummy like Belinda McKenzie – the terror of the school gates – she would have thought nothing of coming right out and cross-questioning Miss Griffin, the slightly bumptious head of Learning Support. As it was, Miss Griffin deployed her usual shiny imperviousness to all Beth's approaches, honed by years of fobbing off anxious parents desperate to get to the bottom of their children's issues. The more you defined the problem, the more people expected you to solve it. Therefore, Miss Griffin was all about ducking and diving, avoiding naming names, and swerving away from concrete pronouncements.

This partly stemmed from the fact that, when Miss Griffin had studied Psychology at Sussex in the 90s, 'ology' subjects had been seen in some circles as a bit woolly. She had learnt to be defensive about her hard-won qualifications. But she was now cresting a wave of newfound tenderness and sympathy for children who were on the autistic spectrum, had processing issues, were dyspraxic, dyslexic, or suffering from dyscalculia.

The reason was not a million miles away from the fact that these children now got up to twenty-five per cent extra time in exams.

It hadn't taken the pushy parents of Dulwich, or the high-performing feeder schools that served them, much time to connect the dots and there were now vast numbers of children trooping in and out of Special Needs departments at all the local schools, while the exam results were zooming ever upwards. Twenty-five per cent more time didn't correlate to twenty-five per cent higher marks – but it certainly didn't hurt. Miss Griffin wasn't about to let this pleasant upswing in her department's popularity change by allowing too much light to fall on its inner workings.

'There is an issue of confidentiality surrounding all staff meetings, as I am sure you are aware, Ms Haldane,' said Miss Griffin with a rubbery smile, a necklace of brightly coloured wooden beads bobbing on her bony chest as she spoke. 'I'm really not at liberty to say whether any of us attended at all.'

'Seriously? There was a meeting but you can't say whether *anyone* attended it? What sort of meeting would it be with no one at it?' Beth smiled, willing Miss Griffin to share the joke.

Miss Griffin, who thought a meeting with only herself present would be the ideal time-saving scenario, did bend her lips upwards, but only the most charitable of observers would have defined what subsequently happened to her face as a smile.

'I'm not sure why you are so interested in a discussion which didn't involve your son or any issues to do with him?' The lilt at the end of her sentence made the words, in them-selves quite harmless, seem more pointed.

Beth thought furiously but she could not come up with a single justifiable reason for Miss Griffin to divulge any informa-tion at all. Luckily, just as she was cursing herself again for her lack of Sherlockian cunning, Miss Griffin's phone pinged. She read the text and immediately got to her feet. 'Excuse me for just one moment, Ms Haldane, this is urgent,' she said importantly, bustling out of the room.

Beth didn't waste a second, but shot out of her seat and peered at the other woman's laptop, quickly jogging the cursor to make sure the screen didn't go dark. She was in luck. A still-open window showed the minutes of the Monday morning meeting. One of Miss Griffin's ways of making sure everything went smoothly was to assume command of all such tasks. History is written by the victors, after all.

Sure enough, there was a list of attendees, and Miss Brown, aka Mrs Jenkins, was on it. But, more importantly, at the top of the document it said in bold: 'Learning Support Meeting, Monday 16th March, 9.30 a.m. to 10.45 a.m.'.

Mrs Jenkins had had a meeting, yes. But it hadn't started until 9.30 and she'd been free from 10.45 onwards. Yet she'd told her friend she was busy all morning, and missed their usual lunch too. The Village Primary was, what, seven minutes' walk from the gates of Wyatt's? Ten minutes, if you were hopping. Five minutes, if you were in a hurry.

Mrs Jenkins didn't have an alibi either.

Beth collected a disgruntled Jake from the playground and left the school just as Miss Griffin bustled back to her office to find it empty. 'Well!' she said. These parents. They were as bad as their children, half the time.

Beth, meanwhile, was meandering home with Jake, wondering if she'd ever get to the bottom of all this. She now had Mrs Jenkins vying with her teacher Prime Suspects for the post of murderer. Was anything she was doing making things clearer, or was she just blundering about, muddying the already dangerously opaque waters?

NINE

Just as well she had resolved to get down to some proper archive work at last, Beth thought the next morning, as she sat on the floor surrounded by piles of documents. Some of the stuff that had come out of the box she'd used for Jenkins' belongings had looked quite interesting, but she'd promised herself she'd clear some of the central floor space first, just to make it easier to get around her lair. She was deep in an old ledger, which seemed to show nothing more exciting than who had supplied Wyatt's with provisions after 1921, when there was a knock at the door.

Even if she hadn't been immersed in her reading, Beth would probably have jumped a mile. It was the first time anyone had come to the door... apart from Inspector York, of course. For some reason, he didn't count as a threat. She leapt up, brushed a bit of dust from her jeans – her outfits had become steadily more casual as she'd realised how little scrutiny she was under – and hurried to the door.

To her astonishment, there on the threshold of the archive office was the deceptively cuddly figure of Mrs Jenkins, looking a little like Mrs Tiggy-Winkle in a capacious-looking mohair coat. The only thing missing was the cheery twinkle in her eye.

She was carrying several of those supermarket bags for life – from Waitrose, of course – and looking grimly determined.

Beth fell back to allow the older woman to pass. 'Mrs Jenkins, it's good to see you again so soon. What can I do for you?' she asked, but faltered when she found herself addressing Mrs Jenkins' back as the woman barged in without waiting for an invitation.

She threw off her coat, covering up Beth's own jacket which had been slung on the back of her chair, and got to work. She clearly knew exactly what she was looking for. She started to move cartons around, trying to reach, Beth realised, Jenkins' old desk – now her own workstation.

'Um, Mrs Jenkins, if I could just give you a hand. I brought all the stuff from your husband's desk round to your house, don't you remember? You've got everything already.'

Mrs Jenkins wasn't listening at all. By now she had reached the desk, and started flinging open the top drawer, taking out several pens, a packet of tampons and some paracetamol that Beth had stashed there, and dumping the lot unceremoniously on the floor.

'Actually, that stuff is mine?' Beth's voice was rising as she tried to get through to her extremely determined visitor. Mrs Jenkins took not the least bit of notice of her and stuck her hand right to the back of the drawer, rooting around, before moving inexorably on to the next.

'Could you just tell me what you are looking for?' Beth asked helplessly, as a couple of her notepads and some sheets of A4 joined the mound on the floor. Honestly, the place was in enough of a shambles as it was, without Mrs Jenkins trashing it even more. Beth edged through the cartons towards her and put her hand on Mrs Jenkins' arm, today clad in another cuddly sweater, this time in a dusty rose shade. Her light touch seemed to do the trick. Mrs Jenkins stopped sorting through the drawer, and slowly turned to face Beth.

Her expression, which had been strangely blank, suddenly took on an alarming vehemence. 'Where have you put it? You've hidden it, haven't you? Where? Where?' Beth let go of the woman's arm immediately and started to back away in fright, but Mrs Jenkins lunged and grabbed at her arms. 'You know, don't you? You know all about it.'

Beth was just stammering out a denial and brushing the clawing hands from her jumper when there was a brisk, flourishing rat-a-tat-tat at the door. Normally, Beth couldn't stand people who couldn't do a straightforward knock but had to personalise things with their own little tattoo. At this moment, though, she positively loved whoever was at the door, and would smother them in relieved kisses when she got half a chance.

'Come in, please come in!' she yelled out, just as Mrs Jenkins charged towards her.

The door opened and suddenly the older woman backed off, becoming once again a cuddly Mrs Tiggy-Winkle lookalike.

Indeed, she looked so shattered by her exertions that when the bursar burst jauntily through the door, he immediately said, 'Beth, get Mrs Jenkins a chair! She looks as though she's about to pass out. What on earth is going on in here?' he added, belatedly taking in the chaotic scene.

Beth, who was already hastily revising her plan to cover her unexpected caller in kisses, wasn't surprised he was taken aback. There were papers and boxes strewn everywhere, not to mention tampons rolling around. So much for the new archivist getting the place in order. And what on earth was the bursar doing here, anyway? She'd been pretty much ignored all week. Now, all of a sudden, it was like Piccadilly Circus in here.

'I think Mrs Jenkins has been a bit... distressed,' said Beth, trying to be reasonably diplomatic yet at the same time keen to apportion blame where it was due. All right, the room hadn't been exactly tidy before Mrs Jenkins arrived, but it looked a hell of a lot worse once she'd started throwing stuff around with bizarre abandon.

'I see,' said the bursar, shooting a highly disapproving glance at Beth and then treating Mrs Jenkins to his most unctuous smile. No one looking at Mrs Jenkins, sitting docile and pale as one of the many sheets of paper strewn on the floor, would ever have thought her capable of creating such disorder.

'Well, it's perfectly natural in the circumstances for Ruth to be feeling a little overwhelmed. Being back here in Alan's office must be very distressing, isn't that the case, Ruth? Perfectly natural. Do take some deep breaths, Ruth, and just rest there for as long as you like, then I'll escort you out. In the meantime, maybe you, Beth, could fetch her a glass of water, cup of tea?'

It was framed as a question but Beth knew it was actually an order. Instantly, she realised she didn't want to leave either of these people alone with her archives. Mrs Jenkins was looking for something. That much had been abundantly clear when she'd been chucking stuff all over the place. And Beth had no idea what the bursar was up to, suddenly 'popping in' on her after making it clear all week that the archives office was rock bottom on his action-packed, super-important agenda. All she knew was that she distrusted him thoroughly, and wasn't any keener for *him* to be alone in the place either.

Mrs Jenkins came to her rescue, rising to her feet slowly. 'No, I'd best be getting along. I've got what I came for,' she said, fixing her beady eyes on Beth with a malevolent half-smile. At once, Beth wondered what on earth the woman had managed to pick up. There was nothing in her hands, but as she shrugged the mohair coat back on, Beth noticed the pockets were bulging. Had they been that full before? She just couldn't say.

Beth resolved to check around and see if there was anything missing, but she knew that was a hopeless task. If this episode had taught her anything, it was that she must make getting on top of the archives a priority. Otherwise, people would be able to make off with anything they liked, and she'd be none the wiser.

But what could Mrs Jenkins have been searching for that was so important? It wasn't anything directly belonging to her husband; all that stuff had, as she'd said, been in the box that Beth had delivered. Apart from the sheaf of bank statements, of course, and those Moleskine notebooks. Luckily, Beth had stashed all those over in the filing cabinets, well away from the area that Mrs Jenkins had searched. Maybe the woman was just trying to freak her out, implying that she'd found something vital just to unsettle her. Well, it was working. She was definitely unsettled.

'Well, if you're sure you're happy, Mrs Jenkins, then I'm sure the bursar would be able to escort you out. So useful to have a strong man to lean on if you're feeling a bit faint,' said Beth in as sympathetic a way as she could manage.

She was hoping that an appeal to Seasons' chivalry would mean he felt obliged to escort the woman off the premises, and take himself a long way away from the archive office in the process. It worked. Seasons proffered an arm, and Mrs Jenkins took it tremulously. Beth marvelled at what a brilliant actress the woman was. One minute, she'd been scaring the bejeezus out of Beth. The next, she was frail, harmless and sixty going on ninety. Maybe this was why her initial impressions of the teacher, as the perfect warm and caring support for Jake when he needed a little extra help, had been so off-kilter.

Three dusty hours later, Beth was still pondering whether she should report that morning's strange encounter to Inspector York. Was there enough there, really, to suggest that Mrs Jenkins had actually been threatening her? Or was the woman just behaving very oddly as the result of her recent bereavement? Beth was not quite sure. She thought she might well end up feeling quite silly if she told York she'd felt threatened by someone who, half the time at least, seemed a cuddly elderly lady.

While mulling it over, she'd managed to get a huge amount done in the small room, she realised as she rubbed filthy hands on her jeans. It felt as though the dust of, not quite a thousand years, but probably several decades, was all over her. She could feel the grit in her mouth, her eyes were itchy, and her hair was begging for a wash. Even her Shetland pony fringe felt uncharacteristically limp.

But the results were spectacular. She wished the bursar would rap on the door now, and see the room as it suddenly was. She blushed to think of how awful it must have looked this morning. Now, instead of an obstacle course made up of cardboard, she had a neatly stacked pile of duplicate copies of legions of school magazines, ready for recycling, while one of each edition had been preserved and shelved.

This crazy doubling up on what were essentially pretty run-of-the-mill publications had accounted for a surprising number of the boxes, though a phalanx of them did still remain to be sorted through. The cartons that had been satisfyingly emptied had been dismantled and folded flat. She wouldn't need them all, but she would retain some in case documents needed to be moved again at some point in the future. She was very much hoping this would never need to happen, but if it did, the school would be prepared and wouldn't have to buy in new materials.

In among all this chaff, however, she had found some very promising-looking ledgers, bound in handsome leather, much older than the rest of the contents of the archive and featuring beautiful, though faded, copperplate writing, which she judged dated from the inception of the school. It would take her a long time to decipher the faded, sepia-coloured writing; she might even, she realised with a bit of a thrill, need to get some of those white cotton gloves that *real* archivists wore. She corrected herself quickly. She *was* a real archivist, and white cotton gloves were an essential part of her kit. She would order some just as soon as she'd made more of a dent on the room.

In the meantime, she had locked the precious ledgers into the filing cabinets, piling some of the most boring school magazines on top as camouflage. They were where she had previously stashed Jenkins' bank statements and notebooks. These, in turn, she had moved into her own briefcase, ready to take home. She was planning to look through them over the next few days, once Jake was safely tucked up in bed, of course, and once she had got through some of her sorely neglected freelance work.

Looking through Jenkins' documents seemed a bit intrusive and would almost certainly be quite boring, she thought. But she realised with a thrill of pleasure that she was really looking forward to inspecting the old ledgers. It was the sort of project she'd thought she'd be involved in all the time when she took the job. That seemed like a lifetime ago. She had to keep reminding herself that less than a week had gone by, and that she would get to her own pet project in good time. There were mountains of other documents that she needed to consult on first, though.

Nowadays, the school's day-to-day records were all computerised, but in the past huge quantities of information had been kept on paper and it was hard to see how even the most dedicated Wyatt's fan would want to delve through centuries of this trivial stuff. There needed to be a strategy for what was kept, as well as for what she could let go. She could see the archives office had become the dumping ground for everything someone else did not want to make a decision on. Records relating to all school matters, from the suppliers of prefects' badges, to every paracetamol currently in the infirmary, to the architect who'd concocted the Grand Hall, and the recipients of bursaries throughout the ages, were lodged here in no particular order at all. Rather like the 'downloads' folder on a laptop, the archives office had become the automatic repository of choice. Everything went in. Nothing came out.

But now, both Mrs Jenkins and the bursar suddenly seemed interested in its contents. She wondered why now, of all times, the archives had suddenly become so fascinating. Had Dr Jenkins been working on something that had stirred up a hornets' nest? Was that the *real* reason for his murder?

Beth found it quite hard to find any trace of anything in the archives that Jenkins had actually been engaged on. Almost everything she'd touched that day had been covered by a film of thick grey London dust, and although she was no expert, it was much, much more than a week's worth of the stuff. The exception, she supposed, might be the contents of the filing cabinets – but most of them had been yawningly empty when she'd looked. What on earth had Jenkins been up to? Well, maybe she'd find out tonight. His papers would tell a story, even if the man himself no longer could.

Later that evening, with Jake finally tucked up, Beth ran her fingers through her thick, freshly washed fringe as she stared exhaustedly at the kitchen table. She was still in her dressing gown, after hopping in the shower the moment they'd got home. What with homework and the rest of the evening childcare cavalcade, she hadn't had a second to shrug on her clothes, and now it was too late to bother.

She'd arranged the bank statements into thick piles, each representing a year. Jenkins might not have had much of a work ethic, but he was an archives man in one respect – he didn't seem to have thrown anything away. Lugging this little lot back home had not been easy, and she was glad that Friday afternoon was CCF time at Wyatt's. She didn't totally understand the workings of the Combined Cadet Force, except that it gave eager pupils the chance to dress up in uniform and rush about pretending they were members of the army, navy or air force. Suffice to say, it meant that people not involved got to knock off a little early on a Friday, which was no bad thing in general, and was particularly helpful when you were trying to drag a bunch of dodgy documents home.

She wasn't entirely sure what the ethics of leaving the school premises with a dead staff member's private documents were, but she was willing to bet that the bursar, for one, would be very keen to stop her. Luckily, he was the Grand Panjandrum of the CCF, so he was fully occupied in getting small boys to run up and down rugby pitches at the crucial moment when she sidled out past the porter with two of Mrs Jenkins' abandoned bags for life stuffed to the gunnels with papers.

Mrs Jenkins, whose home was really not a million miles from where Beth sat, would also be beside herself if she knew what Beth was about to do.

Maybe that was the reason Beth was hesitating. There was also the fact that reading someone else's bank statements was such a taboo. It was a total invasion of privacy. But did that count for anything, Beth wondered, if the person in question was dead?

She remembered how awful it had been after James had died, when the bank statements, bills, and even the junk mail had continued to roll in every single day, all addressed to someone who could never, now, read any of it. Each letter had seemed like a stab to her heart. Even when she had eventually been able to rouse herself to send a round robin to all the companies they had accounts with, informing them as blandly as she could of his sudden death – a letter which had cost her rivers of bitter, hot tears – many had persisted in keeping him on their databases. In fact, she sometimes still made decisions about which utilities to choose based on how efficient they had been back in those dark days.

Now, if ever a piece of junk mail did arrive with James's name on it – and it still did happen – she was actually rather glad. It proved he had really existed, and that somewhere, somehow, he still did – if only in the obsolete memory bank of some cheap, un-updateable, spam-generating computer.

She wondered how it was for people now, when their loved ones died suddenly, leaving such a footprint behind on social media. Facebook histories, showing what seemed like every moment of life, and always featuring laughing gangs of friends (whatever the real truth). Would it be a comfort for those left behind, or more of a torment, to see them forever suspended in the ether: young, carefree, enjoying plentiful LOLs, 'liking' pictures of kittens, and posting inspirational messages?

In some ways, she was glad James had not been that into Facebook. She wasn't sure how it would have felt, looking over his posts now she was growing older, while he remained fixed and static. How did the phrase go? 'They shall not grow old, as we that are left grow old.' It was all too sad. She could feel a lone tear track down her cheek. It fell onto the 2010 pile of Alan Jenkins' bank statements. She pulled the papers towards her, and slid off the elastic band she'd used to keep the sheaf together. But first, she'd just make herself a quick cup of herbal tea... and maybe just do the washing-up...

An hour and a half later, and despite every method of prevarication she could deploy – including a thorough clean of the entire kitchen, sitting room, utility and downstairs loo – she knew an awful lot more about Dr Jenkins. Notwithstanding the orgy of scrubbing and a swimming-pool tang of chlorine bleach in the air, she felt distinctly grubby about this. It seemed so much like prying. She wasn't entirely positive the dead really had private lives, as such, but Dr Alan Jenkins definitely didn't now, that was for sure.

The bank account was his alone, so there was probably a joint account somewhere which paid for heating, lighting, the mortgage if they had one, and all the domestic details from food to council tax. But Jenkins had been assiduous about ensuring that all his statements from this separate account, which were delivered to the marital home like clockwork, did not stay there. He took every single one to Wyatt's and stashed them all at work. There was something here he wanted to hide.

Once she was finally settled at the table with nothing else to distract her, it didn't take Beth long to make sense of the statements. Rapidly, she knew how much he spent on clothes – a surprising amount for someone she would not have described as well dressed; she remembered that jacket with the now regulation shudder. She knew he spent even more on wine, mostly claret, and a fortune on cigars. She knew he made regular, expensive payments to a company which, when she googled it, turned out to be a Harley Street hair loss clinic. She knew he bought books from several antiquarian bookshops.

She also knew he had started to buy increasing quantities of DVDs from some very dodgy porn websites. She knew she really *didn't* want to know more about those DVDs. He also had an Amazon Prime account, Netflix *and* Now TV as well – surely no one could be that interested in mainstream films? She was willing to bet he wasn't watching Disney classics at any rate. She knew that, for the past eighteen months, he'd been spending regular, pricey weekends at a swanky Oxfordshire hotel. And, most importantly, she also knew that, as of June last year, he had started to bank regular sums of money. It had started off with a £200 cash deposit each month. By the time he died, it was up to £600 a month.

Now where on earth was that coming from? And why?

She stared at the bank statements in frustration. Five minutes ago, she'd felt as though they were telling her much more than she wanted to know about this man. Now, all of a sudden, the air was full of question marks and the statements were mute pieces of paper with no voice to tell her what they really held. How on earth was she going to find out more?

. . .

It was a question which preoccupied her over the weekend. Though she did love these unpressured, schoolwork-free days with Jake – free from the tyranny of the alarm clock, the school run, and the regimented bedtime necessary to achieve everything else – she also felt the lack of a partner more at weekends than at any other time. It was easy enough to slip from day to day during the weeks without thinking too much. Weekends gave her a bit more space to ponder, and that wasn't always a good thing.

At times like these, she was grateful for her freelance work. It was rarely enough to have her slaving flat out, but there had always been just enough to keep her ticking over, feeling busy and – if she were totally honest with herself – just a little bit important. She needed to matter – not just to her darling Jake, but also to someone else, somewhere in the working world. If there was an impatient editor drumming their fingers waiting for her copy, that meant she counted. Rewriting company reports, gussying up badly written websites, the odd article for a newspaper if she thought of something clever enough to pitch to one of the terrifying features editors – all these kept the wolf from the door and distracted her from her loneliness.

But she *was* lonely. And taking the football to the park with Jake on a Saturday for a proper kick-about brought it home with a bump. It was always the dads taking the kids to the park. The mums, she supposed, were enjoying a bit of well-deserved quality time with their sofas, while the dads reacquainted themselves with the tiny humans they'd made and then abandoned all week while working. So, she saw dads attempting to post their tiny toddlers into the baby swings, unaccustomed to dealing with so many uncooperative limbs at once. She saw dads struggling with exploded nappies; dads doing their best with skinned knees; dads cheering on the more mobile tinies whooshing down the slides; dads finally relaxing on the benches as their charges grew older; and everywhere, dads retreating behind their smartphones when interaction with their children got too much. Meanwhile, for her, it was business as usual.

She knew that some of the mums at the school looked askance at her, as she was always hanging out at the playground on Saturdays with the dads. To some territorial women, that made her a threat. Belinda McKenzie, the Alpha Mummy, had once joshed to her in a jokey-*not*-joking way that, 'if she ever wanted to remarry, she'd have the pick of everyone else's husbands; they all worshipped her because she was so great with a football'. Belinda, of course, had pronounced 'football' as though saying 'rancid slug', and her implication was that the desperate Beth was only pretending to like the game so she could snare someone else's meal-ticket man – a foul if ever there was one. Belinda was far too dainty herself to play rough games with her three kids, and besides, it would have played havoc with her nails/hair/pristine white jeans. And she employed an au pair and a husband to do that stuff for her.

As she obligingly kicked, ran and yelled with Jake, Beth reflected that football wasn't something she loved; it was just something she had to do. She hadn't loved nappy-changing or Thomas the Tank Engine or Lego either, and she particularly didn't love Minecraft or anything that came in a ridiculously expensive PlayStation box. But here she was; this was the boat she and her boy were in, and she'd do her best, and that was that. The time would come – very soon, she suspected – when Jake wouldn't be caught dead kicking a ball with his mother anyway, and she would be happy to retire then, just like George Best and David Beckham before her. Though possibly, without either the alcohol problem or the aftershave and pants deals.

On the Sunday, she was spared the football as her beloved brother, Josh, tipped up just before lunch. At thirty-six, Josh was her big brother, but he had always operated – so the family said – in reverse dog years and often seemed much younger than Jake. He was naturally carefree and, while he loved his work as a press photographer and had done well, it was by accident rather than design. The rootlessness that came with the territory suited him perfectly.

Though Beth worried about him when he was abroad, she was the first to agree with his own assessment that bombs and bullets would always simply bounce off him, if he even stayed in the same place for long enough for someone to take aim. He was much the same with girlfriends. Magazines were full of articles bemoaning commitment-phobic men and, much as she loved her brother, Beth could see he pretty much ticked every box. He was a nightmare with women. Today was a case in point. He'd arrived with a lovely Swiss girl in tow, who seemed to have been acquired on a recent assignment.

Josh was as careless about her as if she'd been a Toblerone he'd picked up in duty-free, introducing her then promptly abandoning her in the kitchen while he ran out to give Jake a masterclass on headers in the garden. Magpie the cat, who normally shunned all visitors, had a huge soft spot for Josh and deigned to pat the football with a black and white paw when it came near her, and ran after it for a while with Jake. She'd soon had enough of the rough and tumble, though, and stalked back into the kitchen via her cat flap, giving Josh's new girlfriend a very wide berth and flicking her tail in final disdain as she disappeared into the sitting room.

Beth and the girl smiled at each other warily. Beth had been here too many times before. In fact, she did sometimes wonder whether Josh's attitude was somehow putting her off dipping into dating again herself. It had been years now since James had died. Though she still thought of him every day – and Jake growing into his carbon copy helped keep him with her in a way – she knew he wouldn't have wanted her to be alone forever.

She remembered that precious feeling of being held, safe, in a beloved man's arms, and she was sad at thinking that might not happen again. But somehow, it never seemed to be time.

Jake, and life, and now this whole murder business, contrived to keep her busy enough not to feel too bereft. And maybe all men were like Josh now, unable to make a decision. There was always someone new just a swipe away.

She sighed inwardly, rather wishing Josh hadn't brought Marlene with him. It was worse if she got to know the girls, because they were always so lovely (Josh had great taste, she'd give him that), and she really felt for them when things started to go wrong. The poor things would start texting her or, even worse, ringing or dropping round, for advice and comfort. But what could she say? There was no magic formula that was going to make the relationship work. Josh got bored after two years, and that was that. If only he could tell them that at the beginning, Beth thought longingly, catching the beautiful Swiss girl gazing out of the kitchen windows at him with unmistakably goo-goo eyes. She was crazy about him. Soon she would be made crazy *by* him.

Beth should just get a job lot of T-shirts printed with the slogan, 'It's not you, it's HIM' and wear them every time Josh visited with a newbie. She sighed again – this time audibly.

'Is everything OK?' said Marlene, with a tiny frown. 'Josh told you I'd be coming with him?'

'Yes, and no,' said Beth, smiling at the girl but already unable to assuage her doubts. Josh, of course, had said not one single word about poor Marlene, and probably never would. That tiny frown on the girl's perfect creamy brow was already growing bigger. It was going to be a long afternoon.

TEN

With one thing and another, Beth was actually very glad when Monday rolled around. There was a lot to be said for a secure routine. Jake, who'd been delighted and exhausted in equal measure to see his beloved uncle, had slept like a log. Beth, who'd felt the same about Josh but with a massive side order of sympathy for poor Marlene, had not slept nearly so well. The wind had whistled in the little house's chimneys as she'd turned and turned again to no avail in her too-big bed.

She replayed the day, and worried about whether she should have given Marlene a hint. But that would have been so disloyal to Josh, who enjoyed the girl's company as far as that went (not very far in his case). They'd done plenty of snogging, which Jake had looked disgusted at, much to Beth's relief. She certainly didn't want him to get any ideas about love and relationships from Josh. Oh, it was all so tiring. She wouldn't think about it any more. She couldn't do anything to change her brother, and she wasn't sure if anyone could. But she *could* push on with her little investigation.

This, of course, gave her a new set of things to worry over, and chased sleep still further away. Should she, or should she not, come clean to Inspector York about the lumps of cash littering Dr Jenkins' bank account? Would the police find out about them anyway? She had no idea whether they would investigate his finances as a matter of course, or if that only happened when there was a whiff of impropriety in the air. Mind you, getting murdered seemed, fairly or unfairly, to be a moral condemnation of a sort anyway. Unless you were just in the wrong place at the wrong time, there must be the implication that there was something about you that annoyed the perpetrator enough for them to break the ultimate taboo and bash you on the head. Or, in this case, stab you.

Beth had spent quite a lot of the night wondering whether it was possible that Jenkins had come by the cash legitimately. He could have been phenomenally lucky at the National Lottery. He could have been addicted to scratch cards. There were none in the office, but possibly there were giant stacks of the things inside those dark cupboards in his Gilkes Place kitchen. Maybe he just had very, very generous friends, who loved to give him piles of money. He could even, she supposed, be organising some sort of school collection – maybe a really spectacular farewell present for a colleague.

Or he could just be a blackmailer.

Jenkins had not been a nice man, so blackmail – a nasty crime if ever there was one – wouldn't be much of a stretch for him. On their slight acquaintance, she was pretty sure he had the relevant skill set, being sneaky, unpleasant, secretive and obnoxious. And, of course, it gave whoever was on the receiving end of his demands an absolutely twenty-four-carat motive for murder.

Beth wasn't sure whether, if she revealed what she'd found out to Inspector York, she'd get into such huge trouble that she would just regret it. And also, if she did tell the police, how could she then get any further with her digging? They wouldn't obligingly tell her how they were getting on. She'd already had one warning off – York might not be so restrained a second time.

In the end, Beth decided, as she dropped Jake off at school, that she'd say nothing for the moment. It was just easier that way. The decision made, there was a spring in her step as she strolled to Wyatt's. The magnolia trees were starting to bloom now, their waxen petals delicately flushed with pink. Beth thought of Marlene, suffused with blushes when Josh had tossed her a careless compliment. Already, a few petals had fallen, heavy and waxen, to the pavement after a windy night. The air was fresh but not too cold. A night's buffeting had left the new day feeling rumpled but clean, like a sheet fresh on the bed.

She passed the porter with a smile. On the way to her office, she exchanged hellos with the middle school head Alison Lincoln and the combative mathematician Sam Radley – one of her Prime Suspects after that tense lunchtime talk from the bursar. Neither he nor Alison Lincoln was looking particularly shifty or plagued by an uneasy conscience.

Beth didn't know whether to be glad about this or not. It was exactly a week now since her grisly discovery, and a large part of her wanted closure on the whole matter as soon as possible. Meanwhile, she had to admit that a tiny part of her was quite enjoying the investigation and she had a very real anxiety that, as soon as the bursar discovered how little she was doing in the archive office, her lovely job would be gone.

The more time had passed, the more she had realised with crystal clarity that the school did not need a full-time archivist. Goodness only knew why they had so recently appointed a second person as well. She was glad they had, of course she was. And the job, while not bringing in a fortune, was pretty crucial to her – and to Jake. But, even while occupied with a murder investigation, she had more or less got on top of the filing in one hectic afternoon. She hadn't finished, by any means, but she knew now how to get the place in proper order, and it wasn't going to take months, or even weeks. What she would do with herself when that was accomplished was another matter.

Luckily, she had more than enough to occupy her at the moment, puzzling over Jenkins' ill-gotten loot, she thought while she fumbled to get her swipe card ready as she turned the corner in front of the archive office.

Then, she saw, she had no need of a card at all. The door was swinging open.

Beth approached with great caution. If the events of the last week had taught her anything, it was to expect the unexpected. With her phone in her hand, already scrolling through recent calls to get York's number, she edged into the doorway. The storage area, crammed as ever with the bits of sports kit which seemed to have no other home, seemed much as usual.

She climbed the rickety stairs as quietly as she could, cursing the faint unavoidable rattling of the cheap aluminium rungs. The door at the top of the stairs was swinging open, too. She looked in, and only realised she'd been holding her breath when she let it go in relief. There was no sign of a dead body. Thank goodness for that.

But that was all the good news. The archive office, which she'd left in such good order on Friday, looked as though a Wizard of Oz-style cyclone had torn through it. The filing cabinets were overturned, every single box was upended, her desk had been pushed over, each drawer thrown onto the floor, and drifting across the lot was a sea of papers. Her eyes filled with tears. She couldn't help herself. She had spent so much time sorting everything out and bringing a sense of purpose to the little room. She had felt quite peaceful here afterwards, and had been looking forward to building on that good start and really settling into her job – as well as solving the Jenkins business, of course.

Now, all that was wrecked. It was hard, as she walked

forward onto a mound of documents, torn and strewn this way and that, not to take this as a personal attack. She felt great sorrow at the destruction. She also, for the first time since the initial terror of finding Jenkins' dead body, felt afraid. Was this some kind of warning to her? Did someone know what she was up to? And was this their way of telling her, in no uncertain terms, to stop?

'Hello? Hello?' It was York's disembodied voice, cutting in on her thoughts. She looked in surprise at her phone. She must have pressed the dial button by accident. Well, that saved her having to make a decision.

'Inspector? It's Beth Haldane here, from Wyatt's,' she said, her voice trembling.

'What is it?' York's reply was terse, but Beth could feel the concentration in his voice. She had his full attention.

'It's the archives office. It's been... destroyed.'

Two hours later, and with another cup of tea clamped in her hands, Beth knew she had been a little overdramatic. The office had been trashed, yes – but not destroyed. The shelf of Wyatt's school magazines she had organised the other day was untouched, their breathless reviews of long-past productions and speeches of thanks to dead headmasters too boring even to be stamped on by a burglar. It was just everything else that had been thrown on the floor, trampled and torn.

While she was sheltering in the bursar's office, and sitting pretty in his luxuriously padded leather chair while he grumpily took temporary shelter next door with the administrative assistants, Beth reconciled herself to redoing all Friday's work again. It was a task that would be made much more difficult now everything had been thrown out of order, and quite a lot of the documents damaged or destroyed. But what really worried her was those lovely leather-bound ledgers, the ones that had looked as venerable as the school itself and which she had been dying to decipher, just as soon as she'd got somewhere with her investigation.

Now, she was cursing herself roundly. The investigation, such as it was, seemed to bring nothing but trouble in its wake. And the few objects that had seemed worthy of serious study in the archive were, if not destroyed forever, then probably damaged beyond repair. She had been such a fool. Her job was to safeguard those ledgers, not to poke and pry into her dead colleague's affairs. She had missed her chance of really making a difference to the archives.

Her head was bowed over the strong builder's tea as York rushed into the room. 'What do you think they were looking for?' he demanded, without ceremony, dragging a chair up to the desk where Beth sat in state.

'Looking for?' Beth raised her head, surprised.

'Yes. They were searching for something, whoever did this. And they got quite angry when they couldn't find it. You know what was in those records. What was it?'

Beth hesitated. It could have been the ledgers, or it could have been... 'Jenkins' bank statements,' she said flatly.

'What? You had those there?'

Beth flushed a little. 'Not exactly. I... stumbled across them. I wasn't quite sure what to do with them... so I took them home.'

'You took them *home*?' said York, sitting back a little, eyebrows hitting his hairline. 'What the hell? We'd better get them straight away. Tell me where they are and give me a spare key if you can't leave work now. I don't need to tell you those were private property. What did you think you were up to? Is this more of your poking around? I thought I told you that was going to get you into trouble?'

'They're next to my laptop. Under some old newspapers. And there's a key under the mat at home.'

York gave Beth a disbelieving glance and she sat there,

shamefaced. All right, it wasn't great security-wise... but she had to leave one there for Josh. Her brother had a habit of turning up unexpectedly and couldn't be trusted not to lose a key if she gave it to him.

It was probably the first time someone sitting in the bursar's big chair had suffered a ticking off. Usually things were the other way round. She wasn't enjoying it.

York finally spoke again. 'I suppose you had a good look at the bank statements, did you? You might as well tell me what you found, save me a bit of time at least.'

Beth kept her head down and mumbled, 'Blackmail.'

York sat up straight. 'Let me get this right. You found evidence of blackmail, and didn't think to tell me?'

Beth shrugged. 'I didn't know how you would take it,' she said.

He subsided – but only a little. 'Well, I suppose you were right to wonder. And now you know.'

'I didn't know for sure, of course. It's just that he'd been receiving lump sums of cash, getting bigger, over the past few months. It's possible that it was from some legitimate source,' she added, her shoulders rising hopefully. York gave her a sceptical glance and she slumped a little.

'We'd better go and pick up these statements right away. I'll check with the team and then you'll come with me,' he said gruffly, and stalked out.

Beth, left to her own devices and still feeling like a naughty child in the huge, throne-like chair, started to do what a child does when left alone in Daddy's office. She swivelled the swivel chair, she fiddled with the photos on the desk, she pulled at the drawers – and in the top one on the right-hand side, she found a key. Suddenly grown up again, she held it up in front of her. No, it couldn't be – could it? She put it back down on the desktop then reached round to her handbag on the floor. She got out her own key to the inner door of the archive office. She placed it on top of the one she'd just put on the bursar's desk. They matched exactly.

Perhaps it was because she'd just endured such a major bollocking, but Beth remained silent about the twin keys. She felt sulky and uncooperative. She knew it was silly, and she recognised it as childish; it was precisely the behaviour Jake exhibited on the rare occasions when she had to lay down the law. But it was OK, she'd let York in on this newest revelation. At some point. For the moment, she just wanted to get back to her poor, beleaguered office, to start putting it to rights – and to check on the ledgers.

Her heart sank a little as she stood on the threshold. The mess had not been improved by a lot of policemen's feet joining the burglars in stomping on everything, and the further addition of drifts of fingerprint powder here and there just made things all the more grungy. The powder particularly annoyed her, as York had told her more or less straight away that whoever had broken in had worn gloves and managed to keep their DNA to themselves – thank goodness – while they were about their wrecking. So why dust for fingerprints everywhere? It was the icing on a particularly rubbishy cake, as far as she was concerned.

She sighed deeply as she started picking up sheaves of papers. No doubt there were police protocols that were always followed, even when it was obvious they would serve no purpose. Fine for the fingerprint guys – they didn't have to tidy up after themselves. No wonder crime scene cleaning companies were springing up these days, she thought a little crossly. More than anything, she needed to clear a path over to the filing cabinets somehow. So, she might as well work her way across the room by doing a quick triage of all the poor papers flung hither and thither.

She quickly realised the mayhem had looked worse than it

was. She was making good progress. Most of the papers dumped on the floor, she decided after a cursory glance, were fit only for the bin now anyway, so that was easy. She just jammed the lot into plastic bags and stacked them outside the door for the recycling bins. She wasn't that keen to take them down there herself – for obvious reasons – but she was sure she could appeal to the porter or one of the grounds staff to help her out.

It was hot, dusty, dirty work, and after an hour and a half, Beth was filthy and exhausted. It was like Friday, all over again. She didn't know how papers sucked up dust, but they did, and it wasn't until you moved them that they released it – all over you. It was all very well for miners, she thought crossly, they had access to showers after a hard day down the pit – though she was horrified with herself as the comparison crossed her mind. She'd have to walk through Dulwich Village covered in grey smudges until she could take a shower, which probably wouldn't be until after she'd dragged Jake through the bedtime routine. Meanwhile, she would be judged by every other mother in the district, all of whom managed to remain pristine at all times – mostly wearing the regulation Dulwich white skinny jeans. They all had lovely 'little jobs' which definitely did not involve fingerprint dust, policemen, blackmail – and murder.

One thing she was pleased about, though, was that she'd already managed to persuade the porter to attach a temporary hasp and padlock to the inner archive office door. And she was pretty sure, having seen him take the padlock out of its plastic packaging, that she had the only two keys in existence.

Better still, she had finally managed to get the filing cabinets upright and opened just before home time. Inside, battered but intact, were the three leather ledgers, exactly where she'd stashed them the other day, and still covered by a wodge of Jenkins' old cryptic crosswords. Either the layers of yellowing newspaper had saved anyone from even seeing the ledgers, or they hadn't bothered with the filing cabinets at all because they knew what they were looking for was stored somewhere else. That rather begged the question – what on earth had they been hoping to find? Beth had been turning this over all the time she'd been tidying and clearing. Her money was on the bank statements.

She fished the big old ledgers out, cradling them carefully in her arms, and cast around the room, looking for somewhere safe to put them. She didn't want them to be snatched if someone came back for a second go. She was almost tempted to take them home with her. But after this burglary, she realised that someone considered the archives fair game and there was no way on earth she would even consider bringing that danger close to Jake. The last thing she wanted was to drag her son into all this.

She'd probably be hopelessly disappointed when she finally got a chance to read the ledgers properly. For all she knew, they could have been an eighteenth-century version of the coma-inducing *Wyatt's Chronicle* school newsletters that the school seemed to churn out in unforgiveable quantities, and which had been filed by successive archivists with as much reverence as though it were a serialised version of Magna Carta. But some-how, their very air of venerable age gave these ancient books a promise and a mystique that was sorely lacking in ninety per cent of the contents of the archive. No, thought Beth, that was unfair. Ninety-nine per cent.

Yet again, she'd run out of time to see whether her hopes were justified. If she hung around any longer, she'd be late to pick up Jake, and she hated keeping him waiting. Where on earth could she stick these books quickly, where they'd be safe?

She was racking her brains, eyes darting here and there, when she realised that the perfect hiding place had been under her nose all along. The shelf of unspeakably dreary Wyatt's magazines. No one would ever think of disturbing them there.

Even her rabidly destructive burglar had shunned the magazines. She slid the ledgers next to some bound copies of the *Wyatt Wanderer* – a 1930s precursor of today's *Wyatt's Chronicle* – and stood back to survey the effect. Though the ledgers, to her mind, were so much more full of promise than anything else on the shelves, she had to admit that, to the untutored eye, all the tomes looked pretty much of a muchness. Being right in the middle, and squeezed in among so many frankly soporific volumes, seemed like the perfect place for them. Hidden in plain sight.

Despite her best efforts, Beth was five minutes late for pickup. She ran the last few yards, expecting Jake to be loitering crossly in the playground, but realised he was deep in a kickabout with Charlie and a few of the other boys. A straggle of mothers looked on, and she smiled to see Katie among them.

'Haven't seen you for ages,' said Katie, giving the regulation kiss on both cheeks, and smoothing a smudge of archive grime off Beth's face in the process. 'You look like you've had a busy day,' she added, laughing.

'You wouldn't believe it if I told you,' said Beth, pushing her fringe out of her eyes with a tired hand. She'd had a thorough wash in the loos before leaving work, but maybe she didn't have Katie's eagle eye for detail. Her fringe flopped back immediately but she grinned. It was so good to see her friend.

'Come back with us for supper?' Beth found herself asking on impulse. She wouldn't normally suggest it on a school night. She knew her friend had started the rigorous process of tutoring which, in Dulwich, was considered essential before an assault on the endowment schools at secondary transfer time, but it was so great to see Katie and she wanted to bounce around a few ideas on the investigation.

'No, you come back with us. You've been working all day. I'll cook, you can entertain me.' Katie twinkled.

'No extracurriculars tonight?' Beth asked. Charlie was

getting coaching in English and Maths, and Katie had been toying with verbal reasoning lessons too. This wasn't like Jake's little in-school reading sessions with Miss Brown (or Mrs Jenkins, as Beth now had to think of her). Charlie was getting heavy-duty grooming for the entrance exams, which Beth privately did not believe he needed at all.

'This is his night off. Apart from piano, of course.' Katie smiled, but she wasn't joking. Charlie, like Jake, was an only child, and the centre of Katie's world. By Dulwich standards, he wasn't being hothoused at all – he only played one instrument, and he did have this whole day off coaching during the week, for goodness' sake. But his parents wanted the best for him. In the wildly competitive environs of Dulwich, the best meant squeezing him into Wyatt's. And the effort wouldn't stop there. By the time he applied for university, a boy like Charlie would have a Duke of Edinburgh Gold Award under his belt; he'd have a certificate saying he'd dragged his lacklustre piano playing all the way up to Grade 8 level; he'd participate in some form of sport at least once a week; and he'd have a cache of work experience stints at blue-chip companies (usually owned by friends of his mum and dad) on his CV. It was an exhausting prospect, for any boy – and any mother.

And Katie was the *most normal* mother Beth knew. Beth was dearly fond of both her and Charlie. The trouble was that fear was contagious. And the terror that Charlie wouldn't get a place at a good school, and that other boys who were no brighter would because their mothers had forced them through these hoops, was very real. Even Beth herself was now worrying – when she had the time – about whether she was doing poor Jake a disservice by not making him swot away night after night. For the moment, she thought he was doing just fine, and when she was at her calmest, she was certain that he didn't need extra help at all. But sometimes, it was hard to hold the line.

Twenty minutes later, Beth had washed her hands lavishly

again with Katie's Neal's Yard soap in her lovely guest loo, smoothed away the last traces of dust from her face, and even done a quick detangling job on her hair with her hands. She would have loved a shower, but that would just have to wait until later. She was now ensconced at the breakfast bar of a kitchen straight out of *World of Interiors*.

It was a sea of marble, with industrial hints in the bright copper tubing of the bar-stool legs, and the three copper-shaded pendant lights swooping low over the bleached oak dining table. Even the handles on the sleek line of floor-to-ceiling glass doors fronting the garden were burnished copper. In high summer, the doors swooshed back like stage curtains to reveal the beautifully tended garden which, unlike Beth's, seemed impervious to football-boot scuffs, bald patches and weeds. At the end of the lawn, two graceful Japanese acer trees, already showing clusters of the red which would unfurl into flaming leaf in the next month, were backed by the giant chestnut trees of Dulwich Park right behind the house. There was even a narrow door in the fence which led straight into the park. It was probably the thing that Beth most envied Katie for; though the list of possibilities, she was the first to admit, was extremely long.

The boys had scampered off to Charlie's bedroom, where they were no doubt deep in some artificial world by now. Beth and Katie were peeling and chopping vegetables for the boys to push around their plates later. Beth admired the splashy orange of the pile of organic carrots on her chopping board – itself a beautiful thick slab of olivewood, which chimed so well with the kitchen's copper highlights. She marvelled at how her friend got all these things right without seeming to try, while Belinda McKenzie, who lived three doors down on this particularly lush and lovely Dulwich street, had got a designer in to do her entire house at vast expense and the whole thing had turned out aching with soullessness.

'Do you see much of Belinda?' Beth said, idly following her train of thought.

Katie gave her friend a measured look. 'Belinda's OK, you know. Her heart's in the right place.'

'On the transplant list, you mean?' said Beth. 'No, she's fine, she's just... so Dulwich. If you know what I mean.'

'No one's more Dulwich than you, though, Beth, come on. Your family has been here for generations.'

'True. But we're, well, low-key people, I suppose. Belinda is more... headline news. I just find her a bit intimidating,' said Beth, peeling carrots and admiring the vivid orange curls as they piled up beside her on the creamy marble.

'Oh, Belinda's OK. I don't see that much of her, I don't think she considers Charlie a great influence.'

'Why not?' Beth's hackles immediately rose in defence of Jake's friend.

'For a start, he's only doing one instrument. Her three are all playing at least two each.'

Beth thought silently of the cacophony that must entail. Six musical instruments played in one house, each one no doubt practised for at least the mandatory twenty minutes a night. No wonder Belinda's husband travelled so much. Beth was still scarred by Jake having had to play the recorder for two terms in Year Three. Sometimes, on a clear night, she thought she could still hear the mangled opening notes of 'London's Burning'. It would be a while before she could face another instrument, and she was pretty sure most things wouldn't even fit in the house, unless Jake suddenly got enthusiastic about the triangle, of course. Maybe Belinda's lot were musical geniuses. Maybe Belinda used earplugs.

'But I want to know about your job,' Katie was saying as she skilfully sliced up some sweet potatoes. 'What on earth is happening? Is there any word yet on the... you know?'

'The *murder*?' Instinctively, the women lowered their voices and looked around. Neither wanted their boys to be contaminated by such goings-on, though it would have been the one topic both boys were keen to discuss in depth with their mothers, unlike anything to do with school and homework.

'No idea how the police investigation is going. All I know is that I haven't made much progress yet myself,' said Beth.

'What about Judith Seasons? That was quite promising, wasn't it? Any more from her?'

'Last I saw of her was at Ruth Jenkins' place, when she was shutting the door firmly in my face. She doesn't seem to want to make my job easier. Have either of them been at yoga?'

'Only Judith, and she's been quite distant,' said Katie, reaching into a cupboard for a bowl. Into it she glugged a tablespoon or so of soy sauce and added a matching quantity of coconut oil. She then tipped the strips of sweet potato into the bowl and deftly tumbled them in the rich brown mixture.

'The oddest thing happened on Friday. Ruth Jenkins came to my office and started throwing things about... and then when I arrived today there'd been a burglary.' Beth took a baton of organic carrot in her hand and munched it thoughtfully. It was sweet and crunchy, but was it any better than a non-organic carrot? She wasn't sure.

'A burglary?' Katie looked up, shocked. 'That's awful. Why didn't you say?'

'Well, nothing was taken, as far as I know. But everything was messed up. I spent the whole afternoon trying to put the place back together. I still feel grimy.'

'That explains the dust on your face earlier. You look fine, though. But that must have been such a shock.'

'It was, after everything else. But someone's done me a favour, really. I've been able to chuck out a whole load of rubbish that would have taken me months to sort out otherwise.'

'Do you think it was Ruth Jenkins? Come back to finish what she'd started?'

'She is the most likely person... and according to the police, the door wasn't forced, so it was someone with a key. She could easily have got hold of a spare key, if Jenkins himself had one at home – which he might well have done. She could have just borrowed it one day and taken it to that shoe place on Norwood High Street where they do keys, cut a copy.'

Naturally there wasn't anything as useful as a cobbler's shop in Dulwich Village itself. Shopping there was great if you were having a massive cushion-cover emergency or wanted to go to a party wearing something bohemian with tassels, but if you needed a pint of milk you were in big trouble. Even the post office had recently closed down, and bets were already being taken on whether the prime village space left vacant would be taken by a chi-chi café or a bijou boutique. It was rumoured that other types of shop did exist, just not within the hallowed confines of Dulwich.

'What's Mrs Jenkins actually like, would you say?' asked Beth. 'Because I didn't realise she was the *Miss Brown* who takes Jake for reading on Thursdays. She told me she stuck with her previous name because it was easier than changing it at work.'

'Oh yes! I hadn't made the connection,' said Katie, whose faith in expensive extracurricular tutoring meant she was quite vague about the services offered by the school itself. 'Brown's a pretty common surname. I'm not sure I've seen her much around the school, just a couple of times. I recognised her from yoga. Thought she might be an admin helper or something, but she could even have been someone's granny come to pick them up, I never asked. She looks like the grandmotherly type, doesn't she?'

'I would have said exactly the same thing until last week,' said Beth, sitting forward in excitement. 'She seemed lovely. But she's not. She's... weird.'

'I thought you seemed pleased with the way she was helping Jake, though, didn't you?' said Katie, surprised.

It said a lot for Katie that she had never once offered any sort of judgement on Jake needing a little help with his reading. Beth herself was reasonably calm about it – most of the time – and took the school's assessment of the situation at face value. Jake needed temporary help but would soon be up to speed. But at the same time, Beth knew that if *Charlie* had been singled out as in need of support, Katie would instantly have amassed a team of experts who would soon have plunged him back into the mainstream – kicking and screaming, if necessary. Whether this would have ended up denting his self-esteem was a moot point, but Beth appreciated her friend's acceptance of her own, much more laid-back approach.

'The thing is, I thought I liked Miss Brown – oh God, I suppose I should just say Mrs *Jenkins* now – when I thought of her as the cuddly reading support lady. But the woman I saw when I went round to her house was a whole different person. And when she came to the archive office, well, she was worse still – like a woman possessed. I couldn't get through to her at all. It was like I wasn't even there. She was looking for something and she was determined to get it. If we hadn't been interrupted by the bursar, then I don't know what she would have done. She had a really strange look in her eye.'

'Lord! She sounds like your number one suspect, surely?'

'Well, but she doesn't have a motive, as far as I can see... and the other thing is that I made a huge discovery just before leaving today. The bursar himself had a key to the archive office, too.'

'Hmm, Judith's husband... he's quite dynamic, isn't he?'

'In a bullish sort of way, and I hate the way he's always jiggling his leg as though he should be running a marathon. I think he's like a sneaky Labrador.'

'Beth! Labradors aren't sneaky.'

Beth had forgotten what a dog person Katie was. 'Labradors *are* sneaky when there's food around. He's like a Labrador with his eye on your sandwich,' said Beth.

'Fair enough. I never warmed to him. He's picked Judith up a couple of times from classes on Saturdays and he seemed fine, but maybe he didn't want my sandwich.'

'Oh, come on, Katie, everyone wants *your* sandwich!' When they'd stopped giggling, Beth added, 'Seriously, he is the only person I've been able to find a good motive for, so far. There's my Prime Suspects, that's what I'm calling the teachers and staff who were actually in the school at the time Jenkins was stabbed, which includes the head and the school secretary. She's lovely, by the way, but she seems really cosy with the head. The bursar is the one I've always felt a bit iffy about.'

'Hmm, it is certainly odd he had a key. Why would he need one?' said Katie.

'I suppose, in his job, he could have the keys to any or all of the offices and no one would think it was that surprising. I just don't know for sure, though. I'm a bit baffled.'

'Well, don't despair. It's not like you're even supposed to be sorting it out, after all. Leave it to the professionals,' said Katie soothingly, passing over a cup of tea and collecting up what remained of the chopped carrots. 'That reminds me. I saw a plainclothes policeman outside Wyatt's earlier. Tall, wearing one of those nice navy jackets. Blondish hair. Rather gorgeous, in fact,' she said, with a sidelong look at her friend.

Katie hadn't known James. She'd met Beth just after she had been widowed, but she was well aware that he cast a long shadow. That didn't mean that Beth had to be single all her life, though.

'Gorgeous? You're *kidding*,' said Beth, fresh from that afternoon's humiliating ticking off in the bursar's chair. Inspector York was not her favourite person at the moment, by a long way. And the fact that she knew his strictures about the dangers of meddling had been well deserved made her even crosser. She was poking a rogue bit of carrot peel crossly with her knife when her phone rang.

'Talk of the devil,' she said, blushing a little as York's name came up on the screen. 'It's the police. I'd better get it.' She slid off the bar stool and wandered out into the hall.

'You can use the drawing room,' Katie called with a hastily concealed smile.

Beth went in and closed the door carefully behind her. The room had an air of quiet disuse. The furniture was dramatic, modern and luxurious. Beth found herself sitting on the extreme edge of one of the mauve silk sofas, hoping fervently there wasn't any archive dust still on her jeans. This was a room which did *not* have small boys running around in it on a regular basis.

'Is this a good time? Where are you?' asked York.

She could hear a conversation in the background. It didn't sound like an office, though. There was the repetitive click of a camera flash and a strange rustle as someone moved about behind him. Maybe it was one of those forensic space suits? Beth wondered where he was. Maybe at the scene of another horrible crime.

'Yes, this is fine, I can talk. How can I help?' Beth knew that York couldn't possibly guess they'd just been discussing his sex appeal – or lack of it – but she still felt unaccountably awkward talking to him.

'Do you know what they were after? Whoever broke into your office?' York said abruptly.

'What? I thought we went over this earlier. I thought you'd decided it was the bank statements?' said Beth, jerked out of bashfulness, and not sure why they were going over old ground. 'That's why you said you had to pick them up from my house, isn't it?'

There was a long silence from York. Beth was suddenly scared. 'Has something happened? Something else?'

'When you took the bank statements home, was there anything else with them?' As usual, York was not answering her question. But there was something about the tangent he'd taken that alarmed her.

'Look, what's going on? Can't you just tell me?'

'So, there was nothing with the bank statements, nothing else, is that what you're saying?' York was curiously insistent. She could still hear rustling in the background.

It was time for her to come clean. Yes, she'd told York where to find her key, and the location of the statements. But she hadn't mentioned she also still had a pile of Jenkins' Moleskine notebooks stashed at her house which she hadn't even started looking at yet. She was beginning to feel, with a sinking heart, that maybe she should just turn them over to York, as Katie suggested. She didn't want any of this to get any closer to home. She was just about to confess when York broke in.

'The reason I'm asking is I'm standing in your kitchen. There's been a burglary. You might want to get round here straight away.'

ELEVEN

Katie had been magnificent, as usual, giving her shocked friend a hug and, most importantly, reassuring her that Jake would be in good hands. Beth had wondered for a second whether she should ring her brother. Josh would be delighted to have Jake over, but then she realised she didn't even know if he was still in the country. His job as a photographer meant he had to drop everything and take off for the latest trouble spot on the double, and he wouldn't think to let his little sister know. Even if he were around, there was the whole problem of the lovely Marlene. Did Beth want Jake to get close to another of Josh's short-lived girlfriends?

Beth's mother, Wendy, also lived close by, but again that was problematic. Any sudden movements threw her into a bit of a tizz these days, and an unexpected overnight with her grandson, much though she loved him, would count as a major blow to her placid routine. Beth's father was long dead and her mother lived according to so rigorous a schedule that, unless Beth had pencilled in her burglary several weeks ago, there was no possibility at all that her mother could accommodate it in her life. It was a no-brainer, really. Jake would stay over with Charlie tonight – it was easier on all fronts.

'Don't say a word to him. Let him think it's just a normal sleepover,' said Katie sensibly. 'No point worrying him if we don't have to. I'll get the homework done and drop him at school tomorrow, if you're still tied up. Don't worry about a thing, he'll be absolutely fine here.'

Jake had taken the news he was staying at Charlie's, on a weeknight, with incredulous delight. He gave his mother one questioning glance, but evidently her poker face was impressive enough for him not to guess there was calamity behind this unprecedented turn of events. Even ordinary playdates on school nights had become a rarity, particularly since Charlie's tutoring regime had begun in earnest. Sleepovers were verboten until the weekend. But he decided it was not in his best interests to question his good fortune.

Charlie was thrilled, too, because piano was on the back-burner for once and both boys got the huge treat of extra time on the PlayStation.

As soon as the boys were sorted and they had run off to the playroom, where the PlayStation was installed on a dais like the god it was to them, Beth's face dropped and Katie hugged her again.

'Tell me if it's too awful. As soon as Michael gets home, I can leave and come and be with you. Or you can come back here, no probs at all.'

Tears sprang to Beth's eyes at her friend's kindness, but she blinked them back and just hugged harder. There was no time to break down. 'Thanks for everything. I'll ring you.'

With that, she rushed up the path, then instantly doubled back. She'd forgotten her handbag, phone and jacket. Katie ran back to the kitchen to scoop them up, then handed them over. 'Don't worry too much. The police will sort it out,' she said.

Beth's heart started to hammer as she walked the familiar

route back home. It was only a few minutes away, even with Jake at his most wayward. At first, she'd decided she wouldn't run. But then, as she edged onto the main street and got closer to home, she thought sod that, and broke into a jog, which became a sprint. By the time she turned into Pickwick Road, she was out of breath and her hair was all over her face.

She could see a PC at her door, which would have drawn attention in the quiet street anyway, even had there not been a police car double-parked right outside with its blue light flashing coldly. Already this was causing havoc with the traffic. The street was narrow and there was never a place to park at the best of times. The evening rush hour – it was now bang on 6.30 p.m. – was not the moment to plant an obstruction in the road. There was a line of impatient vehicles forming behind the police car already.

Another PC was in the road now, gesturing at the drivers to turn around. There was no room for most of them to pass, as the cars were all the type originally designed for farmers to drive up mountains in, which Dulwich mums had somehow settled on as the perfect conveyance for suburban life. And, as well as being home time for commuters, 6.30 p.m. in Dulwich was also the moment when ballet schools, karate clubs and tennis academies disgorged the last of their little prodigies, and the mothers all desperately needed to get their precious offspring back for supper and bed. Now, if not sooner.

Oh great, Beth thought, traffic would soon be backed up all along the high street. Though most of her mind was taken up with dreading what she would find at home, unfortunately she still had enough capacity to worry about explaining this kerfuffle to the neighbours. The families on either side were lovely, but there were others in the street who would see the police cars and would not care for one second about what had happened to her. They would think only of the noughts dropping off the price of their properties. The equation was simple: police equals crime, resulting in buyers looking elsewhere.

Meanwhile, all the mothers were now backing their 4x4s perilously down the street, like a camel train swaying into ungainly reverse. Despite their phalanxes of urgently beeping motion sensors, not all were great drivers and the street's wing mirrors were in serious jeopardy. These mothers, thought Beth, would hate her unreservedly for causing their children to be up late, which would lead inexorably to reduced performance at school tomorrow. This meant, as night follows day, that they would fail their entrance exams/GCSEs/A levels and end up as dustmen instead of hedge fund managers.

She was doing her best not to look at the cars too closely. There were bound to be mothers she knew at those wheels, and she could imagine all too well the compressed mouths and knotted brows that would be focused on her little house as the cause of all the trouble. At least the village's beauty parlour would be in work for months to come, smoothing out the lines caused this evening, and even injecting a few of the tougher wrinkles with a discreet syringe or two of Botox. Beth almost wished she could afford it herself – and that she was vain enough to want it. She could already feel her forehead doing origami with the stress of her run home, and she hadn't even seen what lay in store yet.

Beth was just beginning to explain breathlessly, 'I live here' to the impassive PC on sentry duty outside her house, when the door swung open and York gestured her inside.

'It's not too bad,' he said, taking a look at her stricken face and flushed cheeks. It was worse.

The whole of the ground floor had been ransacked. Everything that could be thrown on the floor had been; anything that could be broken was. It was spiteful, and thorough.

'Who could have done this? And why?' Beth didn't mean to, but she was shouting. It was such a desecration of her space and, worse than that, of Jake's safe home. She *hated* whoever had done this.

'I was rather hoping you'd have the answers to that,' said York. 'How did they even get in?' she asked.

'Looks like they had a key,' said York. She was aghast. 'A key? *How?*'

York shrugged. 'Not sure. It wasn't your spare, that was still there when I got here and I've put it back. But I would say, for future reference, your under-the-mat system isn't totally foolproof.'

Beth blushed painfully. He was right, she realised. He was being quite restrained about her idiotic key situation. While she'd been pretty much screaming in his face. But she wasn't really yelling at him; she was shocked and angry, that was all. She perched uncomfortably on the arm of the sofa, utterly deflated. It didn't even feel like her sofa any more, she couldn't relax back into it as she would have done at any other time. While her possessions were heaped around her, destroyed, she could not be at home, even in her own space.

'I just don't understand this,' she managed to croak before, to her horror, a single, heaving sob overtook her. It was hard enough to be alone, to be all in all to Jake, to have created a home and a refuge. To have it wrecked with such overt mean-ness was too much.

York hesitated, then sat down next to her. She saw him reach out a hand, then let it fall, as though he felt helpless. No doubt there was protocol and guidelines. There would be appropriate behaviour.

'All I can say is, we'll get whoever did this. Don't you worry,' he said gruffly.

They were both aware that, with the Metropolitan Police's abysmal clear-up rates, it sounded hollow. But Beth appreciated that he was trying to reassure her.

She took some deep breaths and tried to get herself under

control, searching in vain for a tissue in her jeans pocket, or from the box on the sofa table – but of course that was long gone, hurled into the heap of mess in front of her. She tried not to let that thought set her off again, and concentrated instead on York's declaration. It was like a bedtime story. The words themselves might have meant little, but the delivery was curiously reassuring. York then handed over a pack of Kleenex, which was even better.

He sat in silence as her symphony of sniffles petered out. Beth found his reassuringly large presence a surprising comfort. When the sniffs were only occasional, he asked again, 'Any ideas?'

'It must have been the same person who turned over the archive office. They can't have found what they were looking for there. They must have taken my spare key from the desk drawer. Then there was my letter confirming the job in the in-tray – with my address on it,' said Beth, her voice wavering but gradually getting clearer. 'I think they were probably after the bank statements. Either that, or the notebooks. I brought them home with me to study. I'd looked at the bank statements, as you know, but I hadn't got round to looking through the books. God, I've been so stupid.'

'Well, you should certainly have told me about these note-books before—' York started.

'Not about that,' Beth broke in. 'About bringing any of the stuff here in the first place. I should have known... particularly after the break-in at work. It was so reckless. I've been an idiot. I've put Jake in danger. How could I do that, when I'm all he has?'

'Jake's fine. He's come to no harm. He's at a friend's, I take it? Or at your mum's?'

'No, at a friend's.' Beth shook her head at the idea of involving her mother. It had been unthinkable before she'd seen the chaos. Now she was sitting in the wreckage, she knew for certain her mother couldn't cope with this at all. It would have been great if she'd been the tower-of-strength type – but she just wasn't, and that was that. They saw each other often, and were on cordial terms, and Beth had got used to not expecting more. But on nights like this, that seemed a small tragedy in itself. Still, there was no changing things now.

'So, there we are. He's probably having a whale of a time. You've got the rest of the evening to get this tidied up. There are no fingerprints, again, and the door wasn't forced. The SOCOs have done their bit, so they'll be out of your hair once they've packed up. Now, have you had a look around, seen if anything has been taken? Apart from the notebooks. I'm assuming they are long gone?'

Beth nodded. The pile of books had not been hidden away, it had just been camouflaged, again, in plain sight on the well-stocked bookshelves, with several of her own notebooks. She was a habitual note-taker – a hangover from uni days, she supposed, when she'd compulsively taken down everything said by lecturers on a just-in-case basis. She could see that her notebooks, which had been dead ringers for Jenkins' own, were now lying contemptuously torn and trampled on the floor. Whoever had done this had not been fooled for an instant.

Was anything else missing? She cast an eye around the now sad and battered room. There was nothing valuable in here, apart from the telly, and even that was years old and not nearly big enough to satisfy most tastes. The kitchen, she could see from here, was a horrific mess but, again, there was nothing there worth stealing, unless you were very keen on pasta. It was Jake's favourite. She wasn't about to count the bags, but the ones strewn across the floor, some split with the force of their impact, looked as though they roughly tallied with her last big shop at Sainsbury's.

'Have you looked upstairs?' said Beth, hesitating now with her hand on the bannisters, afraid for a moment that whoever did this might be lurking in the dark at the top of the landing, waiting for the police to go.

York nodded, looking a little embarrassed. Beth didn't stop to wonder at his hesitation, but ran lightly up the stairs, opening the door to Jake's room first and seeing with relief that things were just as they had been that morning. That is, a terrible mess – but one created by Jake, not by the unseen hand of an enemy.

Her own small room seemed untouched, too. She realised it would have looked incredibly girly to York – the walls painted a pale pink, the duvet cover a Cath Kidston explosion in a flower shop that she adored. Knowing that he'd been here, looking around, scrutinising all her private things, she couldn't help seeing it with his eyes. Though the bed was neatly made, the bedside table on the right was empty, while there was a novel, splayed face-down, on the left-hand side, together with a drained cup of tea, some hand cream, earplugs and one of those eye masks they gave you on long-haul flights. The thought struck her that York wouldn't have had to be a detective to deduce a single woman with insomniac tendencies. She felt a little embarrassed, but shrugged it off. There was no law against trashy paperbacks and florals, was there? And anyone in the thick of a murder investigation could be excused the odd bout of wakefulness.

As she walked into the small bathroom, she picked up the towel Jake must have dumped on the floor after doing his teeth, then noticed the loo hadn't been flushed. Funny. The seat was down, meaning the culprit was not Jake. Despite her years of effort, he still forgot to return the seat to its rightful place more often than not. And she would have automatically flushed the loo – wouldn't she? Her nerves were so jangled by the evening that she couldn't quite reconstruct the morning in her head.

'Inspector York?' she called out.

He trundled up the stairs. 'Something missing?' he said, his voice sounding a little anxious. He coughed quickly.

'Not missing. Added, I think,' she said, with the first smile she'd managed this evening. She stood in the bathroom, gazing into the pale yellow waters of the loo.

'What is it?' he said, after a cursory glance around the small, white-tiled room. He stood on an Ikea bathmat in bright blue, then shifted a little, as though conscious of his clodhopping shoes. Sure enough, the mat retained the imprint of his large feet, but Beth wasn't bothered.

'I think whoever it was came up here for a pee.' 'Really? Are you sure?'

'Well, not a hundred per cent, I suppose. But I always flush, and Jake, who forgets half the time, usually leaves the seat up. So, seat down and loo unflushed is not a combination we ever have. But here it is.' They both looked.

'OK, then.' He smiled, too. 'I'll get the SOCOs back.'

'For DNA? Can you get that from urine?'

'It's not a great source, but it is sometimes possible,' he said. 'I won't bore you with the science, but sometimes there aren't enough nucleated cells to get a result. It's diluted, of course. And this sample has been sitting around in water all day. But it's worth a try.'

'I had no idea you could do that,' Beth admitted.

'It's not widely known. Maybe the perpetrator was disturbed, or maybe they were so full of adrenaline that they didn't go about their usual routine and flush. There's a high incidence of burglars needing to, ahem, use the facilities,' said York.

Beth, despite herself, was fascinated. 'Really?'

'Yes,' said York, holding up his finger as his phone call to the SOCOs went through. After a terse conversation, he cut the call and turned back to Beth. 'They're on their way back. Thrilled, of course. What was I saying?'

'You said thieves often need to... go,' she prompted.

'Yes, that's what leads to these cases where burglars, erm, defecate on the carpet in the houses they steal from. It's not all contempt and an attempt to add insult to injury – some of it is simply a human response to the amount of stress hormone in the body, caused by the tension of breaking in and having to get out unseen.'

'Hmm, well, I'm not feeling very sympathetic to my burglar's stress problems, I must say,' said Beth. 'Will I have to give a sample, to eliminate my DNA?'

'We've already got your cheek scrape, I think, from the initial enquiry, so you're fine. We'll come back tomorrow and just take a quick sample from Jake too. It won't take a moment, I don't think it'll scare him.'

'Are you kidding?' said Beth ruefully. 'He'll absolutely love it. At his age, it's all just a great big adventure.'

Suddenly, she was overwhelmed again. She wasn't sure if it was sadness, despair at her situation, or just the comedown from the rage she'd felt earlier on first seeing the devastation.

York briefly laid a hand on her shoulder. Seconds later, he'd turned to go.

'So, I'll send someone at some point to do the sample. There's nothing missing, though, as far as you can see?'

'Nothing,' Beth confirmed. She had a long night of cleaning up ahead. Then suddenly, she looked around, startled. 'Wait a minute, Magpie!' York looked blank.

'Our cat, Magpie. She's black and white,' Beth explained hastily, rushing for the garden doors in the kitchen. She struggled with the locks but got them open, and York was soon crouching with her in the dark garden, making 'here, kitty kitty' sounds, and no doubt hoping his colleagues were well out of earshot.

It took nearly an hour and, finally, a brainwave from Beth, who abandoned shaking the cat's bag of dried food and resorted to opening a tin of tuna instead. Once they'd both taken turns to exclaim loudly about the yumminess of tuna, Magpie gracefully unfurled herself from the tree nearest the kitchen window where she'd been enjoying the spectacle, dropped down onto the lawn, and sauntered back into the house.

Beth was surprised to find herself exchanging with York the kind of tiny, rueful smile that bonds the parents of a wilful child. Magpie, presented with a saucer heaped with her favourite treat, scoffed the lot before settling down to snooze on a pile of strewn papers, with an air of virtuous exhaustion.

The next morning, Beth was at the school gates, as usual. But this time she was there to greet Jake, not to wave him off. After a restless night following an orgy of tidying and sorting, she was so pleased to see him that she attempted a hug, but he fought her off good-naturedly. Katie, who'd just been given similar treatment by Charlie, smiled ruefully and enfolded her friend in the hug she needed instead. 'How did it go?'

Beth had called Katie briefly after York had left, once she'd got her emotions a bit more under control. She'd wanted to check on Jake, though she knew full well that he'd be having a fine time and wouldn't have given her a moment's thought, which was just as it should be. Beth had fobbed off Katie's offers to come over and help out, despite Michael being happy to hold the fort once the boys were safely in bed. For one thing, the complete mess gave her an opportunity to have a thorough clear-out, and only she knew what could be discarded and what could stay. With her obsessively tidy streak, Beth had found that, though she was still a bit shaky, the whole process was bizarrely therapeutic. She would never have chosen to dump the entire contents of her bookshelves, which covered two floor-to-ceiling walls of her sitting room, right in the middle of the floor. But now that someone had done it for her, she could see the horrifying zebra stripes of dust on the shelves, where books had lain undisturbed for years. She had sometimes worried that her house was too clean – but this was thick, dark, furry proof that it definitely was not.

Her books were mostly classics, which she had every intention of rereading at some unlikely point when life gave her months, or maybe years, of undisturbed reading time. And quite a few of them bore James's distinctive scrawl on the flyleaf. These would never go.

There was a history section, of course, bristling with Tudors and gold-embossed spines, and then an extensive collection of thick, paperback beach reads, each the size of a brick, which she tended to wedge on top of other, more intellectual, tomes. These, she decided, could be heavily pruned.

Even sifting through the piles of Jake's books on the bottom shelves felt like a long overdue, positive step. Though there were books here she could not part with – the ones that came bound with memories of feverish bright eyes on the sofa, begging for one more page when her boy was tiny and ill – there were also piles of tatty old tomes that were ripe to go to the great bookshop in the sky, or Oxfam. Whichever was closer.

Armed with her trusty Flash bleach spray and some jumbo kitchen rolls, and thanking her stars that she had bought these in bulk just that weekend, Beth had set to. The end result had been a neat row of black bin bags outside her house, and a sparklingly clean home. The chlorine whiff of the bleach spray had done much to purge the evil spirits from her house. Once everything was in order again, Magpie strolled into the sitting room, jumped up onto the sofa, and curled herself up contentedly, shedding black and white fur over the newly vacuumed cushions. Beth wondered if Magpie had seen who had wreaked this havoc on their house. The cat blinked slowly, with a flash of green. If she had, she wasn't saying a thing.

Beth had been physically exhausted by the time she'd got to bed in the small hours, but her mind had still been whirring.

The questions were by now familiar. Who? And why? She

had to find the answers, or she'd be driven mad. And, now that whoever it was had actually had the temerity to set foot in her house, she had to find them, and make herself and her son – and little cat – safe.

The emergency locksmith had arrived bright and early that morning and supplied new fittings, including a Banham lock for the front door and deadbolts for the kitchen French windows, so at least Beth knew that was done. Though the locksmith had breezily told her, as she handed over vast sums of money, that of course a burglar could get into any house past any defences, if they were determined enough.

Some of this was in her tired eyes as she answered Katie at the school gates. 'Well, the mess is sorted. In one way. And thank you so much for having Jake last night. It meant a lot, knowing he was safe and having a fantastic time. I'm so grateful. But I've got to find out who is behind this, I just have to. Before things get even nastier.'

Katie grimaced. 'It's too much for you to take on, you should just let the police get on with it,' she urged. 'That nice handsome officer can sort it all out for you. Was he helpful last night?' she couldn't resist prodding. Beth's reaction had been interestingly fiery the previous evening.

'He was fine,' Beth said dismissively, with a shrewd glance at Katie's innocent face. Katie was an incorrigible matchmaker at the best of times. Her own marriage was so happy that she thought everyone was better off paired up, like the animals in Noah's ark. But this was not the best of times, thought Beth, and she didn't need Katie to be getting any ideas.

Then she remembered York patiently searching the dark garden for her naughty cat. That, surely, had been above and beyond the call of Met Police duty.

'Well, he was great,' she acknowledged shortly. 'But on the other hand, the investigation seems to be going nowhere. It's over a week since the... since what happened, and now there've been two burglaries as well. Someone pretty nasty – probably an actual killer – has been in my house. That's a horrible thought. I just don't think I can hang around waiting for the police to make progress. I can't risk it, not when someone has let themselves into my house and rooted around in there.' She lowered her voice. She wasn't going to let Jake find out there'd been a burglary if she could possibly help it. It was bound to unsettle him – and one unsettled person in the house was quite enough.

'I wish we could just go and discuss it all over a coffee, maybe we would have a brainwave or something,' said Katie, wrinkling her brow.

'I'd love that. But the archives are calling. And don't you have a class, anyway?' Katie was in her yoga kit – long, dark purple leggings and a zip-up top – but managing, of course, to make the get-up look like elegant daywear rather than a trackie-bottomed mess.

'I've got a class at ten. I'll let you know if Judith comes and lets anything slip. And normally Ruth Jenkins would be there, too, but I don't know whether she'll show.'

'Hmm, I don't know what mourning etiquette is these days. It was easier with the Victorians. She'd be in a heavy veil, black gloves, the whole shebang; everyone would know she was officially a widow. Would she be all right today if she showed up all in black athleisure wear, or does she have to wait till next week, for form's sake? It's not like she seems the yoga type anyway,' said Beth.

'I shouldn't really criticise any of my clients, but I've always got the impression that she just comes along because Judith drags her. She can go through the motions, all right, but she doesn't look like she's enjoying it and she never pushes herself. She doesn't smile much, either. Some of the ones who aren't that serious just come for a laugh – which is fair enough,' Katie added quickly, realising Beth herself was firmly in the yoga-as-a-giggle camp. 'Judith, though, she's pretty impressive. But she hasn't been coming as much since the, you know, murder. And she's quite subdued when she does come.'

'Really? Intriguing,' said Beth. It looked as though someone at least was still sad about Dr Jenkins' departure from this life. If not his actual wife.

Mrs Jenkins, she reflected, was remaining quite a conundrum. Was she the cuddly reading teacher, the slightly psycho widow, or the reluctant yoga student?

'Do you think you could let me know if Mrs Jenkins does turn up? And would you mind keeping a bit of an eye on her? I know you're busy with the bending and stuff, but if you do get a chance...'

'Bending and stuff? That's my life's work you're talking about there,' said Katie, mock-outraged. 'Yeah, of course, I'll call you. Now, we'd better get on with it,' she said, as the school bell rang and the children filed into lessons. They'd just turned to go their separate ways when Katie looked back. 'Promise me you won't do anything dangerous, though.'

Beth rolled her eyes. 'As if,' she said.

TWELVE

It wasn't until she was back in the archive office, with her jacket slung on the back of her chair and her bag stowed under the little table, that Beth thought of Katie's words again. She was standing facing the line of criminally dull Wyatt's magazines that she'd painstakingly reassembled. Interspersed among their dreary spines, she could see the faintly gleaming leather of the old ledgers. She slid the first one out and felt its heft in her hands. It was surprisingly heavy, solid, the leather softly grainy, buffed by the years, pleasing to her touch.

She laid it on her table reverently, and wondered. She felt as though she were on the cusp of a discovery. It was extraordinary the way that books could be like depth charges. This had sat around, in boxes or openly out on shelves, in this very office – or one like it – for years, decades, and even centuries, possibly containing the secrets that had sparked a murder and two burglaries. So far.

The bursar, Mrs Jenkins, even the head, Janice, and the suspect teachers might all have reasons of some kind to want to do Dr Jenkins harm. But, despite there being no shortage of flesh and blood possibilities, Beth wondered whether the true answer to the mystery lay before her right now.

She wiped her palms on her trousers, and slipped on the pair of cotton gloves she'd found serendipitously after yesterday's ransacking. She'd been given them by her mother for Christmas – along with a pot of expensive hand cream as a not-subtle-enough hint about the way she was letting herself go. The idea was to slather on the cream at night, pop on the gloves, and hey presto, in the morning her soft palms would soon find her husband number two. Well, they might not have been the proper archivists' gloves she'd dreamt of – with one thing and another, she hadn't got round to ordering those yet – but they would certainly do the trick for now.

Taking a deep breath, she opened the ledger and the heavy leather cover hit the table with a thud. She leant forward to decipher the title page. A minute later, she'd switched on the overhead light, and then craned her desk lamp until its yellow beam was right over the friable pages. It was a bright day, but the ink she was peering at was faded to a pale, watery brown; the lettering, in a lavishly looped hand, leant far, far to the right, as if being blown by a gale. It was going to be hard to make sense of this.

Three hours flew by as quickly as the first morning she'd spent in this office. Back then, she'd been trying to work out the archives themselves – the purpose they served, and her place in them. Now, she was trying to adjust her views on nothing less than the very foundations of the school she was sitting in.

The ledger before her was, to all intents and purposes, a simple record of goods owned by the school in its early years. It wasn't that different from the endless records she'd already come across, relating to matters as mundane as the suppliers of the school-crested ashtrays – very popular items in the 1950s, 60s and 70s, when probably the staffroom would have been as smoggy with cigarette smoke as any pub, but of little use now.

Conversely, Wyatt's crested USB memory sticks had appeared from nowhere and were now ordered in huge bulk. Records of all these trends, their development, growth and abatement, were compiled here and would doubtless serve as a sort of social history in centuries to come.

And that's what the ledger in Beth's hands turned out to be.

So, it was a record of supplies and goods. Nothing extraordinary about that. Until you looked at what the goods, so meticulously noted in such a fine hand, were.

Negro man, 35, one eye, labourer.

Negress, 18, and child of two.

Negro of 15, lame.

And so it went on. It was an inventory of chattels owned by the school but, instead of crested tea towels and Biros, in the 1700s the school had owned *people*.

Slaves.

Beth felt her scalp prickling with heat. She was flushed with the shame and horror of the book. She fanned herself with a white-gloved hand, which suddenly, horribly, reminded her of the *Black and White Minstrel Show* – a 'family entertainment' programme which had run on the BBC until 1978. She had never seen it herself, except in YouTube clips watched through her fingers, but her parents' generation had settled back on their sofas to watch it as a highlight of their Saturday nights. She stripped the gloves off quickly.

In one sense, what she was seeing written down in front of her was nothing new. She understood perfectly well that British landowners in the Caribbean in the 1700s had owned slaves, and had used this unpaid labour to work the land they'd colonised to enrich themselves. The misery of slavery was the bedrock of many a fortune.

And she knew, on one level, that the great Sir Thomas had been a huge landowner. The legend was that, after his rackety youth, he had disappeared off to the West Indies, before eventually returning to found Wyatt's in Dulwich with the spectacular proceeds of his adventures. He had then settled down to be a pillar of the community, lauded even at the time for creating such a successful – and charitable – school.

Beth pushed her chair away from the table and stood up, feeling sick. To think that Wyatt had earned his reputation for charity – a reputation the school still had – at the expense of these people, noted down in the ledger as belongings, nothing more or less than the bushels of sugar cane that filled other columns. It was revolting.

It was an ugly secret, festering at the heart of this beautiful school. She thought of the smoothness of the lawn in front of the Grand Hall, carefully criss-crossed with stripes by the groundsmen. It seemed to symbolise Wyatt's, so carefully tended, so free of weeds, so much a mirror of the tenderly nurtured shoots that were the pupils. They were growing in poisoned soil. The greatest and most evil of imperfections lay underneath the smooth green façade. Everything at this school sprang from tainted money.

Beth sat for a while with her head in her hands. The ledger was open before her, the tally of slaves marching quietly on over page after page. Their voices were silenced, then as now, but she felt their presence somehow in the terse descriptions: 'Boy, 12, wasted leg', 'Girl, 6, and boy, 5'. The only salient features mentioned were physical problems. She supposed that these affected the slaves' monetary value. Ages were often approximate. Names were of no interest at all.

Perhaps Wyatt had not been different from others of his time, in forcing this army to rake in money for him. But that did not change the facts. Wyatt's School was founded on the proceeds of slavery.

Beth wondered how many other people here knew of this. In some ways, now that she had the proof in front of her, she was surprised that it was not more widely known, or suspected.

Wyatt had lived in an age of slavery, he had spent time in a place where slavery was established practice, and he had made piles of money there which he had brought back home with him in triumph. Now that she thought about this story, knowing what she knew, it seemed self-evident that slavery was behind his wealth. But she had lived in Dulwich all her life and had never heard even the merest sniff of a whiff of an inkling of a rumour about it.

Was that because, in the not-too-distant past, there had been much more tolerance of racism by the general public? Landlords had famously posted signs in lodgings, stating: 'No dogs, no blacks, no Irish' as recently as the 1960s and 70s, while even today black actors were more likely to get run over than nominated for an Oscar. She didn't know.

It could be a factor; it could have allowed acceptance. From that point of view, she was a little surprised that Wyatt's hadn't just been more open about the basis of its wealth. If everyone had always known the place was founded on slavery, then people – even those who disapproved – would have got used to the idea. After all, it had happened several hundred years ago and there was no changing the past. It would have taken the sting out of the facts, and no one now would consider it a dirty and shameful secret.

But that was exactly what it was.

Had it been wilfully and deliberately hushed up, or had the school just decided that it was simply convenient to skip lightly over aspects of their founder's past? The fact the ledgers had not been destroyed seemed to point either to this expediency theory, or to something even easier to achieve – a convenient case of amnesia. Skirting around unpleasantness, Beth realised, was something that was always highly tempting for any red-blooded Englishman. And the past, being past, is very easy to forget.

Almost as a way of distracting herself from the unpleasantness of her discovery, Beth let her mind wander over recent events. The ledgers. The thefts. And then, ultimately, the murder. There had to be a connection.

Had Dr Jenkins stumbled across the ledgers, before her? Had he discovered Wyatt's murky past, and been extorting money from someone in exchange for silence? If that was the case, then one other person already knew what was hidden in the archives room. Were the ledgers what the burglar had been seeking, or was he after the bank statements that proved the blackmail? Or Dr Jenkins' notebooks? Or all of these?

Beth had a lot to think about. And she wasn't sure the archives office was the place to do it. As she slid the ledger back into its innocuous place on the shelf, collected her belongings and locked the door carefully, all she was sure of was that she didn't want to be alone with this secret any longer. It didn't feel safe. She had to tell as many people as possible, and quickly.

The first person she went to see was the porter. By this stage, under the sunny influence of Beth's twice-daily smiles on her journeys to and from her office, they were firm friends.

'Do you have a proper lock you could fit to the archives office door?' she asked. 'I know we've put a padlock on, but I'd be happier if there was something more permanent fitted,' said Beth, reflecting that she seemed to be keeping Dulwich's lock-makers in business at the moment.

'Got just what you need right here,' he said, holding up a chunky plastic package containing a fearsomely sturdy-looking Chubb. 'It's a five-lever mortice, this is. Was going to fit it this morning. It's next on my list, soon as I can get someone to relieve me here.'

Beth was puzzled. 'Great. But, erm, if you don't mind me asking, who ordered that?'

'Bursar, of course,' said the porter.

Beth continued on her way, a small frown etched between her brows. If she'd had to put money on who had a motive to lift the incriminating ledgers and keep the slavery secret quiet, it would have gone on the bursar. Yet here he was, apparently trying to protect the whole archive, ledgers included.

She was still looking a bit puzzled by the time she got to reception. Janice held court, as usual, behind the pristine, chest-high countertop which screened her laptop, landline and notepad. She was looking as lovely as ever today in a wisteria purple cashmere cardigan buttoned over a pretty floral tea dress, which Beth had spotted in one of the village boutique windows last week at a price that had made her eyes water.

Today, there were some prospective parents sitting on one comfortable sofa, with their little boy opposite. He was kicking his heels into the underside of his sofa in a way which, Beth could tell, was driving his mother insane. The slight wince crossing her beautifully made-up face showed she was torn between the ills of giving the boy a public dressing-down just before expecting him to perform brilliantly in an interview for a much-coveted mid-term place, or letting the annoying behaviour slip and thus risking being judged as a lax mother by Janice, and now by Beth as well. Her husband, meanwhile, exuded total indifference from behind a copy of the *Economist*. Beth smiled sympathetically and turned back to Janice.

'Just wondered if I could get a moment to see the bursar?'

Janice smiled professionally at Beth. 'For today?' she said, her rising inflection gently suggesting that such an expectation was utter madness.

'As soon as possible. It's urgent,' said Beth.

Janice's smile was bland and reassuring as she tapped a few keys at her laptop and effortlessly brought up Tom Seasons' schedule. Beth knew she was being chided, in a barely perceptible way, for suggesting anything at Wyatt's could ever judder out of well-oiled pathways to become 'urgent'. The feet might be paddling madly, but all that would ever be seen was the crisp white perfection of the swan.

She smiled even more as she scrawled on a Post-it note and passed it to Beth. 'He's free now' it said simply. Janice would never have admitted this out loud. To prospective parents, anyone as important as the bursar must remain an endlessly double-booked Stakhanovite worker, bent double by the pressure of their appointments. To Beth, who knew that Seasons was digging into the mystery for reasons of his own, it was fine to admit that he was desperate to pounce on any scrap of information she could offer.

'So, I'll be sure to let you know,' said Janice blithely, keeping up the fiction, and Beth thanked her, and then smiled generally at the family group. The mother favoured her with a great beaming grin, in case she was someone important. The husband was still resolutely behind his *Economist* tent. The boy ceased drumming for a moment, and fixed her with a surprisingly intelligent stare. He'll probably get in, she thought.

Outside reception, she took a deep breath. In truth, she hadn't been expecting to see Seasons so quickly. She hadn't quite got her story straight yet, so to speak. She needed to collect herself a bit and decide how to present this news. But then she shook her head infinitesimally. Telling people was what counted, not how they were told. She didn't want the burden of this secret upon her a second longer. The more people who knew, the safer she was. And the safer she was, the safer Jake was. Squaring her shoulders, she knocked on the door.

'Enter,' came Seasons' voice, and Beth wondered for a moment why he couldn't just say 'Come in' like a normal person. But that slight pomposity seemed essential to his role as bursar. She opened the door and felt as though she was wading across his thick carpet, before coming to a standstill in front of the imposing desk. Seasons was tapping lightly at his computer, in his usual rather stagey way, and continued to do so for a few moments while she hovered.

Just as she was about to take the plunge and sit herself down without invitation, he broke off from his 'work' and boomed, 'Beth, Beth, do take a seat' in his warmest tones, as though she were his long-lost friend breezing in for a much anticipated catch-up.

She was pretty sure his jovial mood would not last long.

THIRTEEN

It was an uncomfortable half-hour later that Beth left the bursar's office. She had often heard the phrase, 'Don't shoot the messenger', but had never yet felt so close to having to defend herself as the bearer of bad tidings. Seasons seemed to blame her entirely for bringing up the slavery issue, for having found the ledger, and also for suspecting that Dr Jenkins himself might well have stumbled across the matter in the months leading up to his death. If he could have blamed her for the slavery itself, she was beginning to think he would.

The upshot of the interview was that they both, along with Dr Grover who had been hastily phoned, had arranged to meet back at the archives office in an hour, to look over the evidence and decide what should be done with it.

Though it had not been a pleasant encounter, Beth felt relieved. She was glad the matter was now out of her hands, that the knowledge had started to spread. Knowing the rumour mills in both Wyatt's and Dulwich as a whole, it would soon glide by uncanny osmosis well beyond the school gates. At last, the whole issue would get a thorough, and centuries-overdue, airing. She was also somewhat relieved about one other thing.

She was almost sure that, excellent though the bursar was at maintaining a front of unshakeable superiority, she had seen a flash of genuine shock and consternation when she had told him everything. He had not known about the slavery. Which meant, she thought, that he had not been the victim of Dr Jenkins' little blackmail racket.

Who could it have been then? She ran through the list of suspects again in her head. There were the remaining teachers, Janice, Mrs Jenkins herself (though surely he couldn't have been blackmailing his own wife?), and the headmaster. None seemed likely. Was there anyone she was forgetting? Any other connections that Jenkins had? Anyone close to him who might have strong feelings?

As she walked back to her office, Beth suddenly stopped dead. Much as she didn't want to complicate matters, or add to her tally of potential killers, there was one obvious link to Jenkins staring her right in the face. There, at the other end of the playground, was Wyatt's junior and prep school. And hadn't Judith Seasons told her that both she and Ruth Jenkins had had daughters, whose girls were now at the school in their turn? That meant Jenkins' little granddaughter was being educated right here, just a few hundred yards from the scene of the crime.

She wasn't imagining for a moment that the granddaughter herself, whoever she was and whatever her age, had pottered across the playground, knife in hand, on that fateful morning. But if Beth had the victim's wife down as one of her potential killers, shouldn't she also add his grown-up *daughter*? All right, she knew nothing about her yet, but if she were anything like her mum, she'd be quite odd, and if she were anything like her dad, she'd be really, really odd.

And there was also a potential son-in-law angle. In the rigidly conventional world of Dulwich, it was probably at least eighty-five per cent certain that all pick-ups and drop-offs were carried out by the mother. But fathers were becoming less unusual at the school gates. Possibly he had a 'bohemian', but still incredibly well-paid, job which allowed him the leisure to be involved in his daughter's school career? Or maybe he just wanted to be a hands-on dad? Either could put him at the right place at the right time – or the wrong time and place, if you were Dr Jenkins. Beth mentally kicked herself. It was no good at all speculating. She'd have to do some digging. She looked at her watch. Was there time, before her meeting with the bursar and the head? Just about, if she got on with it.

It was quite a stroll to the prep building, which was lucky as she had not a single clue what she was going to say when she got there; she'd just have to work it out somehow as she walked. She set off at a brisk and purposeful pace, her face scrunched in concentration. She had to think of a ruse that would elicit the right sort of information, without raising too many hackles and without, of course, compromising any of the school's rigid ideas about parent confidentiality.

She passed through the reception entrance, thanking her stars that her swipe card worked in this part of the school too, and found herself at a countertop very similar to Janice's. The girl behind the counter was much younger, though, looking barely out of her teens, but as beautifully smiley. Absolutely perfect for her job and, Beth hoped, not wise enough yet in the ways of the world to withstand her wiles.

'Hi, I'm Beth Haldane from the archives office, just popping in about the project I'm going to be doing with the prep,' she said airily, mentally crossing her fingers. That still got you out of telling lies, right?

'Louise, call me Lou,' said the girl, holding out a hand to shake. Each of her nails was painted a different colour. That must take forever, thought Beth, marvelling that anyone had that much free time. Or energy. Or interest in nails. 'Love your manicure,' she said, hoping she was getting away with the fake sincerity.

Lou smiled complacently at her nails, like a parent whose favourite child is justly praised, then wrinkled her dainty nose. 'Um, what's this project?' she asked, a little nervously. Beth immediately seized on this evidence of slight insecurity, hating herself but convinced that the end result was important enough to warrant the manipulation.

'You mean they haven't told you? I can't believe that!' she said, all mock outrage. 'No one's said a single word,' confirmed Lou. 'Is it really important?'

'Well, yes,' said Beth, leaning close to whisper to the girl. 'It's a really big thing. For the anniversary, you know?'

'Anniversary? Right?' said Lou, her smooth brow beginning to pleat with the effort of concentration. Had someone said something to her which she had forgotten? She looked worried now. So many pieces of paper to keep track of. Such a big school. Everything always so important. She started sifting uselessly through the pile of papers on the desk in front of her. Lou was clearly no Janice.

'Look, don't worry too much about the detail,' said Beth, thinking that, thank God, she wouldn't have to be too elaborate in her web of lies. 'The thing is, it's Dr Jenkins' granddaughter that's involved, you know who *that* is, right?'

Lou's relief was palpable. Her pretty face cleared of strain. After the massive fuss last week, even the prep school hamster knew all about Dr Jenkins' granddaughter, who'd been taken home in floods of tears and had a couple of days off for good measure. 'You mean Ellen Fitch?'

'Yes, yes, Ellen. What year is she in, again?'

'She's in Year Two now, bless her. Very upset she was.'

'The thing is, she was supposed to be helping with, you know, the project that very day.'

'Which day?' said Lou. The nose was beginning to wrinkle

again. Beth gave Lou a slightly exasperated look, wondering whether she was going to have to spell it out. 'Ohhhhh, *that* day, riiiight,' said Lou, pleased with herself for making the connection.

Beth nodded briskly. 'So, on that day, do you remember who brought, erm, Ellen into school? It's quite important because it's... all about the project,' she finished. To her own ears, the story she was concocting was the lamest one she'd ever told. Luckily, Lou wasn't joining all the dots. She was just trying to get her own tiny portions of the whole right.

'So, you want to know who dropped her off that day?' Lou was frowning in earnest now. 'I don't know... I can tell you who it usually is, it's her nanny. But the thing is, the nanny changes a lot. That happens with quite a lot of families, you know. I used to be a nanny, so I've been there, totes. Not that I was ever let go. I worked for my families for ages, it was only when they suddenly had to move abroad or whatever...'

Beth, worried now that she might be in for Lou's entire employment history, and feeling a glancing sympathy with any family who had to contemplate upping sticks to shake off the lovely but clearly hare-brained girl, sneaked a glance at her watch. She still had ten minutes, but she'd be cutting it fine unless Lou's memory took a sudden upturn.

'Are you in a hurry?' Lou asked, more observant than Beth had given her credit for. 'Listen, give me your number, I'll give it a good think and I'll text you later.' Lou smiled her beaming smile, and Beth joined in. She might despair of ever getting useful information out of her, but you couldn't help but like the girl.

Though she still had a couple of minutes in hand, by the time she got back to the office both the bursar and the head were already there. There was something about the two grown men in suits, who were both utterly sure of their own tremendous importance, that made the corridors contract around her. The fact they stopped talking as soon as they saw her meant, of course, they'd been discussing her. Probably both wondering what on earth she was doing here and how soon they could terminate her employment, she thought pessimistically.

She felt flustered, and cursed herself for having wasted precious time on what was probably going to turn out to be a wild goose chase over at the prep school. She should have stayed here and polished all her folders, got everything ready for the official inspection she now realised she'd accidentally brought down on herself. She fumbled at the heavy, ugly padlock, which had been put on the door with more speed than finesse by the porter, and finally let the two men in. The new mortice lock couldn't be fitted too soon.

Once ushered into the small space, the two men and Beth barely had space to turn round, and it immediately began to feel just as cramped as the corridor outside. Though the archive office was now clear of all the boxes which, as far as she knew, had been stacked there for years, the men looked around the room without comment. She hadn't been expecting lavish compliments on her organisational abilities – though that would have been nice – but some sort of recognition of all the hard work she'd done would have gone down well.

It didn't come.

'I wish I could offer you both seats, but as you see there's only one chair and a fold-away one over there,' she fussed.

'Ms Haldane, Beth, you take the seat. No, I insist,' said the head, ever urbane even in these cramped surroundings. 'Now, the bursar tells me you have stumbled across something rather... disturbing... in our archives here.'

Beth noted the word 'our' applied to the archives. Was he giving her a subtle reminder that whatever she had found belonged to the school, and was not hers to do with as she wished?

'That's right, it's a very... serious discovery, and naturally I wanted to make you, both of you, aware of it as soon as I possibly could. I think it may have... implications, given the murder of Dr Jenkins.'

The head held up his palm. 'Now, now, Beth. Let's deal with one thing at a time. I don't think any of us need to leap to any conclusions, however tempting that may be. Let us simply consider the facts. First of all, we need to see this information that you have uncovered.'

'Of course.' Beth leapt out of her seat and then realised she was going to have to disclose the ledgers' hiding place. She cursed herself again for wasting time earlier. If she'd come straight back here, she could have had the ledgers on her desk and they would probably then still have been safe to store on the shelves. Damn. All right, the hiding place was not exactly Fort Knox, but it had done its job and the ledgers seemed so at home tucked away, with all the secrets they contained, on her shelves. But there was nothing for it.

She stepped forward and slid the first of the books out of line and laid it reverently down on the little table. The men crowded around it, one on each side of Beth, the three of them peering at the black leather cover with its patina of age. She slid on the cotton gloves and opened the ledger to the page she had marked. Both men leant in closer to make sense of the faded words. Then both leant back. If the atmosphere in the room had been less electric, the synchronicity of their movements would have amused her. But this was serious.

The men looked at each other. The bursar's florid face was for once devoid of its patronising smile but, as usual, one of his legs was jiggling restlessly. The headmaster's shrewd eyes were guarded. Even his billowing Hermès tie seemed less colourful all of a sudden.

'What the hell do we do with this?' said the bursar tersely. The head said nothing, but steepled his fingers in front of his face, bowed his forehead, and thought. Both Beth and Tom Seasons stared at him. Beth felt a pang of pity for the man.

The school was not having a great fortnight.

First, a grisly murder on the premises, now the revelation that the entire school foundation relied upon the proceeds of slavery. The headmaster lifted his head from his hands for a second, and he looked hunted. This was going to be very hard to play.

Luckily for Wyatt's, Dr Grover was a very clever man. He was not going to rush into any revelations, but nor, Beth was sure, would he brush this under the carpet.

'Right. I need to give this matter some serious thought. Thank you for bringing it to my attention, Beth,' he said, with a faint bow in her direction.

Beth was grateful that his reaction was so different from that of the bursar. She glanced at him but, if she was expecting thanks or even an apology from that quarter, she'd have quite a wait.

The bursar slanted a look of dislike at her, swiftly masked with his usual hefty bonhomie. 'Nothing Wyatt's can't deal with, eh?' he joshed, but the words sounded empty and the head didn't respond.

'I'll be calling the board of governors this afternoon. We need to have a properly thought-out strategy on all of this. At the moment, I'd be grateful if you didn't discuss this with outsiders.' Dr Grover addressed the remarks to them both, but she sensed they were meant for her. She was reluctant to respond.

She was convinced that Jenkins' death was linked with the ledgers, and she felt that the greatest safety lay in making sure as many people as possible knew the secret. That way, if the murderer did intend to do away with people in the know, he'd have a packed field to deal with before he got to her and Jake.

She knew it was selfish, but she could justify it with perfect ease every time she thought of her son.

Luckily for her, the bursar piped up with a hearty, 'Of course, of course,' which seemed to cover them both, and Beth smiled gladly.

She shut the door on them both a few moments later. The head was going to have a busy afternoon, on the phone to the shocked governors. Beth didn't know any of them personally, but they were the great and good of Dulwich and beyond. They included bigwigs from the City, as well as a BBC high-up, an MP, an actor on the fast track to national treasure status, and a judge. None would be thrilled, she was sure, to hear they had linked their names with a school founded on the proceeds of human misery. No matter how Wyatt's was flourishing now, it had its roots firmly in muck.

Mind you, there was something of a fashion at the moment for large institutions to wake up, as suddenly as Sleeping Beauty, after long, peaceful interludes of blissful forgetfulness, and be forced to contemplate the actions of their founding fathers. Several Oxbridge colleges were being compelled to consider removing statues of Cecil Rhodes, whose nineteenth-century views on Anglo-Saxon supremacy were now causing as much embarrassment as his lavish endowments had once delighted. Wyatt's would certainly not be the first establishment with a problem reconciling an ancient fortune with today's moral standards. It was the kind of mess that no one wanted to have to deal with.

Beth was full of sympathy for Dr Grover. This was not a problem of his making, and it had fallen squarely at his door. She wasn't sure what the best strategy would be, though for her the most appealing tactic would be a 'mea culpa' approach which did not seek to excuse, even with the justification that different times dictated different standards.

In the meantime, Beth had dilemmas of her own to contend

with. Should she let Inspector York know of this latest development, or should she leave it up to the school to contact him in its own good time? Would that time ever come? she wondered. She wasn't sure that anyone on the administration side wanted to link slavery with murder. She could imagine the lurid headlines even now.

A sharp ping from her phone broke into Beth's reverie. She fished it out of her bag. Why was it that wherever she put it, it was never easily accessible? She keyed in her code and a text flashed up. It was full of emojis. She peered at it in surprise. Though a few of the mothers that she knew – those with children already in their teens – had to speak 'smiley face' in order to communicate with their young, and would occasionally slap an emoticon on an ordinary inter-mother text, hardly anyone of her generation bothered. Then she realised. This came from Lou, the junior school receptionist.

She hadn't really been expecting any news from Lou, who seemed a few colours short of a rainbow. Beth knew that she herself would have had major problems remembering who had dropped a particular child off on a particular day – except that murder had a habit of fixing things pretty effectively in people's minds. In among the little pictures signifying great joy and a brainwave, Lou divulged that she had not only remembered but could positively prove that it had been little Ellen's mother, Dr Jenkins' daughter, who had taken the child to school that day.

Lol mrs fitch dropped ellen, signed lost property book picked up gym kit, Lou had typed, along with tiny pictures of shorts and a T-shirt as if to back up her testimony.

Bless the girl for doing a thorough check, thought Beth, mentally chiding herself for having dismissed Lou so easily. She should have trusted more in Wyatt's. The school would never employ someone who was genuinely as dippy as Lou had seemed. She texted back a fulsome thank you, scattered with little emojis. When in Rome, send an emoji of a toga.

People's behaviour towards others was always such a strong influencing factor. Lou's cheery friendliness was perfect for the junior school. Dr Grover's upbeat, businesslike intelligence seemed to get the best out of everybody, even pompous sods like the bursar.

She thought back. It was only just over a week ago, but already her strong reactions to Dr Jenkins were fading, partly out of respect for the dead, partly just because life moved on. When she thought of him now, she thought of a problem to be solved, not a person. She pressed send.

Beth looked up from her phone abruptly and gazed up at the small square of window. She was having her own lightbulb moment.

FOURTEEN

Half an hour later, having sidled out of Wyatt's again, she was sitting in the Aurora café, idly stirring a spoon in an uninspiring and now rather cold cappuccino. The door banged and she looked up to see the tall figure of Inspector York grappling to shut the slightly warped door of the café.

'It doesn't really close properly,' said Beth, as the waiter bustled forward to fiddle with it himself. He cast an angry look at York as though he was responsible for its state, instead of it being a long-neglected bugbear of all who frequented the place, particularly on cold or windy days.

York gave Beth a rueful smile as he took his seat, then struggled to his feet again as the waiter passed muttering, 'Counter service only.'

'Can I get you anything else? Another coffee? Sandwich?'

Beth shook her head vigorously, wanting to warn him off attempting to eat anything here without aggravating the waiter still further. She heard him ordering a bacon sandwich with his coffee, and sighed a little.

He sat down again and the rickety table dipped towards him. He took a napkin from the dispenser on the table next to them, wadded it up quickly, and slipped it under the short leg, then braced his hands on the cold marble surface. The table was steady.

Beth, despite herself, was impressed. She'd sat here several times now with Katie – against Katie's better judgement – and the tables were always rickety but she'd never done anything about it. She did love a practical person. She found herself smiling up at him, then was horrified at herself, nervously brushing her thick fringe away with one hand, which inevitably made it swing back and all but cover her eyes. Her comfort blanket. She was always more at ease when peeping out from behind this useful portable screen.

Was she upset because she'd felt a stab of disloyalty to her beloved James? But James was gone. Would he have wanted her to soldier on alone forever? Did that mean that she didn't want to, all of a sudden? She didn't even want to begin to think about all that now, with this man sitting in front of her. She blinked as York broke the suddenly charged silence.

'So, you had something to tell me?'

Beth nodded vigorously, glad to be distracted from difficult thoughts. She did, indeed, have a lot to tell. But first, she had a question to ask.

'Have you discovered anything more about the blackmail?'

York looked blank. Beth was exasperated. All right, he made a policy of never replying to any of her questions, but come on. What was the point of pretending he didn't know what she was talking about?

'You know, those sums of money that suddenly started to come into Jenkins' bank account, two hundred pounds, then six hundred pounds a month...'

'You shouldn't really be bandying words like "blackmail" about, you know. Accusations like that have implications,' he said with a frown.

'I wasn't accusing anyone. I have no idea who to accuse,'

Beth pointed out. 'But was it, you know, erm, extortion?' she said, after casting around for an alternative word.

York rolled his eyes. 'No. It turned out to be entirely innocent.'

'You're kidding! That much money, every month? How could it have an innocent explanation?'

'You see, that's the trouble with only having half the information at your disposal,' said York heavily. 'Another reason why you shouldn't have been poking your nose into his private papers. You should have handed everything over straight away and left it to the professionals.'

Beth was rapidly deciding that York was the most patronising man she'd ever met – barring some of the staff of Wyatt's, of course. James's ghost could rest easy.

'Come on, you've told me this much now. Give me the full explanation,' said Beth, controlling her irritation with an effort. She leant forward, just as the waiter approached and slapped York's cappuccino down with enough force to slop it into the saucer.

Both Beth and York looked at him sharply. Seemingly oblivious, he drifted away. York took a quick sip of the coffee, winced, and picked a packet of sugar out of the bowl in front of him, shook it by a corner a couple of times then ripped the top off neatly and dumped the contents in his cup, stirring vigorously. Beth stared at him, eyebrows arched with questions under the heavy fringe. York put the cup down, a decision made.

'Listen, you might find this hard to believe, but there's a poker circle at Wyatt's, involving some of the teachers. Jenkins was one, and it turns out he was quite a gifted player. They met once a month, and he almost always won.'

Beth was astounded. She leant back in her chair for a moment, then burst out, 'Poker? At Wyatt's? Are you sure?'

'Yes, I know, I know. I wonder what those posh parents

would make of that, then? Turns out all those clever-clever teachers they're paying so much money for are more interested in playing cards than in teaching their precious kids.' York laughed.

'I can't believe it's *all* the teachers,' said Beth, thinking of Dr Joyce, head of English, who surely would only contemplate a card game if it were Speculation, as played by Fanny Price in *Mansfield Park*. 'And everyone I've met there seems really devoted to the kids. To be honest, quite a lot of the parents are actually bankers themselves anyway.'

'So?' said York, a bit put out that Beth wasn't more shocked by his revelation.

'So, playing the stock market is all about gambling, it's just a bit more respectable than... poker. And I don't suppose they were playing during school hours. At least Jenkins was *good* at it,' said Beth, who found to her surprise that she now had a little more grudging respect for the awful man. Then she had a thought.

'Do you think anyone would kill him for winning too much at cards? Or cheating?'

'We have thought of that,' said York drily. 'And the answer is no. He wasn't just beating one person, who might have turned on him. He was scooping the pot, month after month, beating the whole bunch he played with. I know, it seems pretty surprising.'

Beth had taken a too-hasty swallow of her cold coffee, and nearly choked on hearing about Jenkins' card-playing prowess. It was true the man had had a certain arrogant swagger. She'd just thought it had come from being a guy of a certain age, in possession of a penis. There was a type and a generation of men who thought this simple appendage made them superior to every woman around them, and also, in some very strange corner of their psyche, convinced that all females desperately wanted them to demonstrate their skills with that specific piece of gristle at the slightest opportunity, whether the women demurred or not. But if Jenkins had actually been *good* at something... that might account for why he so transparently felt he was God's gift. Because otherwise, it was pretty inexplicable.

Despite herself, Beth also felt a bit deflated that there was a simple, and almost innocent, explanation for Jenkins' strange cash deposits. Blackmail had been such a perfect motive for murder. Besides, he was such a loathsome man that she had been all too willing to believe he would be capable of the dirtiest tricks around.

She leant on her elbow, and sighed. 'So where does that leave us?'

'Well, we have to rule out that whole idea, but there's still plenty to follow up,' said York, not seeming downcast at all.

'But that's not good. We want to narrow things down, until all we have left is the explanation,' Beth protested.

'Don't hold your breath. These things can take months to sort out, and loads of cases never get solved at all,' said York cheerily.

'But we can't leave this unsolved,' Beth protested.

'We may not have any choice. Things don't always snap into place, you know. Sometimes you never get the breaks, there's no evidence – or the worst is when there are one or two leads, you have an idea in your head, but there's just not *enough* evidence to do anything with it. That's a killer, that is.'

'But that's not going to be the case here, surely? A murder like this, in Wyatt's – there has to be an explanation. Someone will have left clues, and we'll find them.'

'I wish I had your faith,' said York, smiling briefly. 'But in the real world, half the time we can't get convictions, even if we can get someone in the frame. The CPS – Crown Prosecution Service – has to be sure there's enough there to stick. Otherwise, a court case would just fall apart. The lawyers pick away at any loophole until there's nothing left. And it's right that everyone is entitled to be represented by a lawyer; we're not a police state. So, if the case isn't watertight, the CPS won't touch it. It's just a waste of taxpayers' money.'

'It doesn't seem right,' said Beth, her forehead under the heavy fringe a concertina of lines as she thought her position through. 'This shouldn't be just about the money, an accounting issue. It's a moral thing. If someone's murdered someone, then they should be punished.'

'I quite agree. That's why I joined the force, to make the streets safer. Thing is, the streets of Dulwich are going to be pretty safe whatever happens to Jenkins' murderer. Whoever it was doesn't seem to be on a mad killing spree.'

'Well, that's true,' said Beth, briefly remembering that horrible moment when she'd thought Janice had been claimed as the next victim. 'But there have been the burglaries, too – they've been pretty scary. And the second one, in my house, seemed a lot more... aggressive, somehow. That's what they call escalation, isn't it?'

'Everyone knows the jargon these days,' agreed York. 'And yes, it did seem worse; a nasty attack, and I'm sure it was very upsetting. Don't get me wrong, I'm going to do everything I can to sort this out and get the person concerned, don't you worry about that. I just want you to be prepared for the fact that sometimes things don't have a neat solution, they don't get wrapped up with pink ribbons. This perpetrator is careful. There have been no fingerprints, no CCTV... There's not a lot to go on. Ah, I think that's my sandwich coming.'

Sure enough, the waiter, having thudded about extensively in the back kitchen, now came forth bearing a tray and put down a greasy-looking white bread sandwich, oozing with bright pink bacon, with a single lettuce leaf clinging for dear life to the edge of the plate. It looked as much of an afterthought as the fig leaves drawn by the Victorians on frisky Italian frescoes, but luckily York didn't seem to feel cheated at all. He didn't bother to unwrap the knife and fork which had been swaddled in a cheap paper napkin, but grabbed the butty with both hands and sunk his teeth into it. Despite herself, Beth acknowledged a reciprocal pang of hunger. Bacon might be decried as the devil's work these days, but even served like this the smell was delicious.

To distract herself, she racked her brains for more questions she should be asking York. 'Any news on the forensics from my burglary? I don't suppose you got anything from that DNA test, did you? That would be good, solid evidence, wouldn't it? The CPS couldn't pretend that wasn't real.'

York put down the ravaged sandwich and grabbed a squeezy bottle of ketchup from the next table, prising the two layers of bread apart carefully with his knife, before dousing the bacon with a quantity of sauce even Jake would have deemed generous.

He gave her a level look, which she guessed was another reminder that they might never know the identity of whoever had killed Jenkins and burgled her house. He then picked the whole bacon creation up again and resumed the attack. After a prolonged bout of chewing, he was ready to speak. 'I don't suppose you know much about DNA, but it's difficult to get a match on urine.'

'You said that at the time, but why would that be?' She was slightly hesitant to discuss the topic while he was eating so enthusiastically, but she supposed that if he didn't mind, why should she?

'The thing is that there aren't that many of the right type of cells present in human urine. Like I said, you need nucleated cells to analyse DNA. The nucleated cells that are found in urine are typically white blood cells and epithelial cells.'

'OK,' said Beth. For a second, she considered pretending she knew what he was on about, then gave it up. 'Erm, I'm not sure this means that much to me.'

'Doesn't really matter about all that. The main point of interest for us is that while you might not be able to get a proper DNA match from urine, particularly if it's been lying around for a while or diluted – as it was in the case of the sample from your house – you can tell one thing quite easily.' York paused for a moment to take another huge bite.

Beth found herself waiting impatiently as he chewed as thoroughly as a child instructed to chomp thirty times before swallowing, then washed everything down with a long draught from his coffee cup, and finally wiped his fingers on his napkin.

'Yes? What can you tell?' she asked.

'You can tell whether the donor, as it were, is male or female. But before you get too excited about that, just think about it. Yes, you've ruled out fifty per cent of the population. But you haven't narrowed it down any further than that. So instead of sixty million people in the UK being possible suspects, you're just looking at thirty million.'

It was no good. York's note of caution sailed right over Beth's head. She was hugely excited at this potential breakthrough. If the answer was what she thought it was going to be, it would tie in nicely with the little brainwave she'd had earlier, after receiving Lou's text.

She leant forward and asked breathlessly, 'Really? Which was it in the case of my burglar?'

It had been one of the most productive days she'd spent since the murder, thought Beth later. And if she'd spent quite a chunk of the day outside her office, and pretty much all of the day doing things that had very little to do with the archives – or any of her freelance work either – she felt a little less guilty now that she knew what her predecessor had been up to on the premises, at least once a month. However much she might have been neglecting her duties, at least Beth was not the ringleader of a clandestine gambling ring.

She was going to be looking with new eyes at Sam Radley, the Maths head with his wacky ties, and Geoff Henderson, the sinewy Physics guy. They had apparently been in the poker group, along with the French teacher, Louise Godfrey, and the bursar. Beth didn't know which of these last two names surprised her the most. She supposed it was rather sexist to assume that poker was a game only played by men – she knew that some of the best players in the world were women. Victoria Coren, a columnist she rather admired on the *Sunday Telegraph*, was a demon poker player who'd won millions of dollars and was funny and beautiful too. But still. The French teacher looked so (appropriately) soignée. It was quite mind-boggling to imagine her sitting with the frankly unappealing male members of the little club, all focusing on fleecing each other.

On the other hand, Beth could imagine the bursar richly enjoying intimidating the group with bluff after bluff. Though, surely he would have felt the company itself was beneath him. And she was astonished that he hadn't tired, very rapidly, of being bested by Jenkins.

People were endlessly surprising. And the biggest surprise of all was that Jenkins had been so good at poker. Well, she supposed, he had to have been doing something with his time. He had been in charge of the archives and that, quite demon-strably, had not been holding his attention of late – if it had ever been a priority. He must have whiled away the time before and after games honing his poker skills. There were no books on poker or gambling in evidence in the office, but then that wasn't the only way to get information. There was so much gambling online these days. Beth would not now be at all surprised to hear that his browsing history showed that poker sites took up most of his energy while on Wyatt's premises, once he had vaulted the school's firewalls.

Though she had done absolutely no archive work that day, she decided that 3.15 was not the time to make a start. She made a quick call to Katie to beg another favour, making a mental note that she was going to owe her friend a child-free holiday in the Caribbean and several gallons of decent coffee by the time this mess was over. Then she scooted over to the junior school gates.

Beth would be the first to admit that her plan was heavily flawed. She had not the slightest idea what Jenkins' daughter even looked like, or whether she would be picking her little girl up herself. She didn't even have the faintest idea how to get into conversation with the woman, anyway. She was much more used to keeping herself carefully below the parapet than striking up leading conversations with total strangers. But needs must.

York might be happy to let this case peter out into oblivion, but she was determined to sort things out. She couldn't live the rest of her life wondering which of her dear Dulwich neighbours had broken into her house and brought havoc so close to her son. Nor could she stand to see Jenkins' death unavenged. He might have been a horror, but he had still been a human being and an archivist. She felt a twinge of solidarity with the man, shyster, perv and time-waster though he might have been.

Beth was soon standing with a little gaggle of mothers outside the junior gates, busily pretending she'd known them all since reception class. Some looked at her, a little puzzled, as though trying to place her, but she was hoping most would assume she was a working mother with a temporary staffing crisis, who wasn't a regular at pick-up. If she just acted as though she belonged here, she was hoping she'd be able to wheedle her way into the gang. All right, it wasn't something that had worked out particularly well at the school gates she legitimately had to attend on Jake's behalf. But maybe they were just a tough crowd at the Village Primary. And she had never had a real reason to try and ingratiate herself before. This time, she certainly did. And as it happened, she knew enough about early years schooling to blend in pretty seamlessly.

As it turned out, it wasn't nearly as hard as she had feared to break into the conversation. Everyone was loudly discussing the Year Two spelling test, which apparently had been impossible, despite the best efforts of this bunch of tiger mothers.

'Can you believe it, they had the word "apprentice"? What's the good of that? It's not like any of them are going to *be* apprentices,' said one angry mother, to vigorous nods from the group.

'Oh, Ellen was fine with apprentice,' said another, a tad smugly.

Beth's ears pricked up. Could this be Ellen Fitch's mum? Trouble was, it wasn't an unusual name. In Jake's class at the primary alone, there were two Ellens, an Eleanor, and an Ella for good measure.

Meanwhile, the woman continued, 'I did think we might get stuck on "apprehension". Well, it's that little bit longer, isn't it? But we just did the "look, cover, write, check" once – and she got it first time.'

There were one or two polite smiles, but Beth sensed a distinct lack of warmth towards this mother from the rest of the crew. That would fit in with what she knew of Dr Jenkins and his wife. Though they both had jobs right in the centre of the Dulwich community, and could have commanded affection and respect, they just didn't. Neither was likeable.

Beth took a chance and approached the woman. 'Mrs Fitch?' she said, tentatively.

'Yes?' said the woman, with marked coolness. This wasn't the way one mother would normally approach another at the gates; it was too formal.

'Beth Haldane, I work for Wyatt's. Can I have a quick word?' said Beth, gesturing to a quiet spot under a tree in the playground.

'Oh, of course,' said Mrs Fitch, relaxing. If Beth was on the staff she must be OK. 'Do call me Rachel. But my daughter will be out in five minutes and I have to rush her to ballet...'

Of course, you do, thought Beth. The end of school was only the start of a Dulwich child's activities. All round the gates, the mothers were poised to ferry their little ones off to Kumon maths, clarinet lessons, judo, art classes, or just plain therapy.

'This won't take a moment,' Beth said, all professional reassurance. But then she found herself stumped. She'd succeeded in detaching her prey from the herd a little, but how on earth was she going to broach all her tricky questions?

Luckily, Mrs Fitch took the initiative. 'Look, if it's about my father again, and the effect it might be having on Ellen...'

'Yes? Yes,' said Beth gratefully, glad to have been offered such a lifeline into exactly the topic she wanted to talk about.

'The thing is, she was shocked to start with, and yes, I did give her a couple of quiet days at home just to rest, but,' said Mrs Fitch, lowering her voice and leaning into Beth conspiratorially, 'it's just not going to bother her at all, long-term. We weren't close.'

'You weren't?' Beth wasn't sure where this was going, but it was fascinating. She just wanted to keep the woman talking for as long as possible.

'Not at all. I rarely saw my father, only when I had to.' Mrs Fitch's face was shuttered as she said this.

'Really? You were estranged?' Beth asked.

'You can call it that if you like,' said Mrs Fitch with heavy irony. 'I'm not sure I'd say I was estranged myself, but I would definitely say that my father was strange. *Very* strange.' Their eyes locked.

Suddenly, with horrible clarity, Beth understood something – something ghastly – without any words being said. But she had to check, just to make sure she wasn't jumping to terrible, unsubstantiated conclusions. As York had warned her, accusing Jenkins of blackmail was slander. The crime she was now beginning to suspect him of was infinitely worse.

'Your father was quite... old-fashioned in his attitude to women. A little... chauvinistic, shall we say?'

Rachel Fitch laughed mirthlessly. 'That's one way to describe it,' she said. Again, what she wasn't saying seemed to speak volumes. 'What business is any of this of yours, anyway?'

'I was the one who found the body,' said Beth quietly.

'Oh.' That took the wind out of Rachel's sails, but she soon rallied. 'Well, if I'd killed him, I'd have stabbed him right through the heart and then danced on his lifeless corpse,' she said with chilling vehemence. 'Then kicked him around a bit for good measure.'

'Well, he *was* stabbed...' said Beth. 'But all that? You must have hated him. Why?' She had a very good idea, but she wanted to be sure.

Rachel Fitch, exasperated, stressed by the wait for her child, and longing to be rid of this irritating woman, suddenly let rip.

'Why did I hate him? Why was I sad when I heard he'd been killed, *but only because I hadn't had the bravery to kill him myself*? Because he was a child-abusing pervert, that's why. He made my life a misery, until I managed to get out. He turned my mother into a zombie, and ruined her life, too, but that's *her* lookout.'

At that moment, a stream of children burst through the junior school doors, among them a little girl with shiny hair the colour of a bright new penny, who bounced straight up to Rachel Fitch and flung her arms around her. The woman's face softened as she enfolded her daughter and kissed the top of her head. Then she glared across the girl at Beth.

'Now, if you've quite finished cross-questioning me about that man, let me just assure you that my daughter won't miss him. Any more than I will.'

With that, Rachel Fitch turned on her heel and stalked off, with her daughter's little hand firmly clasped in hers. In her high-heeled boots and tight white jeans, with an outsize expensive bag on her arm and a child in a coveted endowment schools uniform at her side, she looked the epitome of the carefree Dulwich mum. They turned the corner to find their car and Beth saw Rachel's face, which was now alight with pleasure and laughter as she bent to hear a story from her little daughter's day. Whatever sadness and horror lurked in her childhood, it was clear Rachel Fitch had started a new chapter with her own child. She was doing her best to slam the door on the past.

But how far would she go to make sure her future, and that of her little girl, was secure? That was the question Beth was left asking. Though Rachel Fitch had said her only regret was not having killed her father herself, surely that was hyperbole? Could any child really mean that about a parent? It went against nature. But then, thought Beth heavily, so did child abuse.

She wasn't at all surprised to hear that Dr Jenkins had had one last secret which had finally been revealed. To an extent, his very public leching – which she herself had only had brief experience of, but others had told her was habitual behaviour – was quite a good front for an abuser. By seeming to demean all women, he deflected attention from the far worse crime of attacking his own child. The man truly had been a monster.

She'd had a momentary burst of admiration for him when she'd heard how brilliant he was at poker. It was something she'd never played, but it involved not only high levels of numeracy but also the ability to 'read' your fellow players – an unusual skill set. She knew plenty of people who were good at one side or other of this equation, but very few who were masters of both.

But then, abusers were highly manipulative people. To keep a dark secret locked within a family for years was no easy matter. Convincing the innocent that they were guilty, the suspicious that they were deluded, and – perhaps most difficult of all – convincing oneself that the crime you were committing was somehow justified, asked for or deserved, required a level of evil sophistry that Beth marvelled at, despite herself. Poor Rachel Fitch. Poor Mrs Jenkins. And no wonder, again, that Dr Jenkins himself had so little time to spare for his actual job. He was as burdened with extracurricular activities as any Dulwich child, Beth thought with a shiver.

The wonder, as always in these cases, was that he had got away with it, and for so long. Dulwich was such a small place, everyone knew everybody and secrets had a way of worming their way to the light. Well, this was no exception. But it had taken many years to burst out.

Though the sun was bright, Beth couldn't stop shivering. She wrapped her cardigan more securely around her, and then wrapped both arms around that. Darting a look at the handful of mothers left waiting, whose children must have been dawdling somewhere inside, Beth pondered her next move.

FIFTEEN

There was only one thing for it. Beth would have to pay another call on Mrs Jenkins. If anyone knew what the true situation was, it was her. She might be quite frightening, and pretty much away with the fairies, but she was going to be Beth's best source of information.

As usual, she wondered briefly if she needed to bring York up to speed. But, after their long talk this afternoon, she was more convinced than ever that his heart wasn't really in finding a solution. He was a pragmatist, and a policeman. He had to work within the constraints of the system. She, on the other hand, was consumed by curiosity, and more than capable (or so she felt, after this afternoon's revelation) of finding out all she needed to know on her own.

She quickly rang Katie, just to check all was well with Jake and Charlie. 'Yep, looks like they've had a good day,' her friend replied cheerfully. 'But you won't like this, they've been given another project to do.'

Beth groaned down the phone. 'It's only been two minutes since the last one, those blimmin' dinosaurs,' she said.

'Don't tell me, tell the silly school. Anyway, you'll love this, they've only got to make the planets. Again!'

'No! At least we know what to do this time, though.' Beth remembered only too well her last attempt to get Jake interested in modelling the solar system. As usual, he had been in denial about the whole business until the night before it was due in. Then Beth had been up till one in the morning, splotching blue paint onto a green furry tennis ball and hoping the result would pass muster as the earth. It didn't.

As she saw Jake's friends bringing in entire galaxies the next day, she cursed for the umpteenth time the fact that other Dulwich mothers had too little to do and too much time to do it in. This time, she'd buy a packet of balloons and do the whole thing properly, with papier mâché and everything. Really, she would.

'You know what would make a fortune round here? A company specialising in doing kids' school projects. You'd just email them and the next day they'd send round the entire Milky Way made out of yoghurt pots,' said Beth.

'Brilliant idea. *Slightly* missing the point about getting the kids interested in making stuff, but otherwise a sure-fire winner,' said Katie.

'Oh, come on, don't pretend anyone's kids are making these things. Do you seriously think Belinda McKenzie's lot have ever been anywhere near paint?'

Belinda McKenzie was famous for rigorously quizzing au pairs on their crafting skills before hiring. Creative talent, and the type of leaden looks that posed absolutely no temptation to Belinda's erring husband, Barty, were far more important to Belinda than any interest in children. One of her hirelings had been so unfortunate of face that both dogs had taken one look and scarpered. But the girl was a genius with crêpe paper, and stayed two years before decamping with the Physics tutor.

'Fair point,' chuckled Katie. 'Just got home. I'll feed them, and see you later?'

'Thank you so much, Katie, you're a star. I've just got to follow something up with Mrs Jenkins... Be right over when I've finished.'

'Her again? Do you have to? According to Judith Seasons, she's taking the death really badly. She's hardly been outside her front door since it happened. And she's completely let her yoga slip.'

'Must be serious,' said Beth, mentally rolling her eyes. Katie was wonderful but she was obsessed with yoga. A normal person missing an exercise class was perfectly understandable. For a grieving widow, surely it was only to be expected? Katie, though, marked it down as a sign of imminent collapse. 'See you soon.'

Beth picked up her pace a little as she walked the short distance to Gilkes Place, hoping against hope Mrs Jenkins would be in. She wasn't sure what the woman's teaching hours were – apart from the Thursday when she was at the primary with Jake and other reluctant readers in his year – though she was still on leave of absence, as far as Beth knew. But if she was shunning yoga, maybe she was at home. She crossed her fingers.

As she walked up the path, Beth noticed a few little changes since her last visit. The recycling tub had been left out in the garden, though collection day had come and gone, and the lid was askew. Not very Dulwich. And, if she wasn't imagining it, the crazy paving of the path to the front door had sprouted a few weeds. Like errantly bushy eyebrows on an otherwise carefully made-up face, they were a jarring note.

Beth rang the bell, peering at the frosted, textured glass in the pillar-box red door. Within, all was dark, distorted, quiet. She was about to turn away, with something like relief despite herself, when the door was yanked open.

There stood Mrs Jenkins, her stolid, tubular body clad today in comforting dusty blue shades – a floral jersey dress with a droopy cardigan over the top. It was the sort of fashion favoured by women who had given up, Beth thought privately, but it was neat and utterly inoffensive.

'It's you again. You'd better come in,' said Mrs Jenkins.

Beth was surprised. She'd expected that she'd have to come up with some sort of story to get herself past the front door. She didn't seem to be improving at all in making these up, so Mrs Jenkins' relatively warm welcome was a relief.

Wordlessly, Beth followed her hostess. She'd thought they'd make for the dark and somewhat oppressive kitchen, but instead they veered off towards a sitting room which also opened off the square hall. It was patterned in a William Morris print, which she recognised as the heavily ornate 'Lily Green'. It amused her that Morris, a thoroughgoing firebrand in his time who had yearned for revolution, had become the middle classes' go-to wallpaper designer. Patterns which had been cutting edge in his day were now safely classic.

Here, all four walls were papered with wildly interlocking lilies and tulips, with tendrils of foliage curling about them in a restless dance. The effect was claustrophobic in the extreme. Floor-length, forest green velvet curtains, drawn tightly against the light, made the room even more of a dark jungle. Ruth Jenkins snapped on a central light, its shade patterned to match the walls, but it was one of those eco bulbs which gave off about as much wattage as a birthday cake candle.

Beth hadn't realised what a cold colour green could be. Usually, she thought of it as warm and welcoming. Here, despite the hectic fecundity of the wallpaper, the green carpet suggested a frozen pond, the pictures on the walls were uninspiring botanical prints, and even the books in the two bookcases looked unloved and untouched.

Ruth Jenkins gestured to one of the hard-looking Chesterfield sofas, arranged around an empty fireplace. Beth perched on the edge, the shiny leather threatening to slide her off and squeaking rudely whenever she moved. Jake would have laughed himself silly, she thought. But she'd bet no one had ever giggled at such noises here.

'So, you've found out, I suppose,' the woman intoned quietly.

Beth didn't know what to say. Should she pretend she knew what Ruth Jenkins was talking about, to decoy her into saying more? Or should she admit ignorance, and try and get her to explain?

Before she could decide on an approach, her phone pinged. Normally, she would have ignored it. But this could help her play for time.

'So sorry, I must get this,' she murmured. Ruth Jenkins tutted loudly, no doubt having all her prejudices about Beth's phone-obsessed generation confirmed.

Beth fumbled around in her bag, drew out the phone and peered at the screen. Just a text from Katie saying Jake was fine and eating fish fingers. Except, knowing Katie, they weren't really fish fingers, but home-prepared fish goujons lovingly hand-breaded to look like the cheap neon supermarket stuff.

She was just composing a reply when a huge weight thundered onto the shiny glass coffee table in front of her, splintering it completely. Her phone flew out of her hand in shock, and dropped to the floor with a thud, bouncing under the sofa where it lay, neglected. She looked up into Mrs Jenkins' triumphant, mocking face, her homely features distorted with hatred.

'What do you think *that* is, then?' Mrs Jenkins hissed.

'What? What are you doing?' shrieked Beth, frantically brushing her fringe out of her eyes and off her forehead, suddenly hot. Her eyes were wide with shock. The object seemed to be a trophy of some sort, complete with a heavy marble base which had completely shattered the table. 'Your table...'

'Do you think I care about the table? When I've found out what he was up to?' 'He? You mean... your husband?'

'Yes. That swine. That's his poker trophy, there. I should have bashed his head in with that, instead of...'

'Instead of... what?' Beth prompted. Mrs Jenkins looked at her and shook her head, suddenly subsiding into one of the chairs. It squeaked like Beth's had, but no one was smiling now.

'Didn't you know about the poker? Is that why you're angry?' said Beth, searching to make sense of this violent turn of events.

'Of course I knew about it! He used to play for a club down in Eltham, that's how he won that blessed lump of a cup I've had to dust all these years. Then he started playing in secret, up at the school. He thought I didn't know about his stupid sneaky games. Well, I knew, but I didn't care. Anything that got him out of the house, away from me, was fine. I didn't even care about his affair with Judith, that bitch.'

'Were they definitely... an item?' said Beth. 'That must have been upsetting for you.'

'Upsetting? Him inflicting his... ways on someone else? I was glad.' Mrs Jenkins' eyes, that Beth had once thought kindly, glittered coldly. 'The only thing I hated about that sordid business was the fact that Judith pitied me. She thought she had some great secret, had one over on me because she was sleeping with my husband. Little did she know that I set the whole thing up. I knew he'd be keen, not because he found her attractive – she was about fifty years older than he liked them – but because he hated her husband.'

'Tom Seasons? The bursar?' Ruth Jenkins was so deep in her story that she twitched her head at Beth's interruption. Beth hoped she hadn't destroyed the woman's train of thought. But then Mrs Jenkins seemed to turn her gaze inward again, and she went on.

'He hated Tom Seasons. Tom was everything he wasn't –

outgoing, good company... normal. Alan was a horrible little pervert, and he knew it himself.'

'Why did you marry him?' Beth couldn't resist asking.

'I was stupid. I wanted to get away from my own home. I hardly knew him, I had no idea what he was like, what his tastes were – and at the time I was young. He liked them young,' she said heavily. 'Of course, I aged. But then we had Rachel.'

Mrs Jenkins picked up the poker trophy from the wreckage of the coffee table, seemingly oblivious to the danger from all the shards of glass, and suddenly hurled it at the windows beyond the heavy curtains. Beth heard the crack of the glass, muffled by the fabric. The trophy bounced off the heavy velvet and came to rest on the floor.

'Did you know... what was going on?' Beth asked tentatively.

'I did... and I didn't,' said Ruth Jenkins, and Beth could feel the pain of her honesty. 'I suppose the truth is that I didn't want to know. I didn't want the burden of having to do something about it. If I pretended nothing was going on, then everything could carry on. It was too difficult.'

'But it was your *daughter*,' said Beth.

'She never loved me. We never got on, never saw eye to eye. When I had a daughter, when she was first born, my dearest wish was for us to be friends. But we never had that bond,' said Mrs Jenkins, deep in self-pity now. Somehow, in her head, her child had failed in her responsibility to befriend her mother. She absolved herself entirely of any duty she might have had to love the child first, and show her by example how to build bridges. Rachel had paid a high price for not having a better relationship with this woman, thought Beth with a shudder.

'Was that why you... turned a blind eye?' asked Beth gently.

'I didn't know. I had no idea,' said Mrs Jenkins, shaking her head rigorously.

Beth stared in disbelief. It wasn't the story the woman had

told her with her own mouth just two minutes ago. But it was the story she wanted to believe. Beth looked around. The jungle pattern of the walls seemed to close in on her. The weight of secrets in the house pressed in on them both.

'So, what happened? What went on?' Beth probed. 'It was Ellen,' said Mrs Jenkins starkly.

Beth sat upright with a jolt. She had nearly forgotten little Ellen, with the shiny hair and open smile. She was Rachel's daughter, and looked like a miniature, more joyful version of her mother.

She must have been a temptation beyond words to Dr Alan Jenkins.

Yes, she was his own granddaughter. But if that hadn't stopped him with his daughter, why would it matter now? In fact, with another generation as a buffer between them, he would have found it easier, not more difficult, to start his horrible games.

Beth swallowed. She didn't want to ask the question, but she felt she must. 'Did he... touch her?'

Ruth Jenkins seemed to crumple in the solid, unyielding chair. Her body, already soft, sagged in on itself like under-cooked dough.

'He'd started to look. I hadn't known for sure with Rachel.' She risked a quick look at Beth, to see if she would contradict her. Beth decided to remain silent. 'But I knew what that look meant. The glances he'd give her... it was like his hands running right up your legs. It was horrible. He used to give me that look when we were first married, and it always meant he wanted to get me alone and... well, you know. When I first saw him look at Ellen like that, I just froze. I didn't know what to do.'

'You could have stopped her coming to the house. You could have forbidden him to see her,' said Beth, thinking aloud more than anything. There were a hundred ways to stop child abuse. But they all started with recognising it existed.

She could see that Mrs Jenkins, who had based her whole life and her whole comfortable, Dulwich lifestyle around pretending nothing was going on in this house, had simply not been able to confront her husband. If she had spoken up now, she would have had to acknowledge, finally, that she had once remained silent – and thrown her own daughter to the wolf.

Mrs Jenkins was twisting her hands restlessly in her lap, turning her wedding ring round and round on her finger, now and then covering her mouth with her fingers. She burst into speech. 'But how could I say that? He might not have meant... anything by it. And then what would I have said?'

'If you admitted you knew what that look meant, then you'd be saying you were aware of what happened to Rachel,' said Beth quietly.

'And I didn't know! I didn't! But I had to make sure it didn't happen to Ellen.'

Beth was beginning to see the many traps that Ruth Jenkins had made for herself. Turning a blind eye to her husband's activities, sacrificing her daughter for peace of mind and the family's reputation, had already exacted a heavy toll. She had got herself into the position where speaking plainly to her husband would have been more difficult, socially, than murdering him.

It was a perfect Dulwich predicament. Mrs Jenkins had had to stop her husband, before he turned her granddaughter into his next victim. Rather than air the decades of hurt and horror which swirled around this house, she had decided quite simply to shut the whole thing down forever.

'So how did you do it?' asked Beth.

Mrs Jenkins glanced up at Beth for a moment, then went back to twisting her hands on her lap, though this time there was a reminiscent smile playing at the corners of her mouth.

'It was so simple. I went to the Village Primary for the meeting, then, instead of meeting that bitch Judith for yoga, I went to

Wyatt's. They're used to seeing me there. I taught literacy there for a while before changing to the Primary. And I pick Ellen up from school when Rachel's between au pairs. They know me,' she added simply.

'I took my washing-up gloves in my handbag, and a knife from the kitchen. It's the one I use for peeling fruit.' Beth remembered the plate, the apple, the peel, on the draining board, the first time she'd been here. The murder weapon had been right there, under her nose, all along.

'I've watched all those detective shows on TV for years. I know all about CCTV footage, so I came through the playing fields. The groundsmen were on a tea break. I knew Alan would be round by the bins at some point in the morning, he usually went there for a smoke. I was just lucky that he came out quite promptly. It must have been just after nine when I stabbed him. He was surprised to see me there. Not pleased, but surprised enough to come right up to me. Normally, he wouldn't come within three feet of me any more; he thought old women were revolting. He only made an exception for Judith because he liked humiliating her husband so much. God knows how he made himself perform.'

Beth stared in horror at Ruth Jenkins, then shook her head to clear it of any taint of Dr Jenkins' sexual fantasies. Of all the places she did not want to go, that was now at the very top of the list. She concentrated instead on the older woman, who had a faraway look on her face.

'What happened next?'

'When Alan was close enough, I stuck the knife in. It wasn't difficult. It just sank right through the skin, and all the way in, as though he was made of lard, the filthy pig. I think I might have struck a rib, there was a nasty grating sound, but I just angled the knife away from it, gave it a bit of a twist. It was all very neat, hardly any blood,' Mrs Jenkins continued with gentle pride in her voice, as though she'd pulled off a rather clever feat of housekeeping.

'I couldn't believe I'd killed him, really. I don't think he could believe it either. He had a really shocked look on his face,' she said, with a grotesque, mischievous laugh. 'He fell on his back between the bins.'

'I carried on watching him for a while, then he started getting restless, moving his head from side to side as though he was going to talk. I just threw one of his handkerchiefs over his face. He'd dropped it on the floor when I stabbed him. He used to insist on me laundering those disgusting things, years after everyone else had moved to paper tissues. He was a revolting man. As soon as his face was covered up, he stopped moving. Like a parrot when you cover up its cage. I waited for a few minutes, then I went home.

'I kept thinking, that afternoon, that he might come home after all. I was so glad when he didn't,' said Mrs Jenkins, a faint smile on her face.

Beth was chilled to the bone. On one hand, Mrs Jenkins sounded stark, staring mad. On the other, she was utterly composed and in command of herself. One thing puzzled Beth.

'What about those burglaries? What were you looking for?'

Mrs Jenkins chuckled slightly. It was rather a nice sound, like a cosy hen clucking. 'That was more of that detective nonsense. I had Alan's office key, and I found your spare house keys in the desk. You should be more careful. I just wanted to make it look like the killer was hunting for something, that Alan had some dirty secret. Which of course he did, but nothing that you lot would be interested in.' Mrs Jenkins looked up at this, as though she had suddenly become aware of what she was saying, and to whom. Her eyes were suddenly sharp and assessing, narrowing on Beth consideringly.

'I won't say a word to anybody,' said Beth quickly. 'Your secret is safe with me.'

'Secrets, this has all been about secrets,' said Mrs Jenkins, then she seemed to come to a decision. 'Just stay there for a moment, dear, I've got something to show you.' Abruptly, she got up and left the room.

A moment later, Beth heard the sound of a key turning in a lock. She went to the door and rattled it in frustration. Locked in. She had to get help *now*. Where was her phone? She patted her pockets, then checked her bag. Nothing. Then it struck her. She ran back to the sofa, got down on her knees and grabbed it, lying where it had fallen when Mrs Jenkins had lobbed the poker trophy at the table.

Within seconds she was jabbing at the number for Inspector York. It rang, twice, three times... 'Come on, come on,' she muttered, under her breath.

Suddenly it connected. 'I'm not here at the moment, please leave a message...'

Beth nearly shrieked in annoyance, but left a garbled, whispered message, rang off, and was just tapping out the third of three nines when Mrs Jenkins stepped back into the room, a small knife in her hand.

Beth involuntarily took a step back, and came up against the hard edge of the sofa, then flopped down heavily. The leather sofa protested in its usual fashion.

'It's nothing against you personally, dear. I don't really like you but I don't like anyone these days,' said Mrs Jenkins in matter-of-fact tones. 'Alan did that to me, too. I used to be the life and soul, I loved a party,' she said, reminiscing. 'But having to keep all these secrets, all these *nasty little secrets*, it changes you. I just want to be on my own now. It's easier that way. You don't have to watch out to make sure people don't guess. You don't have to worry in case someone lets something slip.'

'It must have been such hard work,' said Beth as sympathetically as she could manage, bearing in mind that the woman she was attempting to empathise with was a killer advancing steadily towards her with a knife. 'You did such a good job.'

'I didn't. I let her down.' Mrs Jenkins' face fell.

'Who? Ellen? But you tried to protect her.'

'Not Ellen. Rachel. Oh, never mind. You'll never understand.'

Beth realised that was true. A secret like this corroded all those who came into contact with it – from the man who had generated its evil, to the woman who had appointed herself its guardian. She, thank God, would never understand either mindset.

'Look, Mrs Jenkins, you're free now. All this can be forgotten. Rachel is fine, Ellen is fine. You don't have to worry about the secret coming out any more.'

'No, I don't. Because the one person who knows it, outside the family, is going to be dealt with.'

Oops, thought Beth. Said the wrong thing there. She shrank back in the chair as Mrs Jenkins approached, the razor-sharp paring knife bright silver in the gloomy cold room.

'I'm not going to say anything. I wouldn't tell anyone, your secret is safe,' Beth said, her voice rising to a shriek as Mrs Jenkins came closer and closer.

'Yes, it's safe. Or it soon will be,' said Mrs Jenkins, with a reassuring smile – the kind she bestowed on Jake when he was doing well with a difficult word.

Beth looked around for a weapon, or something to protect herself with. She picked up a square scatter cushion, a chilly pale green silk, and held it in front of her. 'Don't spoil your lovely cushion, Mrs Jenkins,' she squeaked.

Really, this was going to be the most ignominious death, she thought, if she couldn't head the older woman off. But she was younger, and fitter. All right, neither of them had been exactly assiduous with their yoga lessons, but Beth must have the edge – she was thirty years younger.

She slid along the sofa, away from Mrs Jenkins, and tried to get to her feet. The other woman lunged, and the pristine shot silk of the cushion was suddenly rent in two, curled white feathers leaking from the slash.

'You're ruining it,' said Beth, shaking the cushion at Mrs Jenkins. A cascade of feathers flew out, and suddenly the other woman sneezed. Beth seized the opportunity, leapt up and ran to the door – which was locked. The key was in Mrs Jenkins' pocket. Beth didn't fancy getting close enough to fish it out, not with the knife still shining brightly in the older woman's hand.

She ran to the windows, flung aside the dusty curtains, and tried the sash. Stuck tight. But there was the huge crack right across the windowpane, where the poker trophy had been hurled. The velvet curtain had stopped the glass from breaking outright, but Beth was going to put that right now. She wrapped a handful of the dark green cloth around her arm, shrouding it in the thick fabric, then plunged at the window with the best running downward dog Dulwich had ever seen. Thank God, the pane gave with a satisfying shatter.

In a trice, she had knocked out the jagged remnants of the window and had scrambled over the sill, and into the unloved back garden. Being Dulwich, it was maintained to a certain standard, so the lawn was clipped and there was nothing out of place. But there were no flowers, which hereabouts was tantamount to saying you hated Alan Titchmarsh, *Gardeners' Question Time* and all the other gods of suburbia. Just seeing this sterile garden should have shrieked to the neighbours that there was something seriously awry in Gilkes Place.

Unfortunately, the fences were all intact, with no handy side gate giving onto the outside world and the madwoman-free streets of the rest of Dulwich. Beth looked around the highly desirable mature garden, mainly laid to lawn, in despair. Just then, she heard scrabbling at the window and, as inexorably as a zombie in a *Day of the Dead* movie, Mrs Jenkins' iron grey coiffure peeked out into the garden, shortly followed by her rotund, dusty blue body.

Beth, darting glances this way and that, weighed up her chances. Should she just rush the woman, and hope to wrestle the knife away from her? The only trouble with that idea was that Mrs Jenkins was deranged, desperate, and had form as a murderer. That left only one option. Beth hurled herself at the midpoint of the fence bordering with the Jenkins' neighbours. It immediately started to sag.

'What are you doing? That's our property you're damaging!' Mrs Jenkins shrieked at the top of her voice.

In Dulwich, these were the magic words. Immediately, the back door rattled open in the house next door. Mrs Jenkins' neighbour rushed out into the garden, protecting his land against imminent devaluation, like a knight of old defending his lady's virtue.

'Are you trying to bring that fence down, young woman?' said the elderly, silver-haired gentleman in shocked consternation.

'Yes, I am,' yelled Beth. 'But she's trying to kill me!' She pointed to Mrs Jenkins, who was advancing rapidly with her knife poised to thrust into Beth's jugular vein.

They were about the only extenuating circumstances that could possibly excuse an outright attack on a perimeter fence in Dulwich.

'Elizabeth, call the police!' cried the silver fox, shouting over his shoulder to his wife and winning Beth's eternal gratitude.

SIXTEEN

'So, what on earth happened to Mrs Jenkins?' said Katie, on the edge of her seat.

Luckily, they weren't in Beth's favoured café, the Aurora, or the chair would probably have collapsed.

Both had thought Jane's café – always packed to the gunnels – was a bit too public for this post-mortem on the dramatic events of the past week. So, they had compromised on Romeo Jones, a dinky little deli nestled next to the beauty parlour, like a chick under a particularly well-groomed mama's wing. Though tiny, it had a few tables inside and some outside as well, for the rare occasions when it was warm enough to bask in south London sunshine.

Today, with a blustery wind threatening the magnolia petals and riffling through the tiny new lilac buds, Beth and Katie had decided to squeeze inside. They were seated more or less under the cake counter, which was proving extremely distracting to Beth, though Katie seemed impervious to the sidelong glances of a delicious-looking carrot cake.

'Well, they dragged her off kicking and screaming, basically. I've never been so pleased to see anyone as I was when the police turned up. Thank God Harry had already decided he needed to question Mrs Jenkins again – if he hadn't shown up, I would have been stabbed, for sure.'

'Harry?' said Katie, her eyebrows arching.

'Oh, you know, Inspector York,' said Beth, suddenly finding that she needed to stir her cappuccino very urgently.

Katie said nothing, but Beth was well aware her friend would file this nugget of interesting first-name-terms information away somewhere. She was relieved when Katie's next question was back on track.

'Wouldn't the neighbour have stopped her?' she asked. Beth, palpably relieved to be on steadier ground, laughed.

'You must be kidding. He probably would have killed me himself, if I'd done any more damage to his fence. It was his wife rushing out when she did, waving a broom, that did the trick and frightened Mrs Jenkins off. Turns out, they'd absolutely hated each other since they had some dispute about where to put the wheelie bins back in the 1980s. Mrs Jenkins had run back inside and was packing her stuff when the police broke the door down. God knows where she thought she was going.'

Beth shivered. She could laugh about it now, but it hadn't been funny at the time. Sometimes, in the dead of night, she still felt as though she were in that chill green room, the vines on the walls writhing as the family's deadly secrets threatened to choke her.

Katie had to rush off to yoga, so they finished up their coffees secure in the knowledge there would be plenty to mull over in the months to come. The whole of the village had been agog about the details of the killing. And Beth's standing, she was amused to see, had risen considerably at the school gates; even Belinda McKenzie was now smiling fondly at her and beckoning her to come and chat with the select few.

She hadn't told Katie, but all this chumminess was in stark

contrast to her last interview with York. He had been predictably furious that she had chosen to meddle, once again, instead of calling in the professionals. But she'd been able to point out she had tried to call him, and that he had given her the final clue – pointing irrevocably, in her view, at Mrs Jenkins – when he'd told her the urine sample was definitely female. Anyway, just as well that the case was over now and their paths would never cross again, since he was so angry, she thought with a tiny pang which she carefully decided not to explore.

She had thought that even if York had given her up as a bad job, at least the powers that be at Wyatt's would be rather thrilled with her for clearing up their little murder mystery – and proving that the whole murky business had nothing to do with the school after all.

But, of course, Beth had also managed to present them with an equally horrific crime that couldn't have been more linked to Wyatt's if it had tried – the centuries-old slave-dealing of their founder, the dashing Thomas Wyatt himself.

To give the upper echelons at the school their due, the full board of governors and the bursar and head had immediately entered an enclave ten times more serious than that charged with electing a new pope. When they eventually emerged, it wasn't white smoke which was sent up into the cloudless Dulwich skies, but a new protocol.

Beth remembered well the summons to the head's office, to hear what had been decided. She had been certain, from the queasy pit of her stomach to the suddenly lank flop of her fringe, that this was it. She was finally going to be sacked from her beloved little sinecure of a job. Wyatt's had got round to noticing the inescapable fact that they really didn't need an archivist.

Frankly, Beth thought, Janice the school secretary was perfectly capable of doing the few minutes' extra filing a day which would keep the archives up to date and stop them being silted up again with every bit of paper the school produced. Given her close – very close, if Beth's suspicions were right – relationship with Dr Grover, it was surprising she hadn't already been given the job.

In a way, it would have been a perfect fit for Janice, and it would also have guaranteed she could spend even more time with Dr Grover, whose divorce had just been announced. By a not-so-strange coincidence, it turned out that Janice too had just consciously uncoupled from her husband, and she and Dr Grover were permitting themselves small smiles at each other in public and doing a lot less shouting at each other behind the scenes. Time would tell whether this micro-scandal would dent Dr Grover's dashing reputation and whether the Wyatt's mothers would disapprove – or feel miffed.

As far as Beth was concerned, it explained away that baffling flash of fuchsia she had seen on the morning of Dr Jenkins' death, and also showed why Dr Grover had been so flustered when she'd bumped into him and nearly been sent flying. It was a little absurd, she supposed, that two grown people were conducting assignations behind the bike sheds. But with so many Dulwich eyes upon them, she couldn't entirely blame them.

So, if they did do away with her archivist job, thought Beth, they would surely destroy the ridiculous, rickety shed in the playground, and the last few reminders of a grim chapter in the school's history would be closed forever. She'd just have to go back to her existing freelance clients, and try her utmost to drum up a few more. It wasn't an enticing prospect, but she and Jake wouldn't starve. Not immediately, anyway, she thought bleakly.

It would have been wrong to say that Beth had been shaking in her boots as she stood outside the door, where many thousands of pupils had nervously waited to hear their fates. After what she'd already been through with the school, the head and, most of all, with the bursar, they held no real terrors for her any more. She was braced.

But to her enormous surprise, everyone was all smiles when she cracked open the door and trotted in.

'Ah, Beth, take a seat, take a seat,' said the head, his tie today particularly flamboyant in yellows and bright pinks.

Even the bursar smiled at her jovially, his leg ceasing to jiggle for a moment as she sat down slowly. Janice, who was sitting next to her, gave her a reassuring grin, too. Beth looked at the headmaster, who spread his hands wide.

'Now, Beth, I can't pretend you haven't brought us a bit of a... well, shall we say, conundrum? Slavery. It's a shameful chapter in our history.' He paused to bow his head, and the bursar and Janice did, too, like obedient nodding dogs.

'But, as you know, we've consulted with the board of governors and all put our heads together.' Beth realised this was no idle figure of speech. There must have been an enormous amount of deep thinking going on, by some of the brightest minds in the country. 'And we've come up with a strategy,' said the head, his hands now outstretched to welcome the collective brainwave.

'We're a school, so we are going to make this an *educational experience*,' he said, and Beth suddenly realised that this was the beginning of a spiel Dr Grover would be giving many times in the months to come – to the pupils, to parents, and above all to the media. Immediately, he reinforced the impression by getting to his feet and addressing his words not to his colleagues, but to an imaginary audience right at the back of the room.

'We cannot deny what happened,' he said, his head bowed again. 'Our founder made a fortune on the back of his workforce. His workers were slaves.' Then Dr Grover looked up, gazing above the heads of the three onlookers, staring his imaginary audience right in the eye. 'Today, we are ashamed. Ashamed of the fact that we are here because of slavery. But, lest we forget, in those times, it was standard practice. Many fortunes, and many great educational establishments, are founded on these shameful beginnings. These are facts, and we can't change them. What we *can* do is apologise, unreservedly, for the suffering that was caused by our founder, and pledge that we will never forget that this magnificent institution, which has educated some of our finest minds since the seventeenth century, has its roots in this appalling trade.'

Dr Grover paused briefly, before progressing to the denouement of his speech.

'We will, at Wyatt's, therefore be setting up a research institute into the issue of slavery – a topic which will be studied by all pupils, with a special prize issued every year on Founder's Day, for the best original project on the subject. We will also be removing the portrait of Thomas Wyatt from the Grand Hall,' said Dr Grover thunderously, as though delivering his ringing peroration to a packed hall. 'Although, in fact, we haven't quite decided if we're actually going to do that or not,' he said, glancing at those who were actually in the room.

He sat down again and turned his attention to Beth. She shuffled a little in her seat.

'So, Beth, you can see where we're going with this, can't you?' he said, smiling kindly at her.

This was it. The axe was going to fall. Well, Beth told herself, it was only what she'd been expecting.

Dr Grover studied her gravely for a moment, then spoke in his most serious tones. 'We'd like you to head up the research institute. Of course, in a way, it's just your old job with a different title... but we're hoping you'll step up. We've been impressed with your, er, skills during these difficult times at Wyatt's. And we like to reward loyalty,' said the head, with a magnanimous smile.

Beth had so expected to be fired that it took her a few moments to realise she'd been promoted instead. Astounded, she realised her jaw was hanging open slightly. *So* not a Wyatt's look. She shut it with a snap, and it wasn't at all difficult to pin a radiant smile to her face instead. Finally, it looked as though she had some work here to get her teeth into, and the perfect excuse to give her beloved archives the time and attention they truly deserved. However harrowing the secrets they contained, she was sure now that she was equal to the challenge of bringing them to light. After all, she'd seen worse.

And, if she felt it was a little lame of Wyatt's to pass the blood-drenched issue of slavery off as just another school project, well, at least it was finally one truly worth the time and effort.

Her intelligent grey eyes met the headmaster's shrewd gaze. He'd been right in saying she felt loyal to Wyatt's. She had done, since day one. She'd always admired the school and, now she was part of it, that feeling was stronger still. Plus, this had to mean that her beloved Jake had a chance at a bursary, surely?

She smiled happily at Dr Grover, who looked a little disconcerted. As well he might. This great, grand shire horse of a man had just been outmanoeuvred by a small but very determined sort of pony. Most of the time, Beth knew herself to be a shaggy little Shetland, long of fringe and short of leg, but every now and then she got a glimpse of the pretty little Falabella she might become. Today was one of those times.

Dr Grover peered down at her with new respect, then smiled and shook her hand, as the Grand Hall clock struck the quarter. Which reminded Beth, she'd better get going, *now*.

Taking a quick leave of her colleagues, she raced across the velvety green of the Wyatt's grass, contravening every known law of the school. But she didn't have time to go the long way.

As she trotted through the streets, dodging the afterschool tangles of pushchairs and scooters, she should have been glowing with the knowledge that she was finally on the threshold of a worthwhile and satisfying new career at Wyatt's.

And she should have been luxuriating, too, in the profound relief of never having to deal with that infuriating policeman, Harry York, ever again.

But there was something a lot more pressing at the forefront of her mind. She had to cobble together the entire solar system for Jake.

And she had to get the whole damn thing finished tonight, if they were going to be able to hold up their heads on the streets of Dulwich tomorrow.

A LETTER FROM ALICE

Thank you for choosing my book – I know there are a lot of stories out there and I'm so glad you picked mine. I had great fun writing about Beth Haldane and her first step along the way to becoming Dulwich's premier single mum amateur sleuth. I hope you enjoyed reading it too. If you'd like to know what happens to Beth next, please sign up at the email link below. Your email address will never be shared and you can unsubscribe at any time.

www.bookouture.com/alice-castle

If you liked the book, I would be very grateful if you could write a review. I'd love to hear what you think – I always read reviews and I take careful account of what people say. My aim is always to make my books a better read! Leaving a review also helps new readers to discover one of my books for the first time.

I'm also on Twitter, Facebook and Goodreads, often sharing silly pictures of cats that look like Magpie. Do get in touch if that's your sort of thing. Thanks so much again, and I really hope to see you soon for Beth's next adventure. Happy reading!

Alice Castle

KEEP IN TOUCH WITH ALICE

alicecastleauthor.com

 facebook.com/alicecastleauthor

twitter.com/AliceMCastle

instagram.com/alice_castle__

ACKNOWLEDGEMENTS

I would like to say a special thank you to the brilliant Ellen Gleeson at Bookouture, and Alexandra Holmes, Rhian McKay, Kim Nash and the rest of the amazing team, for their faith in Beth and for all their hard work in bringing out this book.

Made in the USA
Thornton, CO
06/08/23 16:49:29

afec5e17-dac7-46d2-8a41-0c17e02edf6bR01